Losing Streak

Nobody could explain it. Juky was about as straight as they come, smart, articulate, generous, a model Christian athlete who volunteered at his church. Hell, everybody liked him. Who would want to kill him?

Maybe things were worse because last year's star, Jackson Tucker, had never made it to Marquette. He had collapsed and died during a practice game. It was one of those freak events—a kid with undiagnosed heart disease plays hundreds of games, and then plays one too many and gets zapped by a heart attack.

Now, some Northsiders were starting to say that the team was jinxed. Me, I don't believe in jinxes where bullets are involved . . .

TWO POINTS FOR MURDER

D.B. BORTON

BERKLEY PRIME CRIME, NEW YORK

*For Dorothy May Borton
and her daughter,
Mary Jane Borton Carpenter*

TWO POINTS FOR MURDER

A Berkley Prime Crime Book / published by arrangement with the author

PRINTING HISTORY
Berkley edition / October 1993
Berkley Prime Crime edition / April 1995

ISBN: 0-425-13947-6

Berkley Prime Crime Books are published
by The Berkley Publishing Group,
200 Madison Avenue, New York, New York 10016.
The name BERKLEY PRIME CRIME and the
BERKLEY PRIME CRIME
design are trademarks belonging to Berkley Publishing Corporation.

PRINTED IN THE UNITED STATES OF AMERICA

10 9 8 7 6 5 4 3 2 1

Acknowledgments

I would like to thank Murray Sperber, an awesome dissertation director and author of *College Sports, Inc.*, for sharing resources. A 1988 series of articles on high school sports published in the *Louisville Courier-Journal* and written by staff writers, including Alan Judd and R. G. Dunlop, was extremely helpful to me.

Derek Benseler advised me on high school basketball, and, as usual, John Kornbluh advised me on everything else.

For further acknowledgments, you'll have to read the book first.

The Roster

One

"A.J. cat gone."

I wasn't a mother for nothing. Mothers know more than the goddam Shadow knows, seeing as how they've got eyes in the backs of their heads and built-in code descramblers more sophisticated than a Dick Tracy secret decoder ring. That was why I had turned to detective work to begin with. Who was better qualified?

So when Leon stood at my door, holding a grubby, tear smeared little white kid by the hand, and stated his business, I knew what I was dealing with. Leon wanted to be my first customer.

"That A.J.?" I said, nodding at the half-pint.

"Uh-huh," Leon said. A.J. stuck a fluorescent thumb in his mouth and snuffled. I refrained from taking it out and inspecting the stain for toxic chemicals. That much of a mother I ain't.

"Come in."

Leon was a tall, rangy black kid whose fame in my Northside neighborhood was exceeded only by that of Bill, the hardware store owner. Leon was supposed to be mentally handicapped. Aren't we all?

I met him while I was working on my first case, which resulted in a citation for Leon for assisting in the capture of an armed criminal. He got his picture in the paper, shaking hands with the mayor of Cincinnati, who is a total loser if you ask me, but that's beside the point. I'm Leon's hero. I'm also the only detective he knows. He's the only kid I know, my own included, who accepts me as a detective, even though I don't look like anybody on TV. Well, maybe Columbo.

"Why don't you introduce us?" I prompted Leon. He's

not all that mentally deficient, like I said, and generally outdistanced his peers in etiquette.

"This Alfonse Dwayne McManniss, J-Junior," he said, gesturing in the direction of the little person sitting perched on my sofa. "A.J., this M-Miz Cat."

I'm Cat to my friends, and Ms. Caliban to my enemies, but Leon, as usual, demonstrated his originality. Besides, I suspected some of his habits were rooted in old Southern traditions, and who am I to quibble with tradition, as long as I don't have to follow it? Sadie had strolled out to see who was here, and stopped dead in the middle of the room, her nose in the air and that expression on her face cats get when they smell something bad. My kitties liked Leon, but baby humans ranked right up there with flea baths on their list of things to avoid. I edged a box of tissues closer to A.J. He wiped his nose with the back of his hand and pulled his head into his ski jacket like a reluctant turtle.

"So A.J.'s lost his cat." See what I mean? Doesn't take a goddam Philip Marlowe to figure it out, just a mother.

Two heads nodded.

I avoided the dead-end question mothers usually ask, Where did you lose it? I asked the next best thing.

"Where was the cat last time you saw it?"

"At A.J. house," said his spokesperson patiently. Where did I think? Riverfront Coliseum?

"When did it disappear?"

"Tuesday." This was Monday. That meant they could file a missing persons report, but somehow I didn't think it would be welcomed at District 5.

"Did you put up signs in the neighborhood?"

"A.J. too little. He can't write. But I wrote some for him, and we p-put 'em down on Hamilton Avenue, and on A.J. s-street, Apple, and on Cherry, and Colerain, and Chase, and K-Kirby, and—"

"Okay, I get the picture. Did you call the SPCA?"

"We rode over there on my b-bike. It w-wasn't no cats like A.J. cat."

"What's A.J.'s cat like?"

"He black, got some w-white on his chest."

They must be kidding. Half the cats in Northside looked like that, and they bred enough to keep the SPCA well stocked.

"He little."

I began to wonder if I couldn't talk A.J. into the idea that one of the cats at the shelter *was* his cat, only it had grown since Tuesday.

"How little?"

Leon raised his hands and held them about six inches apart. If you're having trouble visualizing this part, let me say that my gray tiger Sophie couldn't squeeze her belly into this space.

"A kitten?"

They nodded.

"Male or female?"

"A b-boy."

Now we were getting somewhere.

"How old?"

Leon looked at A.J. A.J. shrugged. Leon turned to me and shrugged.

"Four months? Six months? Eight months?"

Shrug, shrug.

"What's his name?"

"Blackie." A.J. spoke through his thumb.

Why is it that when I'm with Leon, I always feel that I'm playing the straight man?

"Okay," I said, standing up.

"You gonna f-find Blackie?"

"I'll try."

Suddenly Leon was all business. "Show her you m-money, A.J."

Shorty stuck his paw in his pocket, rooted around, and brought up a fistful of change, in which pennies predominated.

"Keep it," I said. "When I start incurring expenses, I'll let you know."

"W-Where you goin' to?"

"*We're* going to A.J.'s house, so I can check out the scene of the— uh, disappearance."

Now, you might think it would be beneath my dignity to take on a missing cat case. To tell you the truth, I never had much dignity to begin with, and raising three kids put a big dent in it. My two oldest were attempting to continue the process. They seemed to think that since their father, Fred the Frugal, had moved on to that suburbia in the sky, I'd need more of what they considered advice and I considered interference. They had been a real pain in the ass since I moved to Northside and announced my intention of training to be a private investigator. They would have me committed except that they'd lose what little free baby-sitting they managed to squeeze out of me—which, I might add, is more than you'd think if you heard them carry on about what an unsafe neighborhood I live in. Lucky for me, I didn't discuss my cases with them.

My tenant and sometime sidekick Kevin O'Neill was coming in as we were going out.

"On a case, Mrs. C?"

He always says that when I wear my mirror sunglasses.

Hell, I was interested in this case, and sympathetic to boot. It was February, and even though we were having a mild spell, Canada could have sent us the big chill any old day. The last snow had almost melted, but if *I* had lost a kitty, I'd have been worried. And kitties, as everybody knows who's lived with one, can be anywhere. They have that ability to slip into a fifth dimension whenever you need to give them medicine or take them to the vet. When mine disappeared they were usually at Kevin's, scarfing down gourmet cat yummies or snoozing on his Barcalounger. But they'd taken their share of unannounced vacations.

If this kitty was a tom, he might be taking a sex tour of Northside, playing his part in the population explosion. I didn't want to have to explain that to A.J., who was wiping suspiciously wet hands all over my beige cloth upholstery.

A.J. lived on Apple, a block down from the IGA, which opened up all kinds of possibilities I didn't want to think about. It was a three-story two-family house, one of those blocky brick Northside types which make up in basement and attic what they miss in closets—from a feline perspective, that is. The front yard looked pretty neat, but my heart sank when I saw the back: someone appeared to be in the middle of a major home-improvement project, and there was all kinds of crap piled up back there. A kitty kiddyland. We went in the side door and up the stairs.

"A.J.? That you?" a female voice called.

"It's us, M-Miz Hedges."

"Us who?"

"That my granny." On his own turf, A.J. was becoming downright expansive.

"Oh, hi, Leon. Who'd you bring to visit?"

Mrs. Hedges was a mature woman in her prime, about my age. She was on the thin and weathered side, with graying brown hair pulled back in a stubby ponytail. She wore turquoise polyester slacks, a print blouse, and trotters.

"This M-Miz Cat. She a detective. She going to find A.J. cat."

"Catherine Caliban, Mrs. Hedges. The kids asked me to help them, and I agreed—"

"Lord have mercy, A.J. and his cat's fixin' to drive me round the bend. I ain't never seen nobody so attached to an animal. 'Course, we had cats on the farm growing up, mousers mostly, and they came and went and didn't nobody ever pay them no never mind. If they was there they was there and if they wasn't they wasn't. Want a Coke?"

She had a cigarette going in the kitchen, so we sat down at the kitchen table to talk.

"So you're a detective? Do you specialize in lost cats, or what?"

"I'm not licensed yet, so I specialize in anything that comes around. I didn't like to disappoint the kids, and I've found a few lost cats in my day, but you know as well as I do what the chances are."

We both glanced at the kids, who were waiting for me to pull off a miracle. She gave me an exaggerated wink.

"Okay, shoot. You going to interrogate me?"

"How old was Blackie? A.J. didn't seem to know."

"Lord, honey, *I* don't know. He's just a little scrap of a thing. A.J. found him out back, maybe a month ago, during that real cold spell, so we took him in. He was a mess. Full of worms and mites and I don't know what-all."

"But he was eating solid food okay?"

She blew out a puff of smoke. "He ate anything he could get his paws on. And Loreen—that's my daughter, A.J.'s ma—she fixed him one of those fancy little boxes of sand, and he jumped right in it and did his business. So we told A.J. he could keep him."

"Has he ever disappeared before?"

"No, he follows A.J. around just like a little puppy. Cute little rascal, come to that."

"Friendly? Outgoing? Likes people?"

"Loves ever'body, far as I can see. Not a bit afraid, like some cats. Sometimes when A.J. was gone he'd go downstairs to visit poor Marion—Mrs. Kay—now *that's* a woman's had more than her share of troubles. 'Course, that apartment's empty now. But lots of times she would leave the door open into the hall, and he'd just walk right in, like King Solomon, calm as you please. Fact, it must've been Marion was the last one to see him, near as anybody can recollect."

"She saw him on Tuesday?"

"That's right. Says she was kind of distracted, on account of packing and waiting for the Goodwill and all, but she remembers seeing him. Gave him some tuna fish in the kitchen to keep him out from under foot."

I shook my head. It couldn't be that easy.

"So Marion was packing the day Blackie disappeared? Where did she go?"

"She moved in with her sister in College Hill. Said the apartment felt too empty to her, bless her heart."

"Do you have her new address and phone number?"

"Well, yes, I do. What you want it for?"

"Well, cats are naturally curious little beasts, Mrs.

Hedges. They love to explore open boxes and suitcases and bags. Sometimes they climb into something and go to sleep, wake up in a different place."

"You mean, that little rascal might've got hisself packed? But Marion would've called me right away if she found Blackie."

"Maybe she hasn't found him yet. It hasn't been a week. Maybe there are boxes she hasn't unpacked."

"But he'd make noise, wouldn't he? I never knew such a little thing make so much noise when suppertime rolled around."

"Well, but maybe he's in a basement or an attic, where there's nobody around to hear him."

I heard a snuffle from across the table and realized I was waxing a mite graphic for little ears.

"I hate to have you bother poor Marion about a lost cat after what she's been through."

"M-maybe the Goodwill t-took Blackie."

Maybe I should offer Leon a goddam partnership.

"What *did* the Goodwill truck take?"

"Why, I don't know what-all they took. Her sofa and living-room chairs, I guess. Juky's bedroom furniture. Maybe some of hers, I don't know."

"Tell you what. I'll start with Goodwill. If that doesn't pan out, I'll let you know, and we'll have to give Marion a call. Now what's her full name again?"

"Marion Kay. Mrs. Bashford Kay. You know."

"Remember what her living-room furniture looked like?"

"Seems like it was kind of a brown plaid Colonial. Chairs was the same as the sofa."

"All right, I'll start there." I looked at the name I'd written down. "Am I supposed to recognize this name?"

"Oh, honey, her boy Julius was that basketball player they found. You know—down by the Mill Creek, where they're doing all that digging." Her voice dropped as she ground out her cigarette. "He'd been *murdered*, and they still don't know who done it!"

Two

I figured this was one case I could solve on my own—well, not counting Leon's advice and counsel. The last time around, I had ended up recruiting every one of my tenants in the old Catatonia Arms, and lucky for me, nobody had yet proposed a rent reduction in exchange for services rendered. But I didn't anticipate any legal complexities requiring consultation with my resident attorney, Alice Rosenberg, unless Goodwill wouldn't release Blackie into A.J.'s custody. Her roomie Melanie Carter might come in handy if I had to move heavy furniture around, but I didn't expect to need Mel's expertise in the martial arts for the missing kitten caper. Ditto for Kevin's astonishing knack for producing unregistered firearms. If I succeeded in my mission, Kevin could cook the celebration dinner—one of his best skills. Moses Fogg, an ex-cop and our newest resident, I would hold in reserve in case I was dealing with a kidnapping. Of course, if Blackie had been transported across state lines, I'd need to involve the feds. In fact, the animal residents of the Catatonia had more to offer than their human counterparts, and I could envision sending them in as a team to flush out a kitty in hiding. When I left, however, the cats were all sacked out on various heat registers, like little warm piles of dust rags, and there was nary a beagle in sight.

The Northside Goodwill store is where I do most of my shopping for birthday presents. You'd be amazed what you can find there. Old rock-and-roll records. Ceramic condiment pots that look like beehives. Old chemistry sets with only a few of the chemicals missing. Mirro cookie presses—the kind everybody used to have and nobody has anymore. On a lucky day, a poodle skirt. I don't hang out in the furniture section, but that's where I was that day.

Not a brown plaid sofa in sight, either, and that's more astonishing than you might think. The only thing Northside
has more of is black cats with white on their chests.

"Whatcha lookin' for, hon?"

"A brown plaid sofa and chairs. A Mrs. Kay donated
them, Marion Kay. They would have arrived on Tuesday."

"Had your eye on 'em, had you?"

"Well, no. It's just that we've lost something, and we
think there's a chance it could be in the furniture somewhere."

"Uh-huh. Well, I tell you, if they was just picked up on
Tuesday, they might not have left the warehouse yet. They
take everything over there, check it out, repair it, and clean
it up, though you might not think they do, but that's what
they say. You go over there and look."

She told me how to get to the warehouse, and I thanked
her. Something about the way I said it tipped her off that
I was laboring under a delusion.

"Oh, I don't *work* here. I just shop here. They should
pay me a commission for all the stuff I sell, just walkin'
around the store. But I wouldn't take it, anyway. I like to
speak my mind. When I see junk, I call it junk."

The warehouse was only a few blocks away, and I was
turned over to a morose individual who was probably not
playing with a full deck.

"You want a brown plaid sofa? Now, we ain't allowed
to sell anything right out of the warehouse. You can't even
reserve anything. You have to go to the store and buy it."

"I don't want to buy it, I just want to look at it. Some
people in the house it came from have lost something, and
they think it might be in the furniture."

"Oh. What'd they lose?"

I knew he wasn't going to budge until I told him.

"A kitten."

"Oh, well, we haven't found any kittens here."

"Could I just take a peek at the furniture?"

"Well, I guess so. But like I say, we haven't found no
kittens. We would've found something like that. I thought

you was meaning a watch or something. Why, you'd never get a kitten into a divan like that. I mean, not so's nobody wouldn't know it was there."

This guy had obviously never lived with cats.

"Let's see. Callahan, you said the name was?"

"No, Caliban is *my* name. The lady who donated the furniture was named Kay. Mrs. Marion Kay, or Mrs. Bashford Kay."

"How you spell that?"

I told him. He shuffled through a clipboard of papers, then decided it was the wrong clipboard, then set about commencing to find the right clipboard, then asked me how to spell Callahan, then asked somebody in coveralls who had just walked in, and Coveralls, without a glance at any clipboards, offered to take me back to look at the furniture.

It didn't look promising, I admit. A desk and dresser flanked a sofa with two overstuffed chairs piled on top, and two lamps on top of that. A linoleum kitchen table lay on its side, with a disassembled bed frame propped up against it. I sighed.

I got out the can of tuna I'd bought at the IGA, popped the top, and went to work.

Coveralls removed the chairs, eyeing the tuna dubiously.

"Blackie," I called softly. "Kitty, kitty."

From the depths of the sofa, there issued a faint, pitiful squeak.

"He's in there, and he's alive!" I said, almost hugging Coveralls in my excitement. Like I said, dignity was not one of my more prominent qualities.

"Well, I'll be darned. Now, how we going to get the little fella out?"

I yanked off the cushions, and was rewarded by a faint but plaintive wail. I shoved my hand down between the back and the seat, and felt something, but it wasn't furry. I considered leaving it there, but I couldn't. As a mother retired from active duty, I still felt the pull of the old mystery: what long-lamented family heirlooms lurked in the depths of the family sofa? I extricated a small brown note-book, and tossed it aside.

"Help me turn this sucker over," I said to Coveralls. "Just lay it on its back."

Up in one corner, there was a sizeable hole in the black gauzy fabric that had been used to line the bottom. I applied tuna, and a black head emerged. I slid a hand in and extricated one Blackie the cat, looking considerably the worse for wear but alert enough to bury his head in the tuna can. Goddam, I love happy endings.

"Well, I'll be *darned*. Would you look at that?" Coveralls was grinning as if he'd just assisted at a birth. I hated to tell him that the kitten already had a name.

I was almost to the car when he came running after me.

"Hey, lady, you forgot your notebook."

I'll skip the tearful reunion between boy and cat, and let you imagine it for yourself. I had to warn Mrs. Hedges about the dangers of overfeeding a cat who'd been fasting a few days; your first instinct is to empty out the refriger-ator into the cat dish. I also had to explain a few basic principles of feline behavior. I left out the part about Blackie eating bugs in the warehouse at night.

Leon beamed at everybody like a godfather at a wedding. Then he took me aside and assured me he'd make up whatever costs A.J.'s piggy bank wouldn't cover.

"That's real generous of you, Leon, but my only expense was a ninety-nine-cent can of tuna."

Look, I know I should've billed them for my time, but I'm a soft touch. I'm also unlicensed, and illegal if I accept any money at this point. Plus, to tell you the truth, I was a little abashed when I realized that it was Leon who'd come up with the Goodwill truck angle.

I was halfway home when I remembered the notebook. I admit, I could've taken it back to A.J.'s, but hell, I'm a detective in training, and here was a genuine artifact out of a house where somebody lived who'd been murdered. I decided to take it home and practice detecting on it before returning it to Mrs. Kay. It was probably her grocery list.

"What do you make of this, Watson?"

Moses had come down, looking for a game of gin rummy. I kept my eye on Winnie as I tossed the notebook to him. Winnie, the beagle world's answer to Michael Jordan, had been known to execute a steal and fast break with vital documents. Moses fished his bifocals out of his pocket and settled them on his nose.

"It's a notebook."

"Mmm-hmm."

"It's smaller than a bread box, and brown."

"Mmm-hmm."

"It's got writing in it. Blue ink, probably a Bic. Looks kinda young. Adolescent, maybe, probably male."

This was worth something, coming from Moses. He'd spent thirty of his years at the Cincinnati Police Department working Juvenile.

"Basketball player?" I asked.

"Now, how would I know that? I'd say if he's a male adolescent in this town, he's a basketball player. But if you asking me does this notebook smell like a locker room, I'd say it smells like a house that's been closed up awhile— musty-like, like used furniture stores."

I hadn't even thought of *smelling* the damn thing. I had a lot to learn.

"Look like he's been taking notes. Homework assignments, dates and appointments, and some kind of mumbo jumbo in the back, look like secret code to me. Rows of numbers."

"Doesn't any of it look like it has to do with basketball or practice or scouting reports or workouts?"

"Damned if I know. I'm an old man, Cat. I ain't been inside a locker room since I had to pass my last police physical. You going to have to ask the resident expert that question." He meant Mel, Ms. Martial Arts, who was off at some martial arts convention in Skokie.

I waited, knowing the mystery would intrigue him. He adjusted his glasses and frowned at the page.

"If you were a high school basketball player, would you keep a notebook like that? I mean, take notes on your games, or the plays, or your workouts or anything?"

"I might. Lots of athletes do, those that can write, that is. We talking about any high school basketball player in particular?"

"Juky Kay."

"Oh," he said, giving me a look over his glasses. "An ex-basketball player."

"Yeah," I said. "But he didn't choose to retire."

Three

I got Mrs. Kay's number from Mrs. Hedges, who gave it reluctantly. Mrs. Kay herself sounded on the wary side, as anybody would be who's been involved in a murder, especially when the victim is famous. She said she'd be home that evening, and gave me the address in College Hill.

Julius Abraham Kay, according to Moses, had been the closest thing Cincinnati had had in years to a candidate for superstardom on the basketball court. He'd landed in the most unlikely place, Oscar Robertson High School, which, in spite of its name, boasted the worst win-loss record in the state. That is, until a new coach arrived. This coach, name of Biggs, had turned the program around so dramatically that the previous year, when Juky was a junior, the team had gone all the way to the regional finals. Juky himself had made the all-state team since his freshman year, and the team's center, a senior named Jackson Tucker, had landed an athletic scholarship to Marquette. Juky hadn't been the only other talent on the team, of course, but he had been the most naturally gifted; the others had been poked and prodded, dragged and shoved and intimidated into becoming the heroes of Northside, so that even without Tucker, Northsiders were planning their trips to Dayton in March. In a neighborhood with a tenuous self-image, all of a sudden there was something to cheer about besides the annual five-minute Fourth of July parade.

Then Juky's body had been found along the Mill Creek, right around Christmastime: he'd been shot in the chest. The whole neighborhood went into mourning. Men wept openly on the streets and in the bars. Women organized memorial fundraisers. Kids wore black arm bands, or laced their athletic shoes with black shoelaces. Stores closed on the day of the funeral—the biggest in Northside history.

Worst of all, nobody could explain it. Juky was about as straight as they come, smart, articulate, generous, a model Christian athlete who volunteered at his church. Hell, everybody liked him. Who would want to kill him? When folks couldn't think of anything else to say, the rumors of drug involvement started. They were kept pretty quiet, though, because any hint of impropriety on Juky's part could start a fight in any bar in Northside. Alive, Juky had been a great kid; dead, he was the Incarnation.

Maybe things were worse because last year's star, Jackson Tucker, had never made it to Marquette. He had collapsed and died during a practice game in the late spring. It was one of those freak events—a kid with undiagnosed heart disease from a family with a history of heart disease plays hundreds of games, and then plays one too many and gets zapped by a heart attack. His athletic scholarship went to a boy from New Jersey.

Now, some Northsiders were starting to say that the team was jinxed. Me, I don't believe in jinxes where bullets are involved.

Mrs. Kay lived in a substantial frame house with gray siding and white trim. Two rows of squat white styrofoam cones along the front walk testified to the presence of a careful gardener. The tall, square-shouldered woman who opened the door turned out to be Mrs. Shielding, Mrs. Kay's sister. Mrs. Kay wasn't as tall as her sister. She was what the books call overweight, but solid, like me, dressed in a shirtwaist. Her medium brown face had a worn look, and a few wisps of hair the color of ash-covered charcoal hung over her forehead like they'd given up the effort to stay put.

She looked a little surprised when I entered the room. I have that effect on people. I think they're expecting one of Charlie's Angels. I like to think of myself as Margaret Rutherford crossed with Lana Turner.

"I spoke to Mrs. Hedges," Mrs. Kay said as I settled

myself on the sofa. I resisted the impulse to slide my hand behind the cushions and check for evidence. "She told me you found Blackie. I'm so glad. A.J. was so attached to that cat."

"I was glad to help," I said. "But, as I told you on the phone, I found something else, too, and thought I should return it to you. I'm very sorry about your son, Mrs. Kay."

I handed her the notebook. She opened it, and bit her lip.

"Yes," she said quietly. "That's his handwriting. It must have fallen out of his pocket while he was watching TV."

Her voice quavered, and a tear slid down her cheek. Mrs. Shielding put an arm around her.

"Did the police search the house on Apple Street during their initial investigation?"

"Oh, yes, they seemed very thorough. Of course, they were looking in his room, mostly."

Score one for the Cat.

"And you emptied out all the furniture before you sent it to Goodwill?"

"*I* did that," her sister said. "Marion wasn't up to it. And I can tell you all the drawers were empty." She relented. "Well, I can see now how I might have missed something; maybe we'd better tell the police to look again."

"I still can't believe he's gone," Mrs. Kay said softly.

"It must have been quite a shock for you." Goddam, Cat, I said to myself; who wrote your dialogue? "Days of Our Lives"? To be fair, though, if you haven't been there, you don't understand the temptation to fall back on platitudes. What do you say to a mother whose only child has been murdered?

"You said on the phone you were a private investigator."

"Sort of an investigator-in-training, Mrs. Kay. I'm not licensed yet."

"But you *are* an investigator."

"You could say that." Hell, I did. Only not when the cops were around.

"Would you be willing to investigate Juky's murder?"

I took a deep breath, but Mrs. Shielding didn't let me get anything out.

"Oh, now, Marion, I'm sure Mrs. Caliban is a busy person. She doesn't have time to take on a big job like that. You'd best let the police handle it."

"But they aren't getting anywhere, Emma. Maybe we need someone else."

"Now, you don't know that, Marion. The police don't tell you everything they know. They keep working away on all that evidence they have, like they do on 'Hill Street Blues'. And they've got all those crime laboratories and experts to work with, like Quincy. And anyway, Mrs. Caliban already said she wasn't a licensed investigator." Translation: if this old white lady is a detective, I'm Magic Johnson.

"Actually," I ventured, "since I *am* in training, I *would* like your permission to look into your son's death. I'd promise to stay out of the way of the police." Okay, I admit I had my fingers crossed when I said it. "And I'm not completely inexperienced. I've already successfully completed one murder investigation." Like Kevin says, it's all in the marketing.

"You have?" Mrs. Shielding looked skeptical.

"Yes. Maybe you know Leon Jakes." Silly question. "He helped me out on my last case, the murder of Leda Marrs."

Mrs. Kay's eyes widened.

"Were you the lady who solved that? I remember reading all about it. Leon was so thrilled to get that citation. Well, Emma, I think maybe the Lord sent Mrs. Caliban to us this evening."

Maybe He did. If so, He hadn't let me in on it, but then we weren't exactly on intimate terms.

"How much will it cost?" asked the ever-practical Emma.

"Oh, I can't accept any money for my services, Mrs. Shielding, since I'm not licensed." Not even the proverbial dollar the boys got. "If I ran into any extraordinary expenses, I might ask you to pay them, but I'd clear them with you in advance. I can't imagine what they'd be, though." If I had to set up a drug deal, I sure as hell wasn't using *my* money, or hers either, for that matter.

"What do you need from me?"

"Well, for starters I need to ask you some questions. Doesn't have to be tonight; I can come back another time."

"Can't you read the police report?" Mrs. Shielding asked. "She's already answered more questions than you can shake a stick at."

"It's not the same, Emma; you know that." She sighed. "It won't get any better tomorrow, Mrs. Caliban, or anytime soon. The only thing that will help a little will be to see my boy's murderer caught. And it's not just because I want vengeance, though I don't seem to be able to purify my heart of that, no matter how much I pray to Jesus. But I don't want to see some other mother have to go through what I've gone through." She paused to straighten out her voice. "So why don't we get started, and Emma, why don't you go on in the kitchen and make us some coffee?"

Mrs. Shielding departed reluctantly as I pulled out my notebook. I tried to think of an easy question to ask first. There weren't any.

"Tell me about Juky, Mrs. Kay. He was a senior at Oscar Robertson, right? So he was, what, eighteen?"

"Seventeen. He would have been eighteen next month, at playoff time. Well, I don't hardly know where to start. You know he played basketball, of course; that and the church were the most important things in his life."

"Which church?"

"The Northside Holy Temple of God. Reverend Cain can talk to you about Juky. He'll tell you the same thing I'm telling you. Juky was a good Christian boy. He accepted Jesus into his life before he was ten, and he has never done anything that would make me or the Reverend Cain or his Savior ashamed of him. He volunteered with the young people at the church, taught Sunday school and sometimes Bible study classes. And I know what they're saying about him, but Mrs. Caliban, that's nothing but envy. I pray every night for those people who are spreading rumors that my son took drugs, because he never touched drugs in his life, and he never would! Never!"

"Tell me about the basketball team, Mrs. Kay. Is that where he found most of his friends?"

She shook her head sadly. "Seems like Juky had friends everywhere, Mrs. Caliban. And I'm not saying that just because he was my son! But yes, some of his closest friends were the other team members, particularly Butch and Cal. I'm sorry, that's Butch Frisby and Cal Sepeta. Cal's family also belongs to Reverend Cain's congregation."

"And Juky was on good terms with the basketball coach?"

"Oh, yes, certainly he was. Coach Biggs was so generous with his advice during recruiting. I don't know what we would have done without him. You see, Juky knows— knew—about basketball, and he knew what he wanted to study, but these things are so much more complicated than I realized. When Juky finally chose Indiana, Coach was very pleased, and thought he'd made the right decision. And afterwards—well, Coach Biggs has been very kind to me. Some people—you know—avoid you. They don't know what to say, and so they say that they don't want to intrude on your grief. But sometimes, you just want to talk about it, and talk about *him*, about Juky, I mean. Emma's been a real help, of course, but Coach has given me another shoulder to cry on from time to time. Everybody else avoids talking about Juky, and they want to think you're getting better all the time so they don't have to worry about you anymore. I guess I'm not explaining it very well, am I?"

"You're doing okay. Tell me what you know about Juky's death."

"Well, I don't know much. He'd been missing four days when they found him. It was the week before Christmas. I— I'm sorry, this is so hard." She stopped to blow her nose. "It was a Friday night. We had dinner at six, just like we always did, unless he had a late practice or a game. I was washing dishes when he left. He said, 'Catch you later, Good-lookin'.' A-and that w-was—"

"—the last time you saw him?"

She nodded.

"Where was he going?"

"Oh, I don't know. I assumed he was going off with his friends. Sometimes they played a little pickup at the park, or at the gym, if it was too cold, or—I don't know—went over to somebody's house or drove around or went to Graeters for ice cream or someplace. You know, at that age, they're always hungry. Or they went to the movies or walked around the mall. You know, just the kind of thing boys do at that age."

"What did the police find out about where he was?"

"They say that he and Cal and Butch were over at Butch's shooting baskets for a while, then, when it started snowing, they went over to Sight in Sound on Colerain to look at some car stereo equipment, then they came back to Northside and went to Tower Hamburgers, there by the viaduct, and then Juky looked at his watch and said he had to be going, but he wouldn't tell them where, and he left on foot. That's all they know."

"What time was that?"

"Close to eleven-thirty."

"What kind of mood was he in? Did they say?"

"They said he was quieter than usual, but he gets— got—like that sometimes. I told the police that he'd had something on his mind all fall, but I just assumed it was his college decision. If there was something else, I guess he couldn't talk to me about it, but I know he took it to the Lord in prayer. If he talked to Reverend Cain about it, Reverend Cain hasn't said anything to me."

"So he was worried about something?"

"Yes, that's right. Of course, he was also concentrating on basketball, and hoping the team would make it to the playoffs again. And at the same time, there were all those recruiters calling him up all the time."

"Did you get the impression that whatever was bothering him, it had something to do with the team?"

"I really couldn't say. It might have been his school-work, or anything, really."

"Romantic troubles? Did he have a girlfriend?"

She nodded. "LaTania Talbot. A real sweet girl. Be-longed to the same church. I don't really think LaTania ever gave him a moment's worry. But I guess he might have worried about what would happen when he went to Bloomington. LaTania was going to stay here and attend UC."

"But he didn't have a date with her that night?"

She shook her head. "LaTania went to a wedding with her family in Newport. She was supposed to go out with him on Saturday night."

During a fresh surge of tears, I pondered what I had so far, which wasn't a whole hell of a lot, in case anybody was interested. Maybe Juky just bumped into a drug deal. Maybe he was an innocent bystander who saw something he shouldn't have.

"Was Juky a friend of—" I had to check my notes. "—Jackson Tucker?"

"Well, not a friend, exactly. They knew each other, of course, and played together. But he wasn't one of Juky's close friends on the team. Still and all, poor Tuck's death really upset Juky. He was there when it happened, and tried to perform CPR, but it didn't help. It was such a shock to all the boys. You know how it is when you're young—you never think death will touch you. But you don't think Tuck's death had anything to do with Juky's, do you? Tuck wasn't murdered, you know."

"I know. But we always have to examine any coincidences. Two deaths within a year on one high school basketball team is pretty long odds, you have to admit."

I thanked her for the information, and Mrs. Shielding, too, in an attempt to get on her good side.

As we stood at the door, Mrs. Kay asked, "Do you have children, Mrs. Caliban?"

"Three."

"Then maybe you can understand. I'm waiting to hear that he didn't suffer, but I know I probably won't ever know for sure. I want to believe that it was so fast, he didn't even have time to be surprised, much less frightened. I pray to the Lord every day that he didn't die in fear."

I nodded.

"Oh, I almost forgot, you'd better take his notebook." She handed it to me.

I beat Mrs. Shielding to the punch.

"Well, actually, Mrs. Kay, we need to give it to the police. But I'll make a photocopy before I take it down to the I.B."

I didn't want to admit that I already had.

Four

I can't say that I was welcomed with open arms at the Homicide Squad office of the Investigations Bureau, and me a Joan Q. Public type of gal, just trying to do my goddam duty. It was my luck to run into my favorite member of the Criminalistics Squad on my way in. Actually, it was more than a run-in; I smashed him in the face with the door, and when he howled I tromped on his foot.

"*You!*" he sputtered.

I think it's safe to tell potential clients that I have a reputation with the local police.

"Good morning, Fricke," I said. "Sorry about the door. How come it always sticks like that? You guys take money out of maintenance and put it into vice again?"

"Lissen, Caliban, I was having one hell of a day even before you fractured my skull and broke my foot. I don't want it should get no worse. One crack outta you and I'll have you up on a 245."

I shrugged. "Okay by me. I'd love to see the judge's face when you identify the deadly weapon."

He worked his chewing gum even faster than usual, but settled for giving me a look. He executed an abrupt about-face, and was in mid-stalk when I stopped him.

"You wouldn't be working the Juky Kay case, would you, Fricke?"

Of course he would. That's the kind of luck I have.

"Lissen, Caliban, I don't want to see you within a hunnerd miles of that case—"

"So you don't want Juky's notebook, is that what you're saying?" I held it out in front of me, and he snatched it. That's why you always photocopy first; you can never trust a cop's good manners.

"How do *you* know it's Juky's notebook?"

"His mother told me it was."

"And how come his mother didn't tell us nothing about it?"

"She didn't know about it. I found it in a sofa she sent to Goodwill."

He glared at me. "I ain't gonna ask how you come to be snooping around in Mrs. Kay's sofa at Goodwill, 'cause I don't wanna know."

That was okay. I wasn't about to tell him.

"But if I hear you been pestering that poor lady—"

"I haven't been pestering her. She has asked me to look into her son's death, for your information."

"Well, for your information, I'd be tickled pink to run you in for practicing without a license."

"Did I say she was paying me? Any concerned citizen has a right to investigate anything."

"Yeah, just like I got a right to re-investigate what happened to the second gun witnesses heard the day you and that retarded kid had that little encounter with Prescott in the alley behind Len's Lounge. And when I find out, you can kiss that little private investigator scheme of yours good-bye. You'll get licensed over my dead body!"

"You already know what I think about that." Retarded kid, hell. I refrained from saying it takes one to know one. That was beneath my dignity—and Leon's.

Well, I never thought detective work would be easy. But I wouldn't want to give you the impression that my face wasn't welcome anywhere between Central Parkway and the river. My next stop was at a place where I was treated with the respect due to a regular customer.

The Public Library of Cincinnati and Hamilton County (found in your phone book under "public," not "library," "Cincinnati," or "Hamilton County," for those of you who are still looking for it) is housed in a spiffy new building a few blocks off Fountain Square. It prides itself on its state-of-the-art computer and security systems, microform equipment, and audiovisual department; its educational programs and exhibit space; its rare book archives. Its shelving system is something else again, but luckily I didn't have to deal with that today.

No, I only had to wrestle with the damn microfilm readers. That meant finding a machine that worked, finding a microfilm, threading it and hoping the end stayed on the reel, checking to make sure the thing hadn't been rewound backward, and watching tiny print go in and out of focus. If I found something I wanted, I would wish I'd remembered to bring a roll of dimes, plead for change at the cashier's counter, feed money into the machine, pray that the paper didn't jam, and extricate a negative copy too blurry to read. If this is the wave of the future, it can wave without me.

I'm always ambitious at the beginning, before my eyes give out, which takes about ten minutes. So I'd pulled maybe six reels apiece of the *Enquirer* and *Post*. I started with the previous season, when the Robertson Rattlers had made it to the regional semifinals. Don't ask me what I was looking for; I didn't know. But clearly, Tucker and Kay were the men to watch. Sometimes Tucker led the team scoring, sometimes Kay did, but nobody else came close. They had their off nights, which accounted for three losses before the regional tournament. I noticed that the lineup changed—sometimes a name would disappear for a while and then reappear—but I didn't know what that meant. The coach was still experimenting? Punishing a goof-off and rewarding a hard worker? Giving somebody playing time in an easy game? Scholastic problems? Injuries? I don't know if you've ever tried to read high school sports coverage in your local newspaper, but thorough it ain't.

I skipped ahead to May 27, when Jackson Tucker, Jr., checked out of the lineup permanently. I know everybody kept saying he'd died a natural death, but I was still suspicious. I can't help being suspicious; I'm a mother.

Jackson "Tuck" Tucker had collapsed in the gym at 4:35 P.M. during a team practice. Even though he was graduating, he had continued to practice with the team—to "keep in shape," he said, and in preparation for some upcoming international all-star game. By 4:37, he was in terrible shape, by all accounts, and Julius "Juky" Kay was attempting to resuscitate him. By the time the paramedics arrived, he was dead.

My guess is, the autopsy started before the body was cold; nobody likes to have a dead eighteen-year-old basketball star on their hands and no explanation. Even the first accounts, though, noted that Tucker's mother had died at age thirty-two of a heart attack. The coroner confirmed that the autopsy showed advanced atherosclerosis. I remembered how the press went into high gear on this heart disease business, dragging out anatomical models and diagrams and shit, interviewing every expert they could get their cameras and microphones on. Hysterical mothers were hauling their kids to the doctor for blood pressure checks, and scrutinizing the family tree to figure out if Aunt Millie really died of a heart attack instead of a broken heart. It wasn't such a bad idea, really, when you consider that some of those kids really *could* have been walking around with undiagnosed heart disease. Let's face it: when I was in the full flush of motherhood, I was worried about measles and tonsillitis, not heart disease. In those innocent days, we thought only old geezers had that.

Still, there's a big difference between eighteen and thirty-two.

From the picture of Tucker, he didn't look too bright. And the kinds of things people said about him made you think he wasn't all that popular, either, because they were all too trite. His father seemed pretty broken up, but managed to make a statement to the effect that Tuck had gone the way he would have wanted to go. Mr. Tucker, a college All-American who had played football for Notre Dame, was sure about that. Me, I want it on the record now that I do *not* want to die hot and sweaty on a gym floor, surrounded by the smell of gym socks and sneakers.

I skipped ahead to Juky's death. The first article appeared in the *Post*, on the morning of December 21. Apparently, Juky had been missing for four days by that time, but we'd been hit with an early snowstorm, and that had evidently slowed the search, if there had been a search. When two-year-olds disappear, the police search the area; but a seventeen-year-old? Mostly they canvas the local motels and teenage hangouts, and talk to the kid's friends.

Juky's body was found along the banks of the Mill Creek, which runs under the viaduct connecting Northside and Clifton. In case you think it sounds like one of those charming park areas with a jogging trail and a bike path, allow me to enlighten you. The only folks who frequent the banks of the Mill Creek are members of the Army Corps of Engineers, who like to move dirt around with heavy equipment. Some people like to think that the city sometimes sends inspectors down there to analyze the water in an attempt to guard the public health against what the Procter & Gamble plant is putting out upstream, but these tend to be the same people who rank EPA pronouncements right up there with the Word of God; they never think to ask why nobody employed by the Cincinnati EPA drinks Cincinnati water. All in all, I guess it was pure luck that Juky's body was found at all. He'd been shot in the chest twice. He was fully dressed except for his shoes: they were missing.

Well, the press had a field day, interviewing everybody who ever knew Juky, and this time the comments had a more sincere ring to them. I copied down the names of some of the people they talked to, who included not only LaTania Talbot and the team members and coach, but Reverend Cain and some of Juky's teachers. They all said about what you'd expect: Juky was a hell of a kid, and nobody could imagine any reason why anybody would want to murder him.

My eyes were getting bleary, and I got tired of reading that the police hadn't made any progress, so I skipped ahead a few weeks. Actually, I mashed the button so hard that when the tape stopped, I was already in early February, but since I'd landed in the middle of sports in a Saturday paper, I looked for anything on the Rattlers. Sure enough, they'd made the headlines for a big win over Forest Park, 65–63. The writer, a guy named Maury Schwab, was calling them a Cinderella team that had overcome numerous setbacks to achieve a surprising win-loss record of 12–3. Former center, now forward, Cal Sepeta had led the team in scoring, followed by forward Sky Skuyler, center Reggie Odum, and guard Corky Corcoran. Coach Biggs had drawn a technical in the second half. I scanned the box scores, and copied down all the names. I cranked it forward; hell, it was no fun reading the earlier ones now that I knew how they'd come out. The Rattlers won their next game, led by Sky Skuyler this time, then dropped a close game to Western Hills. Center Reggie Odum and guard Corky Corcoran led the team in scoring in that loss, though Corky had drawn a technical, and so had Coach Biggs. Forward Sky Skuyler was reported out with an injury, replaced by a kid name of Shellenstein, and guard Butch Frisby was benched with a twisted ankle in the first half. That brought me up to date. The Rattlers had a 13–4 record.

I cranked the thing backward and read about the four games I'd missed. By now I had a list of the starters: guards Corky Corcoran and Butch Frisby, forwards Cal Sepeta—Juky's replacement—and Scottie "Sky" Skuyler, and center Reggie Odum, who'd taken over when Cal was switched to Juky's position. There was some variation, but the patterns were pretty obvious. Apart from the scoring, it was evident that Biggs and Corcoran both had tempers; you don't usually see that many technicals, especially in a high school game where everybody's supposed to be promoting sportsmanship. These kids played aggressively, too, from what I could gather, and seemed to be in foul trouble every game. Was any of these guys as violent off the court as on? Would he be willing to commit the ultimate foul in a one-on-one situation?

• • •

Cat, I said to myself when I'd rewound my last micro-film and tucked it away in its stiff little cardboard coffin, you need a drink.

Kevin worked at Arnold's on Eighth Street, which prided itself on being the longest continuously operating bar in Cincinnati. It boasted a mixed clientele that in any other setting would have been highly volatile—artsy types, old-timers from the neighborhood, university folks, yuppies, and City Council members. When you walked in, the bar was right there on your left, so even if you wanted a booth or a table, you got to cruise the length of the bar and see who was there. Holding up one end of the bar when I arrived was none other than that legal eagle, counselor of the poor and defender of the down-and-out, Alice Rosenberg herself. She was four sheets to the wind, a highly unusual state for our Al. Kevin gave me some mysterious high sign and rolled his blue eyes at her, but you didn't need a neon sign to tell you she'd had a bad day. Her blunt-cut black hair was sticking out all over the place like she'd been trying to yank it out by the roots. Usually, when she's had a bad day, she gets these delusions of grandeur and contemplates dumping Legal Aid and taking up what she calls "real law," which involves suing the shit out of everybody and their uncle.

"So then he says to me, he says, 'I'll thank you to remember who's employing who here.' So I says—"

" 'Sir, a man who knows the English language as imperfectly as you evidently do is not fit to blacken my boots, much less cast shadows on my client files.' " That was Kevin, putting in his two cents, as usual.

Al looked at him in an unfocused way, and hiccuped. "No, I said, 'I'll thank you to remember that you're not paying me a dime for my services. If you're not satisfied, fire me.' And you know what he said *then*?"

"Yes, honey, you told us already. Five times." Al's friend Christine was the only woman I knew who could wear horn-rimmed glasses and make them fashionable. Of course, she had a few other styles to choose from, but today it was the horn-rims, earpieces buried in her elaborate beaded braids, tight black skirt two inches above her knees. Didn't she feel the draft off Eighth Street every time somebody opened the door?

"Cat hasn't heard it, have you, Cat? So he says to me, he says, 'Oh, no, you don't get off *that* easy. I know my rights.' "

Christine patted her hand absentmindedly. Personally, I thought that Christine's fingernails, sharpened to a point and painted a shocking pink, should be kept away from Al's wrists when she was in one of these moods.

Kevin said, "Why don't you just send Mel over to break his kneecaps?"

"She only uses her powers in self-defense." Al shook her head sadly.

"She won't defend *you*?"

"Maybe if he came after me with a tire iron or something. As it is, she'll probably just tell me to work on his karma." Al started dropping tears in her beer, and I turned to the guy sitting next to me.

"How *about* those Muskies?"

It wasn't all that easy to work up a basketball conversation in Cincinnati these days. The eighties were proving to be as disappointing in sports as they were in politics, from my perspective. There was a time it would have been easier, when the University of Cincinnati Bearcats were national contenders, but lately the closest thing we had was the Xavier University Musketeers. I was testing the waters to see if it was worth working the conversation around to the Rattlers.

The guy next to me shrugged. "They drew an easy schedule. They're still pretty young. I look for them to fade at the finish. They might draw an NCAA bid, but if they make it past the first round, I'll be *real* surprised."

"Oh, George, don't be such a wet blanket," said the redhead sitting next to him. "They may be young, but they got a lot of talent, and a first-rate coaching staff."

"Nah, George is right," said the guy next to her. "Young

team like that, they make stupid mistakes. They been in foul trouble all season. They play aggressively, but they don't play smart, know what I mean? That's how you get injuries."

"Speaking of injuries—" I said.

"They don't have a bad record on injuries," said the red-head. "They've had, what, two starters out, and never in the same game. Parker can still play, if they put enough tape on him."

"Speaking of injuries—" I said.

"Nah, Tom's right," said George. "Thing is, when you don't have the experience, you can make mistakes that cost you more than points on the board. Gets worse at tournament time, 'cause the play gets rougher, so mistakes cost more."

I tuned them out and tuned in the conversation in my other ear. Al was saying she knew of four local law firms that would interview her tomorrow if she expressed any interest, and Christine was promising to do her hair for the interviews. Kevin was down at the other end of the bar, swapping secrets with the mayor, who, as I said before, is a real loser, but even losers drink at Arnold's.

"That kid, whatshisname, the center—you know who I mean, the Polack—"

"Wershevski."

"That's him. Now there's a perfect case in point."

"He's six-nine, for crissake. How many college centers you know who are that tall?"

"That's my point. He's tall, but he's skinny. Kid needs more meat on his bones. Tall's not the issue. Kid's got no court sense, and no muscle. He's going to go up for a rebound some day, take an elbow in the chest, and get decimated."

"Speaking-of-injuries-how-about-the-Robertson-Rattlers?"

Six astonished eyes swung to meet my gaze.

"We ain't talking injuries there, we're talking massacre," Tom finally said.

"You mean, you think somebody's responsible?"

"Now, I didn't say that." Actually, he did, but if you're looking for precision in the use of the English language, you'd better pass up sports as a topic of conversation.

"Hell, *I* think the coach is responsible," said George.

"You think the coach shot his own star player?" asked the redhead.

"No, Marlene, I don't mean *that*." He gave her one of those exasperated looks men give women when women misunderstand them because men aren't making themselves clear. You know the kind I mean. "It's that other kid that died—whatshisname—the white guy."

"Tucker."

"Right, him."

"But he had heart disease. The coach couldn't have done anything about that. It said so in the paper."

"Well, you don't think the local press is gonna make a local coach look negligent, do you?" George asked. "Trouble is, the coaches drive these kids too hard. It was post-season, for crissake. The kid was just practicing with the team to keep in shape. He had a scholarship to play at Marquette."

"Well, I *still* say that heart disease is heart disease, and if he hadn't died then he would have died when he started up again in the fall."

"What about the murder?" I asked.

"Drugs," said Tom darkly.

"Oh, come off it," Marlene said. "The kid was an officer in some fellowship of Christian athletes."

"Doesn't matter. I still say it was drugs. Maybe it was his first time, maybe not. These kids, they get to be neighborhood heroes, you know? Everybody offering them things, even giving them fancy presents—all under the table, of course. They got more money than they know what to do with. What've they got to spend it on, I ask you? They want an expensive pair of sneakers, they go down to the local shoe store, and bingo! Just like in that movie with the red slippers—"

"The Red Shoes?" George scowled in his concentration.

"No, he means *The Wizard of Oz*," said Marlene.

"Yeah, that one. Poof! New sneakers. So they got all this money, and nothing to spend it on except the only thing nobody's giving away."

"Yeah," I said. "Except he didn't die of an overdose. Somebody plugged him."

Speaking of overdoses, when I finally pried Al off her barstool and took her home, the sun was long gone. Moses was sitting on the stairs in the hall, surrounded by fur people.

"You-all have any idea what time it is?" He frowned at us.

"H-h-howdy Doody time?" said Al, and shattered my eardrum with a shriek of laughter.

What he wanted me to say was that it was two hours past the kitties' suppertime. He wanted me to feel guilty and act contrite. He wanted the kitties to stare at me accusingly: another mother gone bad.

Goddam, it's hard to look offended when you're licking salmon off your whiskers.

Five

Oscar Robertson Senior High School featured a respectable two-story brick main building, with modern appendages and satellites in a loose orbit around it. These additions ranged from cinder-block wings to metal trailers that looked like they could take off in the middle of the night. The most solidly built structure apart from the main building was the gym, home of the Robertson Rattlers. It was built out of white limestone. A local artist of some imagination and less talent had painted a giant rattlesnake, coiled around the building, with his rattle on the south side and his head, complete with enormous fangs dripping blood, on the north side. He looked kind of like a cobra to me, but when you walked around to the other side and reached his tail, you could see he was a rattler. It occurred to me to wonder if they'd picked the mascot and the school colors at the same time. Maybe you've seen a blue-and-white rattlesnake in *your* neck of the woods, but I never have.

I was dressed in corduroy jeans, a pullover, boots, and a down vest. My object was not to be mistaken for somebody's mother, much less somebody's grandmother, and to inspire confidence with my hip, youthful air. I'd left my earmuffs at home. You know how insensitive the young are to cold.

In fact, most of the kids I saw outside the gym were wearing shorts and T-shirts and carrying athletic equipment. I didn't think my disguise was working too well, because whenever they saw me, they went all silent and sly-looking. I'd sat in my car long enough to have figured out which building was the gym, since I'd already decided to act like I knew what I was doing. I strolled in. My plan was to sit inconspicuously in the bleachers and wait for practice to end. I can only say that bleachers are not designed to be mounted inconspicuously by short-legged sixty-year-old women. For one thing, they make a hell of a racket. By the time I'd settled in, ears burning, I'd caused two errors and a missed free throw on the court, and drawn every eye in the joint.

Every mother in America who's seen three kids through high school knows something about sports. My son Jason, now a business executive, had put in one year as a third-string football player. My oldest daughter, Sharon, now a stockbroker, had been a cheerleader for the longest year of my life. My youngest, Franny, who has devoted the last ten years of her life to moving from college to college in search of the perfect major, had played, at various times, basketball, softball, volleyball, and bassoon, and run track. Name me a sport, I know the basics.

Since the boys were running plays against other team members, it was hard to tell who was who, unless the coach yelled at them. He did a lot of this, though. He was a barrel-chested, muscular guy who stood a head shorter than the two shortest players on the floor and looked ridiculous in gym shorts. He had a military haircut, which I thought was a bad idea because he was balding. Not that I think bald men are unattractive, but when what little hair you have is only a half inch long and standing straight up, it makes for an odd effect.

After a while, I thought I had a pretty good idea who was who. The tallest of the black kids on the floor must have been Reggie Odum, the center, a skinny kid with jug ears—too skinny for a center, really. The tall black kid with the wide, flat forehead was former center, now forward, Cal Sepeta; he was heavier than Odum, more muscular but not as tall, a good perimeter shooter, I noticed. Sky Skuyler, the other forward, was even more muscular, about the same height as Sepeta, with prominent cheekbones and quick hands. The short redheaded guard I had figured for Corky Corcoran; his temper tipped me off. The other guard, Butch Frisby, was a little taller than Corcoran, and quick, with dark skin, lots of muscles, and big hands. All in all, high school players had changed a lot since my kids were younger. Or maybe it's one of those evolutionary things, you know? The way the human race keeps getting taller over time? These were *big* kids. Maybe they didn't do homework any more; they just hung out in the weight room all night.

I wasn't the only one in the stands, though I was probably the oldest one. Maybe a dozen kids were watching practice, sometimes calling out to the players, mostly talking to each other. Some of them were in gym clothes, and some appeared to be in civvies, but it's hard to tell these days. Off by himself, a stocky short guy sprawled, about my size, with black curly hair and glasses, wearing cords and a loosely tucked shirt with a clip-on tie dangling off one side of the collar.

After a while I noticed a gradual increase in the number of tall, healthy-looking girls around me. Pretty soon they were joined by a woman with short brown hair and a whistle around her neck. When Biggs called it quits, they took the floor. I watched them shoot baskets for a few minutes before I went looking for Biggs. I love this part of practice anyway—balls popping up like lottery numbers, making graceful arcs and sliding through the net or caroming off the rim. That's one thing about being an unpaid employee: your time is your own.

Now I had to break down and ask for help. After all, I didn't want to end up in the boys' locker room by mistake. I asked the guy who appeared to be the team trainer, a short but muscular kid with a fake tan and contact lenses that made him blink.

The coach was on the phone as I stood at the door, hesitating. His office looked like a coach's office—that is, like one of those wandering garbage barges had found its home here. The walls were covered with photographs, some framed, some just tacked up. Boxes stacked on top of each other threatened to topple over onto an ancient coffee machine. Trophies graced unlikely corners. The typewriter, buried under piles of purple dittos alternated with old *Sports Illustrated*s, hummed in unison with the fluorescent light, from which hung the remains of some long-dead bouquet of balloons. Balls of dirty socks cozied up to dust bunnies under the desk. Athletic shoes of various sizes stood guard over heaps of unopened mail. Basketballs, some more inflated than others, were scattered around the room like antimacassars. On the back of the doorknob hung a jock strap and a pair of shoelaces.

"Aw, give the kid a break, Marge," he was saying into the phone. "He had practice every night last week. How was he supposed to read this whole book, what was it? *Hard Times*, yeah, this *Hard Times* book—a whole novel—in one week and practice every night?"

He listened.

"Now, Marge, don't give me that, now. You know I'm the first one to defend academics. But lighten up! The kid's a senior, for crissake! This is his last high school season. He's gonna remember this year for the rest of his life. How important is it *really* that he's read this, uh, *Hard Times* book? He read the Cliffs Notes, he knows what the book's about. And I don't agree with you there. I know this kid. He did not think it was cheating to read the damn Cliffs Notes."

He listened again.

"Okay, look, how about we compromise? Let him take the exam again. That's all I'm asking. He can even read the book, if you insist, though it'd be better if you could find a shorter one by this guy Dickens for him to read."

He listened again.

"Okay, listen. I'm not going to discuss this with you anymore, Marge. We'll let Dave decide. I'm gonna talk to Dave tonight, and see if we can't get this whole thing resolved."

He hung up.

"Can I help you?" It was brusque, on the verge of being impolite, but not quite there. He didn't know if I was somebody's mother or not.

"Coach Biggs, I'm Catherine Caliban. Do you have a minute? It's about Juky Kay."

He eyed me suspiciously.

"Mrs. Caliban, I'm approaching the end of the season, two days away from a very tough game with Taft, I've lost one starter and I'm about to lose another one because of some goddam novel a hundred years old, I've got a forward with weak ankles, and a guard coming down with the flu. I'm a very busy man, and—"

"Good. I knew you'd help." I plunked my butt down in a chair. Actually, I was sitting on some file folders, which was pretty uncomfortable, but there weren't that many options.

"Mrs. Caliban—"

"Mrs. Kay speaks very highly of you. She says you've been a real help to her since Juky died."

"Yeah, well, I loved that kid. God, what a natural talent that kid had! He could've been one of the great ones." His eyes scanned his walls, as if searching for great ones there. "He had ability *and* brains. You don't see that too often, especially if you're a high school coach. God, what a waste! What a goddam waste."

"Mrs. Kay asked me to look into Juky's murder."

"You?"

Maybe I *would* tell him about the hair. He looked especially ridiculous wearing an expression of astonishment.

"What are you, some kind of social worker?"

"No, I'm a detective."

"Let me see your license."

"I'm not licensed yet. The paperwork hasn't gone through." It doesn't sound quite as phony as "the check is in the mail," but close. "I'm doing this as a favor to Mrs. Kay."

He'd already started shaking his head.

"Oh, no. Listen, I'm sorry, lady. I don't want to offend you, but the only people who have any business looking into Juky's murder are the cops, and that's just what they're doing. Marion's a nice lady, and I respect her reli-

gion, I do, but it makes her do some funny things sometimes, and I'm not gonna get involved. She calls me, I'll
tell her that."

He was the second person who thought that the Lord
had something to do my sleuthing. I ask you, do I look
like an angel of the Lord to you?

"I'm not asking for your involvement, Mr. Biggs. I'm
just asking you to answer a few questions."

"Lady, I already answered a few questions and a few
more than that, and if you can talk somebody down at the
Cincinnati PD into showing you their report, you will have
the benefit of everything I know on the subject of Juky
Kay's death. Meanwhile, you are wasting my time and
yours."

He walked out of the office. The coach had a strong defense, accent on the *de*. But impenetrable?

I retreated to the back court.

When Cal Sepeta emerged with Sky Skuyler, Butch
Frisby, and Reggie Odum, I was waiting for them in the
parking lot. I knew Cal had a car, because they were riding
in it the night Juky died.

"Cal Sepeta?"

"That's me."

"And Butch, Sky, and Reggie, that right?"

"Right on."

"I'm Cat Caliban. I'd like to talk to you boys about
Juky Kay. I've been asked by Mrs. Kay to investigate his
murder."

"You come to the wrong place, then. 'Cause we done
already give our statements to the police."

"Yeah, and Coach say we don't have to talk to you."

"Reggie, you lie. What you tell her that for? What he
said was, our ass be in hot water if we so much as give her
the time of day."

"Why's the coach afraid to let you talk to me?"

"He ain't afraid. It ain't about afraid. It's about winning
the championship." Cal was marginally more polite than

the others. Good religious training always shows, one way or another.

"Yeah, we be concentratin' on that state title." Butch favored me with a wide grin.

"Boy, you ain't never concentrated on nothin' in your life. Ain't got the brains, so how can you be concentratin'?"

"Don't need brains, Reggie, just my smooth, soft touch." He mimicked making a shot.

"Wouldn't you boys like to help solve Juky's murder?"

"Sure we would, lady. But Coach say the police going to do that." This was Sky's first contribution to the conversation, and it seemed more forceful than it needed to be.

"They don't seem to be having much luck."

"Look, lady, we feel bad about Juky, real bad," Cal said earnestly. "Me and Butch, we was with him the night he disappeared. But we just don't know nothin' about that part. He was okay when we saw him. Wasn't nothin' special about that night, like the cops keep askin' us. It was just a regular ol' night, like any other Friday night. We don't know nothin', we ain't seen nothin', we don't know nobody who'd want to hurt Juky Kay."

"Come on, Cal." Butch was pulling on his arm.

"Hey, guys, wait up." It was the team trainer.

"I *told* you we had to split, man." Butch grumbled under his breath.

"Come on, Eddie. We leavin'," Cal shouted at him.

Eddie barely made it into the Jeep before it shot off.

Now where does a high school senior from Northside get enough money to buy a goddam Jeep Cherokee?

Six

Kevin always said that having a retired police officer on the premises would come in handy, and he was right. Popular as I was in certain quarters downtown, it was damn tough to get the information I needed about the Juky Kay case. Reading the papers told me that there was no official progress to report, but that didn't mean there was no progress, just nothing the cops were willing to share with the general public, including me.

Randy Waltrip from Criminalistics stopped in at the Catatonia Arms on his way home from work, at Moses's request. He was an impeccably dressed, light-skinned, slender guy in a full-length camel coat. He didn't look like anybody on "Hill Street Blues."

"These kids have it easy coming up," Moses said. "Twenty years ago, a black cop could expect to spend his career in one of two places: walking the beat in black neighborhoods, or sitting on his ass in Juvie."

"Yeah, that's why we come whenever one of y'all call us," said Randy, " 'cause we so grateful to our elders for putting us where we are today." He popped the top off his beer and turned his attention to me. "So—Moses says you're looking into the Juky Kay murder."

"Unofficially, of course."

"Hey—do I look official?" He leaned back and propped his feet on the coffee table, ankles crossed. "Far as I'm concerned, anybody want to take a crack at it, they're welcome. So what you want to know?"

"What've you got?"

"A whole mess of nothing that adds up."

"Tell me about the night he died—or, rather, the night he was last seen by anybody who's admitting anything."

"It's like his mother says: he went out with Cal Sepeta

and Butch Frisby. They thought he seemed a little quiet, distracted, but otherwise it was a normal night for them. They ended up at Tower Hamburgers about eleven, and he left about a half hour later."

"What did he say when he left?"

"He said, 'I got to go.' " Randy shrugged. "They asked if he didn't want to rent a video and watch it over at Butch's, but he just said no, he had to go. No explanation. They assumed he was expected at home."

"But he *did* look at his watch first?"

"That's what they say. Then he walked out the door and that's all we know."

"Where was everybody else that night? I mean, the people who you'd consider as suspects?"

He fished a spiral-bound notebook out of his jacket pocket and flipped it open, running his eyes down the page.

"His mother was home, making pies for a church sale." Naturally, I hadn't even considered her. Like most mothers, I'd wanted to murder my teenagers more times than I could count, but I hadn't done it. "I'll skip the student council officers, and the officers of the Association of Christian Athletes, for now, and give you the basketball team, okay? Corcoran—the other guard—took his girlfriend ice skating in Eden Park and then to a late movie that let out near midnight. She confirms that she didn't leave him until one, so you can use your imagination to guess what they were doing between midnight and one."

"Must've been a cold night to be doing it in a car."

"Yeah, well, your circulation's better at that age. Sky Skuyler says he wasn't feeling well, and stayed home and watched television. His father was at some medical meeting and banquet, so we didn't get a real confirmation from him; parents divorced, so the mother's not around—"

"Is that the Dr. Skuyler who has an office up on Hamilton?"

"That's the one—a GP. Anyway, Corcoran and Frisby

saw Skuyler at Tower Hamburgers on Saturday night, and he told *them* he hadn't been feeling well on Friday night."

Shit, if I'd hung out at Tower Hamburgers as much as these kids did, I wouldn't have felt too terrific myself. Thing was, their moms—maybe even their dads—were probably cooking them healthy, nutritious meals at dinnertime, and by midnight they had a load of grease in their bellies that could lubricate an armored tank division.

"Coach Biggs was home watching basketball on ESPN. He's also divorced, so no confirmation there. We could ask him for a play-by-play, but he could've taped something and watched it later, if he didn't read about it. The girlfriend, Talbot, was at a wedding with her family, so we've got lots of witnesses there."

"Did you talk to Juky's minister?"

"Yeah, we talked to him. He spent Friday night visiting members of his congregation—some at the hospital, some at home. His wife confirms that he got home at eleven, and then the two of them went up to the Big Boy for ice cream."

"In *December*?"

"Hey, I just write 'em down, I don't make 'em up. You start trying to apply logic to the things people do, you may as well pick you another profession, right, Mo?"

"You got that right, brother."

"What about Juky's father? Where is he?"

Randy shook his head. "Dead. Helicopter pilot in Viet Nam."

"Okay, so who else is there? Teachers? Friends outside of basketball and church? Any unsavory characters in his life?"

"Recruiters, but there weren't any in town, far's we could make out. Now, maybe Judd Heathcote plugged him 'cause he signed with Bobby Knight, but we ain't exactly had a run of that kind of thing, and ain't nobody seen Judd snooping around the locker room, waiting for his opportunity. And Juky didn't even hang out at a gym, so he didn't run into that crowd."

I didn't know what he meant. I had once had a brief membership in a health club, and the only unsavory people I ever met there were the ones who locked me in a room until I bought the damn membership.

"He means gamblers, pimps, prostitutes, and pushers," Moses supplied.

"Oh," I said. "What about the drug angle?"

Randy shrugged. "Nobody believes that Juky was involved with drugs."

"Could he have witnessed a drug deal?"

"Sure, anything's possible, especially in that neighborhood. The last time anybody saw Juky, he was leaving Tower Hamburgers, which has quite a reputation as a distribution center."

"It *does*? *Tower Hamburgers*?" Know your neighborhood.

He nodded.

"But what happened to Juky's shoes?" Moses asked. "If you dealing drugs, and you got you a dead pigeon on your hands, you don't stop to steal the shoes."

"That may depend on whether the body's wearing Jordans," Randy responded. "Times've changed, man."

"Wearing what?" I was so confused.

They looked at me as if I were a debutante refereeing the Final Four. Even Winnie had raised her head on that one.

"Jordans. Air Jordans. It's a new basketball shoe being test marketed by Nike."

"Oh, you mean like Reeboks." I didn't want them to think I was totally clueless, as my daughter would say.

"Well, not really. Reebok makes mostly running shoes, and they're hotter with women than men. Jordans are red and black—Bulls colors—and they're only available in a few cities. That makes 'em in demand and hard to come by. Juky had a pair, was wearing them that night."

"So you think somebody might have stolen them?"

Randy nodded grimly. "Unfortunately, kids have been known to kill for them."

Seven

I never did get a handle on this sneaker business. I mean, was it just hype, or was this shoe the Michelin of sneakers? Both Moses and Randy thought it was more hype than anything else, but they said that the Jordan ad campaign was dynamite.

Randy didn't have much else to tell me. The postmortem on Juky hadn't found any signs of drugs, much less drug addiction, and the body was pretty well preserved because of the cold. When I asked about Jackson Tucker's death, Randy said the same thing everybody else said: heart attack, natural causes. Atherosclerosis ran in the family on his mother's side.

I grabbed Mel in between her martial arts conference and her next kiln firing, and showed her the pages I'd copied from Juky's notebook, calling her attention to the section in the back.

"Yeah, I could see where parts of it could be related to basketball, Cat, but it doesn't really add up."

"How come?"

"Well, lookit. The first number here: 606. What is it? It's not somebody's weight. Could be their height, if you got a Magic Johnson on the team."

I made a note to myself to check Juky's height and weight.

"It's not a bench press number, or a dead lifting weight. It could be a running time, but for what? A mile? Could be. And if we look down the page, we see that the number in this column goes up, not down, so running time doesn't seem right." She frowned at it and tapped it with a clay-encrusted fingernail. "Maybe it's a date: June 6. That would make sense, since the numbers keep going up but—yep, I was right—the last two don't rise higher than thirty-one when the first one changes. So, a date somebody went out of their way to keep from looking like a date. No wait, here's a 295 on down the line.

"But then what? 1919. Looks like a year. Is that what it is? Again, it's easier to say what it *can't* be than what it is. Does it go with 606—as in, June 6, 1919? It's not a weight or shooting percentage, probably not a time, doesn't look like a pulse rate. So what the hell *is* it? And what about the next four numbers: 72, 180, 380, 650? Seventy-two *could* be a shooting percentage, or even a career high. It could also be a final score. Three-eighty could be a bench press figure. Six-fifty could be a time on the mile, or a height—six-five, but only if 606 isn't a height. But the next figure, 319, isn't a bench press because it's not a multiple of ten, and it's not a mile time, either. It could be a date, except it's not lined up at the margin under these other numbers, like 606, that *do* seem to be dates. Is it related to 1919?

"See what I mean, Cat? I'm only guessing the way I'm guessing because the kid's a basketball player. But you said he was also committed to his church. For all we know, they could be Bible verses or hymn numbers. Or anything else, for that matter. The secret code of an underground organization of Christian athletes. A coded list of drug deals."

"So do you think I'm wasting my time with this notebook?"

"Did I say that?"

"Okay, I'm wasting *your* time with this notebook."

"I didn't say that, either. Look at it this way, Cat. Why would a seventeen-year-old kid go out of his way to write something nobody could read but him? If you asked me that about an average seventeen-year-old boy, I'd say he was living in some kind of spy fantasy. But *this* one went out and got himself killed. Whatever that was, it was no fantasy."

• • •

Both Moses and Randy said that if I wanted to find out anything about high school basketball in general, and the Rattlers in particular, I should go see the local guru, who turned out to be the same Maury Schwab whose articles I'd read in the *Post*. Which was why I was cruising Court Street, looking for a place to park the beige bomber. Since I wasn't making any money off this case, and since I'd just as soon have had my car stolen as not, I wasn't about to pay parking garage prices.

Today was market day, so parking wasn't going to come easy. I was circling the block for the third time when a shrill whistle attracted my attention to a ruckus up ahead. About a block up on my right was an open parking place. Lying sprawled in the middle of it, cocooned in what appeared to be a voluminous cloak, was a figure, probably female, arms and legs spread, surrounded by a barricade of bulging shopping bags and groaning so loudly that I could hear her from my car. In front of her, a man was waving traffic past.

"Just go on by, y'all. Just go on by."

"They're saving it for you." The snarl in my ear made me jump. Next to my car stood a man wearing camouflage and a flak jacket, addressing me out of the corner of his mouth as he studied a building across the street.

I pulled up, and the traffic-directing man waved me into the space as the woman—it *was* a woman—scrambled to collect herself and her shopping bags.

"Miz Cat." Curtis grinned at me. "How you been keepin'?"

"Pretty good, Curtis. Thanks for the help. How you been?"

"The Lord taketh away, and the Lord *giveth*! Bless His holy name!" This from the cloaked woman in a voice that probably woke up judges hearing cases on the third floor of the courthouse.

"Amen, Alma, honey, you done real good." Trish was helping Alma rearrange herself. "Hey, there, Cat. Long time, no see."

Didn't I mention that I had a few fans within the city limits? It's nice to have friends in low places.

"Hey, you see in the paper where Betty's daughter bought one of them big apartment houses on Twelfth Street, and she's gonna fix it up real nice and turn it into a residence for street people?" Trish asked. All my rescuers were members of Street People United, so they were obviously elated by the news.

"Yeah, and she's divorcing that low-life she was married to, so he can't get none of Betty's money." Curtis nodded in satisfaction.

"I *still* say, if it was me, I'd wait until he wasn't looking, and sneak up behind him with my blade, and—" The long-haired man in camouflage thrust a clenched hand forward so violently that we all backed up a step. "Like we did it in Nam."

"Steel, will you put that thing away before somebody gets hurt?" Trish had dropped her cigarette.

"It's just my hand," he said.

"That's what I mean. Put it away."

"So, how's the detective business, Cat? Caught any dangerous criminals lately? Hey, I bet you on a case right now!" Curtis's eyes lit up. He and the others cherished fond memories of my last case. They ate off the victims' memorial service for months.

"As a matter of fact, I'm looking into the Juky Kay murder."

"Oooh-ee, that was somethin' *else*, that was." Curtis shook his head sadly.

"You sure as shit live in a rough neighborhood, girl." Trish said this with a straight face.

"Say . . ." I said slyly. "You guys ever hear of Air Jordans?"

"Why? You know somebody want to *give* some *away*?" Curtis narrowed his eyes at me. "You surely do hang with some mighty peculiar folks, Cat."

If you want to find out about the latest fashions, you

don't need to go all the way to the Garment District. Your local street people know everything there is to know.

"No, but what I want to know is, can you buy them on the black market?"

"Hot Jordans? Sure. Was a guy I know—white dude— told me he got hisself a pair for a hunnerd dollars."

"Where?"

"Didn't say. I didn't see no point in axing him, 'cause where I'm going to get a hunnerd dollars?"

"Is that how much they *really* cost?" I asked, aghast.

"Not at the sto'. But you not axin' 'bout no sto'-bought Jordans, which is good 'cause you couldn't find 'em at the sto', nohow."

"You guys know anything about the Tower Hamburgers on Hamilton Avenue by the viaduct?"

"Shit, girl, that's way out of our territory," Trish said. "Used to be drugs there, though. Don't know if it's still true. Ain't heard nothing lately. But if you ask me, that Juky Kay kid wasn't no junkie. He mighta seen somethin' goin' down, and they took him out because of what he seen, but he wasn't no junkie."

"God in His wrath and righteousness will rise up and punish the iniquitous!" That was Alma, getting rolling again.

"That's right, Alma, honey." Trish tipped me a wink. "But Cat's gonna give Him a little help."

God, I wished people would quit comparing me to a damn angel. Made me feel like I ought to clean up my act.

As it turned out, I'd laid eyes on Maury Schwab before. He was the guy sitting by himself at the Rattlers practice, the one taking up three rows of bleachers with his five-foot-four frame.

He had this little cubicle, about half the size of the entry hall at the Catatonia Arms. It looked like a dump truck had backed up to the wall and let loose over the top—kind of like Coach Biggs's office, except that the collection was more eclectic. The space was dominated by a life-size cardboard cutout of Larry Bird. Stuck to the Birdman's arms, like pigeons on a statue of St. Francis, was an odd assortment of clip-on ties in a range of types and colors. I was contemplating this vision when I first heard Schwab's voice, so it was like hearing the voice of Oz the Great and Powerful before Toto pulled the curtain. Schwab was squashed in a corner, eyeing me over a computer monitor like a Munchkin behind the wheel of a Lincoln Continental.

"So, you're Caliban? Yeah, I saw you at the Rattler practice and wondered who you were. You didn't look like the usual crowd. Pull up a pew. Oops, not there, that's my lunch. No, wait, maybe it's yesterday's lunch. If it's yesterday's lunch, what the hell, you can sit on it. Just dump that crap on the floor. What can I do for you? You want to talk Juky Kay, right?"

"That's right." I took a breath and lost my opening.

"Hell of a kid. Hell of a talent, too. God, what a waste."

"That's what everybody says."

"Everybody's right, for a change. Decent, hardworking kid, smart as a whip. Great hands, incredible concentration, impeccable court sense. They ever catch the bastard who shot him, I'll withdraw my opposition to the death penalty. So, what else you want to know?"

"To tell you the truth, I don't know what I want to know. It seems pretty amazing to me that two members of a high school basketball team could die within a year—two of their best players at that. Does that seem odd to you?"

"Hell, yes, it's odd. If this was New York or Los Angeles or Chicago, then it might seem logical. But this is *Cincinnati*, for crissake. Still, it's hard to make any connection between Tucker's death and Juky's. Unless you think Tucker's old man went after Juky because Juky didn't save his son when he gave him CPR. But that's pretty far out. Knowing Old Man Tucker, I'd say it was more likely he didn't like the idea that a black boy gave mouth-to-mouth to his boy."

"Did the Tucker kid have problems with race?"

"The Tucker kid was an arrogant son of a bitch, but I don't think color was one of his hang-ups. The old man played football for Notre Dame, and you can bet he thought God was on his side. Thinks back fondly to the dawn of time when all the games that counted were between white Catholics and white Anglo-Saxon types. My people didn't play. Vaudeville, yes, but not football. Talk about tough competition!" He waggled heavy eyebrows at me in a Groucho Marx imitation. "Well, who knows what the old man thought the kid was going to do if he hit the NCAA, much less the NBA."

"There's a Jewish kid on the Rattlers now, isn't there?" I was practicing my interview skills, pretending like I was directing the conversation.

"Shellenstein. Yeah, poor bastard. He's not bad, but he doesn't exactly give me hope that the Chosen People were chosen for the NBA. Kid needs some breathing room, and that's not the Biggs style."

"Look, let me put it this way. Here's a team that's lost two starters within a year, and those guys aren't lost, they're *lost*, thrown out of the old game of life. Retired permanently from the lineup. Do you think there's something seriously wrong with the basketball program at Robertson?"

"Do I think there's something wrong with the basketball program at Robertson?" His chair creaked as he leaned back in it, the seat dipping perilously close to the floor. He studied the ceiling for a minute. "Hell, yes, I think there's something wrong with the basketball program at Robertson, I think there's something wrong with the athletic programs of seventy-five percent of the high schools I can think of, and I can tell you what it is in just one word: professionalization. Maybe you don't know what I'm talking about."

"Not really."

He nodded sadly. "Not really. You want to know why? Because the newspaper I work for doesn't want me to criticize the high school programs. I am not supposed to be negative. I am supposed to be dramatic and forceful and enthusiastic and upbeat. The public, according to my editor, does not want an exposé of high school sports because the public loves high school sports. The people who make money off of high school sports don't want an exposé because, in the long run, it might shut down their business. And my editor doesn't want an exposé because it would embarrass some of the pals he eats lunch with at the Cincinnati Club, because some of their kids would be implicated. That's why you don't know what I'm talking about."

"So what are you talking about? Go ahead—make my day. Educate me."

"Okay. Professionalization. That means a lot of jokers want to treat high school sports like college or professional sports. Let's ignore, for the sake of the present discussion, those people who believe that a distinction exists between college and professional sports; that's another argument. So, what've you got? You got coaches who are praying for a spot in the Big Ten doing some major recruiting for their high school players, with all the possibilities for buy-offs and corruption that recruiting at any level entails. You got school officials, some of them former coaches themselves, who want to put their school on the map any way they can, and it turns out that the easiest way, though probably not the cheapest way, is not to hire more teachers or buy more computers or outfit more science labs, but to put together a winning sports team. You got parents who want Junior to win an athletic scholarship and rise to national prominence and secure the cover of *Sports Illustrated* so they can pass it around the office. You got kids who've never been taught to think, much less to think that they can think, dreaming of fame and fortune in the NBA or the NFL. You got teachers who are overworked and underpaid and burned out, and they don't have the strength anymore to stand between Junior and academic eligibility, especially since all the heavy hitters are standing on Junior's side waving pom-poms and singing the school fight song. I think I mixed a metaphor in there. Did I mix a metaphor?"

"*Hard Times*," I muttered under my breath.

"Damn straight it's hard times. And last but not least you got people who will bet on any outcome from arthroscopic surgery on up, and people willing to take advantage of those people. I probably left a few out, but you get the picture."

"Sounds like a mess," I said glumly. To tell you the truth, it was damn disheartening to realize how many things could go wrong, and how many people could be involved. It was sort of like opening the door on "Mister Roger's Neighborhood" and finding yourself on "Dallas." "You didn't even mention drugs."

"Oh, yeah," he said. "They're in there, too. In the category of taking advantage of a bad situation. The kids are under a lot of pressure to perform, so either they're taking drugs to perform better, or drugs to keep them from caring how they perform, or both. And they're being supplied not just by street-corner pushers but by coaches, family doctors, parents, you name it."

"But you've never heard specific allegations of a drug problem on the Robertson team?"

"No, can't say that I have. Wouldn't surprise me, though. Nothing would surprise me."

That I could believe.

"No, I take that back. There *is* something that would surprise me."

"What's that?"

"If somebody proved, beyond a shadow of a doubt, that Juky Kay took drugs. Now that *would* surprise me."

He pitched a crumpled wad of paper at the wastebasket near the doorway across the room. It bounced off the rim and dropped into a heap of identical wads on the floor. Patrick Ewing was not losing any sleep over Dr. M.

Eight

By the time I left Maury Schwab's office, I felt as if I'd taken a charge from the *Sports Encyclopedia*. I had a hell of a lot of notes, but damned if I knew what they added up to. Gambling, dope, bribery, corruption: it was like somebody had pulled the plug on the Easter Bunny. My street pals had split for greener pastures—or whiter sidewalks, whatever. They were probably in line at St. Francis, waiting for the soup kitchen to open.

I must have been feeling light-headed at that, because I decided to run by the Rattler gym to see if practice was still going on. It was, but not for me. Unfortunately for him, Coach Biggs sent a boy to do a man's job.

"Excuse me, ma'am. Coach says you gotta leave. Sorry." It was the trainer again—Eddie, I think his name was. His canned tan looked more unhealthy the closer I studied it. The kid was built, no doubt about it, but he was still shorter than me, and lighter, so if it came to hand-to-hand combat, I figured I could sit on him. I'd learned from Mel that leverage is everything.

"The coach is welcome to come and tell me himself," I said evenly. No point in shooting the messenger.

"Well, he's pretty busy, with the practice and all." He blinked at me nervously—or maybe it was his contacts acting up again.

"I'm busy, too. I took the time to come see him. Seems like he could do me the same courtesy."

He looked at me doubtfully. "Well, I'll tell him."

Biggs turned around and glared at me when he received this report. I waved and smiled.

He got distracted by a bad pass from Butch that slipped through Corky's hands. Corky's expletive was nothing compared to the Coach's accumulated wrath. Poor Butch got what was coming to me. His face took on that mask-like, impenetrable look that kids wear when they're being raked over the coals on a coast-to-coast broadcast. Cal was on the bench with a bloody nose—head tilted back, towel over his face. I found myself wondering if Biggs had popped him one.

When Biggs was finished with Butch, he glanced in my direction, and sent the team to the showers. He headed for me with a scowl, but I stayed put. I knew that clambering over the bleachers would put a damper on his dramatic entrance.

"Mrs. Callahan—"

"Caliban."

"—maybe I didn't make myself clear when we had our little chat the other day. I don't want you around here, getting the boys all riled up."

"I wasn't doing any of the yelling. Was I?" I turned to one of the groups of kids sitting near me on the bench and appealed to them in mock innocence. They stared at their toes. I heard a suppressed giggle from somewhere behind me.

"I won't have it, Callahan."

"Aw, you know I don't care about the boys, Coach. I come to see you." I bit my tongue before it let loose with a comment about his shorts. "See, I've just been to see Maury Schwab, and he told me the most scandalous things about high school basketball. I'd really be interested in knowing your opinion."

His eyes narrowed, then closed. He sighed.

"Look, Callahan. Schwab's a guy with a bee in his bonnet. He don't want to be a sportswriter, not really. No, what he wants to be is an investigative reporter, only, he don't have nothing to investigate. So he makes up a lot. He's okay as long as he sticks to game coverage. But he wants to be noticed by some big outfit, like *USA Today* or ESPN, and he'll never get that unless he digs up some kind of dirt to spill. You can't go around believing everything everybody tells you. See, that's the thing. You don't know what you're talking about, but you go around asking questions and spreading rumors, and first thing you know my kids are going to be jumpy as fleas. I'm not standing for that."

"Don't you care who murdered Juky Kay?"

"Hell, yes, of course I care. But right now, what I care most about is getting *this* goddam team to the goddam playoffs, and I'll be goddammed if I'm going to let some female who thinks she's Mike Hammer get in my way. So from now on, Rattlers practices are closed to you. Got it?"

I made like I was studying him, making up my mind about something. That always drives them crazy—reminds them of their mothers, sizing them up when they were kids. He stomped off, spoiling his exit by missing the last step on the bleachers. He nearly flattened the poor trainer, who was trying to help him up.

The girls' team, which was congregated near the door, applauded as I approached.

"Don't mind him," a redhead commented. "He's a prick."

"Plus, he got some thing about females," a black girl said.

"He's a total dickhead," a blond girl agreed. "Hey, are you really a detective? That's so cool!"

"I'm unofficial," I said. "But I've been asked by Mrs. Kay to look into Juky's death."

"Wow!" This from another blond, by all appearances the twin of the first. "Do you get to, like, carry a gun and everything?"

"I've been known to." I didn't want to tell them I'd lost it during my first caper. I figured they needed a role model.

"Awesome!"

"Hey, you talk to LaTania yet?"

"Not yet. You think I should?"

"Well, if it was me, I go ask her why she been sick ever since Juky died."

"Aw, girl, you know she got mono. They done had the doctor there and everything."

"Well, I still go ask her. 'Bout that and other things, too, like they do on television. LaTania know Juky better than anybody."

"That's right, miss. She did."

"You won't get anywhere talking to those morons on the boy's team anyway. I mean, they're, like, total mental incompetents."

"Uh-huh. Been hit in the head too many times."

"Clueless, totally clueless."

The woman I'd identified as the coach broke through the knot of girls, clapping her hands.

"Okay, Indians, let's go."

"We got to go. But listen, you need anything—information or anything—you come ask *us*. We all liked Juky a lot, and we'd do anything to help catch the guy that killed him."

"Yeah, and you want the real lowdown, you ask Coach Driscoll. She'll give you the score."

"Yeah. She's awesome!"

As they trotted off in the wake of their coach, I heard the redhead exclaim.

"Shit, a gun! That's what *we* need around here. Next time those jerk-offs took up our court time, pow! We'd blow them away!"

"Can we take out Atterbury while we're at it?"

"Sure! Mr. Muscles and the Big Bopper, too!"

That was two surprises in a row. One, Biggs was literate enough to know about Mike Hammer. Two, an eighties teenager had heard of the Big Bopper. Will wonders never cease?

It took me several hours to figure out what was bugging me. I was lying in the bathtub, surrounded by bubbles and fur, drinking a margarita and singing along with an old rock-and-roll album that had belonged to one of the kids. It was one of those Golden Oldies albums given out as twentieth prize in some contest, and I was singing with the chorus at the top of my lungs: "Doc-*tor!*—Mr. M.D.— Doc-*tor!*—Whoa, can't you tell me—Doc-*tor!*—What's ailing me?" The kitties were used to this kind of shameful display on my part. I'd given Sidney, who was sitting on the edge of the tub, a punk hairdo made out of bubbles.

That's when it hit me: I'd just discovered another sick person who needed a doctor. Okay, she wasn't dead. But didn't I feel just a teensy bit uneasy that she had developed a serious illness after Juky's death?

What if I was wasting valuable time looking for a killer, when what I should have been looking for was the next victim? If Tucker had been murdered, there had been two victims already. Who was next? The injuries I knew about didn't seem that serious, and probably not even unusual for high school basketball. And how likely was it that someone would die from tripping, or taking an elbow in the chest? On the other hand, how likely was it that an apparently healthy teenager would die from practicing basketball on a hot day? Tucker had appeared to die from natural causes. Juky's death had been obviously unnatural, but perhaps the killer hadn't planned that one. If the next death were going to follow a pattern, it was at least possible that the pattern was one of death by apparently natural causes. Why anybody would want to pick off Northside's answer to the Fab Five, I didn't know, but I should at least consider the possibility.

The bubbles in my bathwater went flat all of a sudden, and I felt a chill creep up my backbone.

But LaTania wasn't part of the team, so was she a prospective victim? Maybe she wasn't sick at all. Maybe she was being kept out of the way—of what? The investigation? Juky's murderer? Mononucleosis wouldn't be very effective in preventing police interrogation, but I suppose it might keep her off the witness stand, at least during a grand jury investigation.

What if she was sick? Was it really mononucleosis? Maybe somebody was slowly poisoning her. Or maybe— Nah, I couldn't see it. She was probably the type of girl that wore a little gold cross around her neck. I should probably be shot for even suspecting that her virtue wasn't intact. Not that the younger generation sees things that way, but I was willing to bet Juky's mom did.

On the other hand, a baby Juky would be welcomed in Northside like the Second Coming. I could see it now: local business owners falling all over one another to be present at the bronzing of his teeny-weeny little mini-Jordans.

Nine

Just to ease my conscience, I made a visitation to the sick LaTania Talbot the next afternoon. Her mother, a worried-looking woman distracted by the church committee meeting she was holding in the living room, sent me up to LaTania's room. If you've seen one teenaged girl's room, you've seen them all: white frilly bedspread, flowered wallpaper, plush animals, and rock. Judging from the wall decorations, LaTania's Holy Trinity consisted of Michael Jackson, Michael Jordan, and Jesus, not necessarily in that order. I was gratified to note that she was wearing a cross around her neck, but it was Michael Jackson, not the Mormon Tabernacle Choir, that was drowning out my knocks.

"Oh, hi, I didn't hear you come up."

LaTania had a set of cheekbones some women would kill for, smooth milk-chocolate skin, and large, almond-shaped eyes. She had medium-length straightened hair, pulled back from her forehead, coaxed into a long curve and tucked behind her ears. And even though she was dressed and sitting on her bed rather than lying in it, she looked like somebody who'd been sick.

"Thanks for seeing me," I said.

"Oh, that's okay," she said. "It's pretty boring being sick. I mean, it's gotten where I actually *want* to go back to school. Do you want a Coke or anything?"

"No, thanks. So I hear you have mono."

"Yeah. Can you believe it? I mean, here I am a senior and all, and if I don't go back to school soon, I won't pass my classes and I'll have to go to summer school to make up the work. And the doctor says two more weeks *at least,* and I ask, like, well, does that mean two weeks or three weeks or five weeks or what? And he goes, well, we'll just have to wait and see. I'm a varsity cheerleader, and I'm *totally* missing the whole entire basketball season!"

"Is Dr. Skuyler your doctor?" Subtle, Cat, very subtle.

"Yeah." She paused for a minute, then apparently worried that she had cast aspersions on him, and added, "I mean, I *like* him, and he's a good doctor, and everything. I'm just tired of being sick."

"I can understand that. Well, I appreciate your willingness to talk about Juky. I guess it's been pretty hard on you."

"Yeah." She looked down. "Me and Juky, we go way back. I mean, even when I was with Cal, I knew it wasn't right. But after me and Cal broke up and I started going out with Juky, well, I knew he was the one. You know how you feel that way?"

Actually I didn't, but I nodded anyway. "So you and Cal Sepeta were going steady before Juky came along?"

"Well, it's not like Juky came *along*. I mean, me and Cal had been going together since junior high, but it was like a habit, you know? And Juky—he was like my brother. Plus we all went to the same church, you know. So then, I finally made up my mind to break up with Cal. And then Juky calls me up, and he goes, I guess you don't have no date to the junior formal, so I'll take you. So me and him went to the junior formal, only it was like brother and sister at first, you know? But then afterwards, it was more than that. And now—" Her voice broke. "Well, I just don't know who would do a thing like that to Juky. He was just so special." Tears slid down her cheek.

"I know. Nobody seems to think he had any enemies."

"Well, I guess there might have been some people jealous of him, I don't know, but to shoot him that way . . . And I feel so bad for Mrs. Kay. She's just this completely wonderful person."

I handed her a hankie. I seemed to be giving away a lot of them on this case.

"Mrs. Kay thinks maybe Juky was bothered by something this fall, kind of distracted."

"You mean, like the recruiters?"

"No, she thought there was something else."

"Seems like he had a lot on his mind, but he didn't tell me anything special. He didn't talk a lot about his troubles if he had any. He was all the time trying to be a good Christian, you know—like, smiling all the time and making people feel good. Like, this summer, he worked at that church camp for the handicapped. And he's the one got me and Cal involved in the after-school youth program."

"Tell me about that."

"Well, we had a bus go to the schools and pick up kids, mostly kids whose parents were working. And then we'd, like, you know, help them with their homework and their reading, or play games with them, or sometimes Reverend Cain would take us somewhere—like a skating rink or something. It was supposed to keep kids off the street and, hopefully, off drugs. Not during basketball season, though, of course."

"Sounds like a good program."

"It was Juky's idea. He was all the time thinking up ways to help other people."

"Do you think if he was worried about something, he would have confided in Reverend Cain?"

"Maybe he would've. I don't know. He could be real private."

"Did he ever talk about Jackson Tucker's death?"

She frowned. "What do you mean?"

"I don't know. Did he ever bring it up this fall?"

"I don't think so. I know he was real upset at the time, but I don't think he talked about it lately."

I showed her the photocopies I'd made of Juky's notebook, and told her where I'd gotten it.

"Recognize this?"

She nodded tearfully. "He always wrote down everything. I asked him once if he was planning to write his life story someday, on account of he was always taking notes. Aw, look—here's where he wrote down our anniversary!"

"Can you read his notes in the back—those last pages there?"

"Oh, look! It's all in numbers! I wonder what it is. I don't think it's his math homework, 'cause there's no pluses or minuses or anything and those, you know, *x*s and *y*s."

LaTania's grasp of higher mathematics exceeded my own. If this case was going to require math skills, I was sunk.

"Tell me about Juky's friends."

"Well, let's see. He was friends with all the guys on the team—"

"Anybody in particular?"

"Well, him and Cal was real close, and Butch, but they all went around together. And then there was Greg Wertz, the class president. Juky was vice president—maybe you know that. And him and Charles Cantrell worked at that summer camp together. And, oh, I don't know, Phil Mott and Jake Heimlich and Pete Piscatello were in lots of his classes."

I decided to step in before I got trampled by my own suspect list.

"What about Sky Skuyler?"

"Well, yeah, they were friends, I guess. I mean, not *real* good friends, like him and Cal."

"Why was that?"

"Well, him and Cal went to the same church, and I don't know, like, they really just got along great together. Sky was kind of—I don't know."

I waited for the words to catch up with her, which takes a while when you're dealing with the televisual set.

"Sky is, like, real competitive, and kind of stuck up. I mean, not *real* stuck up, just a little bit. Maybe because his dad is a doctor. He isn't real popular at school. He isn't that smart, either; Cal told me he can't hardly read. Not that you'd hold that against him or anything. He hangs out with Eddie Atterbury—you know, the team trainer? They're all the time working out at the gym and then going around, showing off their muscles like they think they're really something. But the girls—we all just think it's kind of cheesy."

I couldn't think of any more questions, so I thanked her, but she stopped me on my way out the door and fingered something hanging on the wall.

"Look. Juky gave me this on our last anniversary."

"What is it?"

"It's the net from the last game he won in junior high." She spoke reverentially. "He said at the end of the season this year, he'd give me another one to match it."

Ten

"*Rat—Rat—Rat—Rat—Rat-Rat-Rat-Rat-Rat-Rat-Ratratratratrat—Go, Rattlerrrsssssss!*"

The bleachers vibrated under my feet. The combined scent of drugstore cologne and after-shave and mutant chrysanthemums assaulted my nose. Horns blared, drums boomed, tubas tilted and bellowed. The girl next to me, who appeared to have reversed her under- and over-wear, cranked a noisemaker. The girl next to her shook a large blue-and-white rattle. Something slid along the back of my neck; the kid behind me was waving a plastic snake. The three kids in front of me sported blue streaks in their hair. Check that; two of them were old enough to be parents. The loudspeaker droned beneath the roar. High school basketball.

To my left sat Moses, calmly studying the program through his bifocals. Kevin, who had taken the night off, was winding his way through the crowd, bearing a cardboard tray full of drinks; here was where his waiting skills counted for something. Mel and Al were on their feet, hissing with the best of them.

I reached for the program.

"Let me see that a minute, Moses. I can't hear the starting lineup."

"No." He tightened his grip. "Now, Cat, I told you if you wanted a program to get you one. You can't be borrowing mine all the time."

"Aw, come on, Moses. Didn't your mother teach you to share?"

"No. I mean it, now, Cat. Get your own."

"I'll get you one, Cat," said Al. "You know how I hate to see you pout."

The Rattlers were playing Hughes, a particular rival because it was located in an adjacent neighborhood, Clifton, across the viaduct from Northside. The Robertson gym was filled to capacity.

The Rattlers were in white with blue trim, wearing black ribbons pinned to their jerseys. Reggie Odum and another tall kid were facing off at center court. Reggie got the tip, the Rattlers controlled the ball, and I thought the woman in front of me was going to pass out and miss the first quarter.

The play was pretty ragged in the first few minutes, on both sides. Corky was called for traveling, Butch made a bad pass to Cal and turned the ball over, and Sky missed an easy layup. To tell you the truth, they looked like the Keystone Cops. Their only salvation was that the other team didn't look any better. Full of advice, the guy behind me rained spit on my head.

Then Butch grabbed a steal and scored on a fast break. With a surge of confidence, he then stole the inbounds pass and passed it off to Sky, who went back-door for an easy two. Sky swaggered to the free-throw line and sank it. The crowd was delirious. I could have floated a goddam yacht in the waterfall I was getting from the rear.

Hughes answered with a quick two, and I could see Biggs fuming on the bench. He pulled Corky and sat him down for a talk. Corky's replacement lost his handle on the ball, and Hughes picked it up. After three attempts, they scored. Cal missed his perimeter shot, Hughes rebounded, and scored. On the next trip down, Butch got the ball to Reggie in the lane, but Reggie missed his shot and Hughes rebounded. On the other end, the center put the ball up, and Reggie went up with him, but the shot was good and Reggie drew the foul. Words were exchanged between Reggie and his counterpart, but Cal pulled Reggie away before anything came of it. Corky returned to the lineup.

As the play progressed, I began to notice the patterns.

"They're killing us on the boards," I muttered to Moses. Notice how I'd begun to identify with the Rattlers.

He nodded. "Our rebounding stinks. Lucky our shooting is as good as it is."

"That Hughes center is all muscle." Kevin had squeezed in on the other side of me. "Ours is no match for a powerhouse like that. Skuyler's the only match for him on the inside."

Fortunately, Cal's perimeter shooting picked up, and Hughes was having a tough time defending against it. They called time, and the Rattlers cheerleaders took center court. Beneath the din of the fight song, Kevin spoke in my ear.

"You want to see what Air Jordans look like, Mrs. C.? That kid's wearing a pair."

I craned my neck to see where he was pointing. Atterbury? I thought about that for a minute. Was Atterbury wearing Juky's Jordans? Good thing it was too noisy to voice my thoughts out loud. This way, I avoided having Kevin and Moses point out that Juky Kay had stood at least a foot taller than Atterbury, and Atterbury could probably have taken a bath in Juky's sneaks. But I studied his feet anyway. From this distance, I couldn't see what all the fuss was about. They looked like sneakers to me.

Hughes switched to a zone defense, which seemed pretty futile to me, since Cal just shot over the zone. And every now and then, just for variety, Corky did a head fake, passed off to Butch as the zone collapsed around Cal, and Butch took it to the hoop. But our defense wasn't foolproof, either, and Hughes had some good shooters. Cal was really skirmishing for position, and I saw some elbows thrown when the refs weren't looking. At one point, Cal's opponent went down, and I saw him look up at the refs in disbelief. The Hughes coach saw it, too, and gave the refs an earful.

Reggie blocked a few shots, but he didn't seem to be good for much else tonight except obscuring the shooter's view of the basket. Corky was going one on one with a guy who was a good four inches taller than he was, and his frustration was showing. He was trying to make up in muscle what he lacked in height. By midway through the second quarter, he was already in foul trouble. Biggs benched him and substituted a taller but slower kid named Schindler.

Biggs did a lot of shouting, and he seemed to have the loudest voice in the place, which was saying something. I was thinking about giving him a Tark towel for his birthday. I hoped somebody had already given him blood pressure pills, and I hoped it wasn't Dr. Skuyler. I studied the crowd around the Robertson bench to see if I could spot the doctor, but I didn't know what he looked like, and nobody was clutching a little black bag or wearing a white coat or anything. The boys behind me began to smell of something besides after-shave, sweat, and hormones, and I wondered where they were hiding their stash. I also considered asking them to share; my watered-down Coke didn't have much kick to it.

With three minutes to go in the half, Hughes scored six unanswered points. Biggs pulled Corky off the bench, and sure enough, he drew his fourth foul trying to block a shot.

There was a skirmish on the floor as Butch dragged Corky away from a Hughes player, who was also being restrained by teammates. In the tangle of players and refs, it was hard to tell what was going on. Then we heard a gasp from the bleachers opposite.

"What is it?" Al asked, on her feet and straining to see.

"Oh, my God," I said. "It's Cal."

As Cal turned, we saw the gleam of bright red against his white jersey. He covered his face with his hands, head tilted back. I held my breath, waiting for him to go down. I was swamped with remorse: Cal had been the next victim, and I hadn't acted quickly enough to save him.

I scanned the players, benches, and spectators quickly, looking for a glint of metal. Nothing. If someone had used a gun, it could be anywhere by now—probably under the bleachers.

"Got a nosebleed," Moses muttered.

"What?"

"Nosebleed."

Sure enough, when I looked again, he was walking to

the bench under his own power, and Atterbury was waiting with an ice pack. Biggs looked frustrated, but not worried. Cal sat down, and Shellenstein replaced him.

"How come they didn't call a foul on that? Somebody must've hit him."

"I don't know," Moses said. "I didn't see it. Maybe he just gets nosebleeds—some kids do."

With thirty seconds to go, I heard a sound like a radiator leak. Then it grew: sssssssssss. The crowd was on its feet. After the Hughes free throw, Corky inbounded the ball to Butch, and the two of them and Shellenstein passed it around the perimeter awhile. Then, with ten seconds left, Corky went up with a pump fake and passed the ball to Sky. Sky and Reggie executed a textbook pick, and Sky hit the basket at the buzzer. The score was 46-45, our favor.

Blue and white snake streamers sailed through the air as the teams headed for the locker rooms. I collapsed on the bleacher, then winced. It had been years since I'd had to sit on a plank of wood this long at a stretch. Two sets of skinny girls in miniscule skirts, boots, and hats were lined up courtside waiting to perform. I decided to take a walk and look around. Maybe I'd bump into a drug deal in the women's john.

What I bumped into in the women's john turned out to be a scene that looked like backstage at Oscar night. A wall of hairspray and cologne hit me just inside the door, and I nearly gagged. Crowded in front of the mirrors, mum to mum, a swarm of girls elbowed for space to apply another layer of makeup, but the defense was tough inside, and I saw one girl go down in the scuffle for a loose lipstick. A space opened before me, and I slipped into a vacant stall and kicked over a beer can. I looked around guiltily, but nobody seemed to notice but me.

"You got paper?" a voice demanded, and a hand appeared under the partition. I put some paper in the hand, and it went away. The graffiti was mostly pretty standard, though there was a new public-service slant to it in the form of a statement that condoms should be used when performing any of the acts described on the walls of this stall.

The voice on my other side was enthusing about Sky's last shot.

"I can't believe it went in! I'm, like, oh, no, it's not going in, closing my eyes—"

"I *know*! I go, why didn't they let Reggie take the last shot under the basket?"

"I *know*! And then it goes in! I couldn't *believe* it! I start hugging everybody, you know—"

"I *know*! It was *so cool*!"

On my other side, a new voice was saying, ". . . when Corky get his ass fouled out of this game."

"I know it, girl. I love to see him hustle, but I hate to see them fouls."

"I wish Cal get his nose fix. Every time that motherfucker start to bleed, I think he been shot."

"Maybe he puttin' somethin' in there he ain't s'posed to."

Now there was an interesting comment.

"Jimmy take you out to eat tonight?"

"Uh-huh, at Frisch's."

"Girl, you got to get you a man with some class, give up these Big Boy-and-fries types."

"It's something to be said for big boys, though."

I flushed and emerged, stepping into the line of fire of a wild woman with an aerosol mousse.

"Oh, God, I'm sorry. You okay?" You could see she thought I was one of those fragile elderly types.

I drove up the middle and found a sink. Somewhere behind me, a voice was saying, "You talk to LaTania today?"

"Yeah," somebody answered, "and she was *so bummed* to be missing the game tonight."

"If it was me, and Juky was *my* boyfriend, I don't think I be going to no games. Be too depressing."

"I know. But she thinks he would've wanted her to go."

"Yeah, I guess he be wanting her to watch Cal scoring all them points."

"Well, I don't know. I mean, Juky and Cal were best

friends, so I don't think Juky woulda minded. I mean, it's
not like it was Skuyler or something."

"Well, that ain't too likely, now he goin' out with that
college girl."

"Yeah, maybe they ain't got no muscle men in college."

"Well, all I know is, they ain't got no better men at college than Skuyler, I ain't goin'."

I was washing my hands for the fifth time when someone interrupted this fruitful conversation.

"Oh, no! I can't *believe* I left my mascara at home!
Jenny, let me use your mascara—please? Please, please,
please? I'll let you borrow that awesome new nail polish
you like."

"*I* don't think it's very sanitary to pass makeup around
like that."

"Aw, girl, you cold. What you think—you going to get
AIDS from mascara? Somebody ought to tell you the facts
of life."

I ducked out before I was nominated. I'm not a suitable
adviser to the young, anyway. Too jaded.

I sauntered around, studying feet and faces and keeping
my ears open, but I didn't learn anything interesting. The
halftime show was over so I went back up to find my seat
and compare notes with Moses and crew.

"So what's your read on the chalk talk?" I asked.

"You mean, what would I do if I was the coach?" Moses reflected. "Well, I can't make Schindler move faster,
'less I slip him some speed, and Corky's on the bench. I
could put a taller man on Murphy, but I couldn't guarantee
that they'd play him as tight as Frisby's playing him. If
Shellenstein stays in, he needs to help out with Murphy so
he and Frisby can box that guy up. Frisby's got to concentrate more; he's caused a few turnovers just because he
wasn't paying attention. Can't do much with Odum until
he gets some more experience and gains some weight.
Sepeta's our best hope over the long run, and in the end
we'll probably need some good free throwing from him
and from Frisby, who has the second best percentage on

the team. But we need Skuyler to keep scoring, too, and his free-throw percentage is lousy."

"I'd say we've got one advantage, though," Mel offered.

"What's that?"

"Judging from the looks of things, I'd say the Rattlers have more stamina than Hughes. They're looking a lot tireder than we are."

"Hey, Miz Cat."

It was Leon, making the rounds, greeting the folk like the emperor on holiday.

"Hey, Leon. You enjoying the game? Say, I'll bet you could tell me something. Is Dr. Skuyler here tonight? You know what he looks like?"

"Yes'm, he *was* here, down behind the b-bench. I don't know where he's at n-now. Oh, there he is! He t-talking to Mr. Odum, d-down there."

Leon pointed, and I spotted the two men. I didn't have any trouble picking out Reggie's dad, who looked like Reggie. The other man was distinguished-looking, wearing a tie and shirtsleeves. He looked like what he was: a family practitioner, competent, genial, reassuringly alert.

The game started up again, with Corky on the bench and Butch guarding Murphy, who was indeed being double-teamed whenever possible. Cal's face was clean, but his shooting went cold. Hughes started fast, racking up eight unanswered points before Skuyler banked one in. At the other end, Reggie was called for goaltending, and Hughes added two. Butch pushed the ball up the floor quickly, and I suspected Biggs had indeed encouraged the Rattlers to wear Hughes down. Butch lobbed one at the basket, and Reggie popped up, miraculously, for the alley-oop. Then Cal stole the inbounds pass and converted it for three.

Things had seesawed back and forth for a while, when Butch was called for a five-second violation. On the next trip down, frustrated, Butch tried to take a charge and went down. To a collective groan from Rattlers fans, he writhed on the floor, clutching his ankle. Dr. Skuyler and Atterbury, the trainer, helped him to the bench. That

brought Corky in, carrying four fouls. When Reggie lost
his man three plays later, Corky left his feet to block a
shot and was called for his fifth.

Corky spun round in a rage and spat something at the
ref. Then Skuyler exchanged a few words with one of the
Hughes players, and he and Corky actually charged three
of them. When the dust had settled, Murphy had sunk four
points—two for the original foul, and one each on the two
technicals called on Corky and Sky. Corky was on the
bench, where he'd practically been dragged by two of his
teammates. Biggs looked dangerously apt to explode, but
at whom, I couldn't tell.

The explosion came with five minutes left on the game
clock. Reggie was called for a three-second violation, and
Coach Biggs shot off the bench like a pea in a wind tunnel. What with all the general hubbub, you couldn't tell
what he was saying to the ref, but you got the gist of it
through his gestures. When he returned to the bench, only
to hurl a chair into the backcourt, you could see he was
not a happy camper. The Bobby Knight school of basketball coaching; no wonder Juky had signed with Indiana.
Murphy shot the technical, and made both shots.

Still, the Hughes team was looking pretty ragged. Cal
found his perimeter shot, and Reggie discovered a sky
hook I didn't know he had. One of the substitute guards
pulled off a steal, and scored two on a fast break. A couple
of weary Hughes guards sent Cal and Sky to the line several times, and they made most of their free throws—a big
surprise where Sky was concerned. For some reason, we
were leading by four with a minute to go, when the Rattlers shifted to a four-corners offense.

Astonishingly, none of the subs lost the ball, and after a
long forty seconds of free throws, during which the crowd
had started to stream up the aisles, Robertson won it,
76–65.

The band struck up, the rattles rattled, the pom-poms
swished, and I sat considering the implications of the volatile tempers on Juky's team.

Eleven

Still, it's one thing to throw a chair if there's one handy, and another thing altogether to pick up a gun, or even to have one handy. Not that guns are hard to come by, as I knew from experience. But how many high school kids pack one in their book bag, along with their Walkman and their math homework? Okay, call me naive, but I just couldn't see it. A knife would be safer. But a gun? Wouldn't you risk shooting yourself in the butt running to catch a bus? Or taking out your best friend if you slammed the bag down on the lunch table?

I knew from Randy Waltrip that Juky wasn't killed where he was found. The body had been moved, but of course, nobody could say how far. So here's how I had it figured. Juky left Tower Hamburgers that Friday night because he had to meet somebody somewhere. Butch and Cal say he left at eleven-thirty, so I figure he was either a little late for a meeting close by, or he had a walk ahead of him—say, between fifteen and thirty minutes. Let's face it, who schedules meetings for eleven-thirty-five or eleven-forty? Even in mystery novels, off times like those only show up when there's a train schedule involved, and there were no trains to Northside. In fact, the city fathers had canceled the half-finished subway back in the twenties when it was pointed out that nobody wanted to go to Northside, and even if they did, they certainly weren't in a hurry to get there. I thought I should check out the bus schedule at Knowlton's Corner, two blocks from Tower Hamburgers, but it still seemed more likely that Juky's meeting was local, since all my suspects so far were local. So, let's say he had a meeting at eleven-thirty or twelve o'clock (probably no later, since he was a good Christian athlete in training, with a mother at home to worry about him). Whoever was meeting him brought a gun either to intimidate Juky or to kill him. Or, alternatively, they met someplace where a gun was available.

If X was a high school student, then he—let's assume it was a "he" since high school girls are even less likely to pack pistols in their purses than high school boys in their backpacks—either had a gun, probably illegal and unregistered, or used his father's (or mother's?) gun. Surely the police had already tracked down all the potential murder weapons in the case, and eliminated them, but I made a note to ask Randy Waltrip. A smart high school student who anticipated that the meeting with Juky would be a stormy one would surely not invite Juky over to his house, even if his parents were gone. Northside houses weren't built on sprawling suburban lots, and the neighborhood is pretty lively on Friday nights, though the cold that night probably kept people indoors. Still, surely somebody would have seen—and recognized—Juky Kay. So that limited the potential meeting sites considerably. The high school was at least a twenty-minute walk from Tower Hamburgers, and it probably would have been deserted at that hour. The closer possibilities included all the stores and offices and other buildings up and down Hamilton Avenue, which constituted the business district of Northside. Among these was Dr. Skuyler's office and, I noted, after a quick peek at the Yellow Pages, Reverend Cain's church. Of course, the Mill Creek was only five minutes away, but even if the body hadn't been moved, who would've called an outdoor meeting on a cold night in December?

So I had to consider that X had moved the body back to the Mill Creek from some place else. If he'd carried the body by himself, he wouldn't have wanted to carry it far, though he might have been eager to stash it someplace where it wouldn't be found soon. But December 16 had been a cold night, with snow by morning. On the other hand, Cal was probably not the only teenager in this case to own a car, and all the adults probably owned one, so distance wouldn't have been a problem. Juky's body

wouldn't have been easy to manage alone, but unfortunately everybody implicated in the case so far, with the
possible exception of Reggie, seemed to have plenty of
muscle, even Biggs. And Reggie only looked puny compared to his muscle-bound teammates and opponents; he
was hardly the Tidy Bowl man. I resolved to take a close
look at the physiques of Dr. Skuyler and Reverend Cain.
Hell, maybe I could challenge them to arm wrestle.

I had my Adidas propped up on a desk full of junk mail
in what would become the office of Caliban Investigations
if I ever landed my license. I was studying a plaster replica
of the Maltese Falcon that Kevin had given me after my
first case. Actually, to be precise, he wrapped it in newspaper and string and staggered in one night, dumped it at
my feet, and collapsed on the floor. Kevin is nothing if not
theatrical. I recognized that the moment had arrived when
I had to undertake the kind of grunt work we detectives
usually edit out when presenting our thrilling exploits to
the general public. So I trotted out to the car and fetched
the map from the glove compartment. I spread it out on the
desk, using Sidney as a paperweight, and opened the White
Pages to the first name on my list: Biggs.

There were fifty-seven Biggses in Cincinnati, fifty-six
of them male. None of them was named "Coach." Ten of
them had Northside or College Hill exchanges. My problem became even more self-evident with Corcoran: eighty-
two Corcorans, none of them admitting to the moniker
Corky. I needed help.

The Talbots I could find, with a little hunting, because
I had been to their house. Luckily, LaTania was home,
which told in her favor as far as the claims to mono went.
Yes, she had a high school directory, and yes, it included
faculty, staff, and students.

She was wearing yellow nylon shorts over purple tights,
eating popcorn and watching television when I arrived to
borrow the directory. I cagily worked the conversation
around to the bad tempers on the team.

"You know, I went to the game last night. Coach Biggs

and Corky Corcoran sure do get into a lot of trouble with their tempers. Skuyler was called for a technical, too."

"Yeah, I know. Juky used to get bummed out about it, and say we lost five points a game because of that—you know, technicals and fouls and mistakes and stuff. I guess the Coach can't help himself, but it's kinda embarrassing, on account of Juky won the city-wide sportsmanship award, and was supposed to be, like, a sportsmanship ambassador or something. And it was kinda embarrassing for us cheerleaders, too, 'cause we're supposed to be leaders and, you know, congratulate the other team and all. Juky said he thought sometimes he took pills for it—the Coach, I mean. But I guess he forgets a lot of times."

"How about Corky? Is his temper as bad off the court?"

"Oh, well, Corky, I don't know about him. He used to be this real sweet, easygoing guy. Back in junior high I remember how nice he was. But I guess it's like Juky said, guys get closer to college and the big time and it does things to them. You know, they get more competitive and uptight about everything. Now he's just so intense all the time, like totally into basketball and working out and everything. It's kinda sad, really. Juky thought it was."

Competitive, huh? And the coach takes pills? On the way home in the car I thought about the part I hadn't considered yet: why X wanted to meet Juky at eleven-thirty or twelve o'clock on a Friday night. What did they have to talk about that Juky couldn't mention to his friends? Something that would keep another player out of competition, maybe even out of college? Something that would cost the coach his job? Drugs? Sex? Gambling? Murder? Violation of training rules? If X was Biggs or Corcoran, it wouldn't take much to rouse their anger. But if he was somebody else, the subject under discussion had to be serious enough for X to be willing to kill over it.

Suppose Juky had figured out somehow that Jackson Tucker had been murdered, and who was responsible. Suppose he'd decided to confront X. More importantly, how long would it have taken for someone else to figure out

what Juky had, or for X to convince himself that someone
else needed eliminating?

Always assuming, of course, that Juky hadn't just stum-
bled into a drug deal and been taken out by a perfect stran-
ger on his way to meet X, who was too terrified to come
forward.

An hour later, I had finished my map. Every goddam
suspect in the whole goddam case lived within a half
hour's walk of Tower Hamburgers.

Twelve

You have reached the Northside Holy Temple of God. We surely are eager to talk to you personally, brothers and sisters, but right now we're out doing His work. Please leave your name and telephone number, so we can return your call just as soon as we can. God bless you, and have a nice day!

I guess the Reverend Cain wasn't expecting a call from one of His emissaries, so I left my name and telephone number when the organ music died down at the beep. I wondered whether the good reverend wasn't being just a tad untruthful, but I suppose when you're a minister, even grocery shopping and shoveling snow are God's work. I was pretty eager to talk to him, now that I had enough background on the case to know what I wanted to ask, and I was hoping Juky had said more to him than to anybody else. I knew the police had already questioned him, but Fricke was hardly a master of subtlety. I figured what was needed was the light touch of a Cat.

The night before, I had called Mrs. Kay to report in. I told her that I had collected lots of information, interviewed lots of people, and expected a break in the case any day now. She's probably heard that one before. But she was one of those women who can't stand to hurt anybody's feelings, and she ended up cheering me up and boosting my self-confidence. After all, she'd been praying up a storm on my behalf.

By now it was three o'clock Saturday afternoon, which meant I had a few hours left if I wanted to hunt down any high school boys before Saturday night hit. Of course, I could probably find them late tonight at Tower Hamburgers, but they'd be traveling in a pack by then, and I was hoping to talk to them individually. The element of surprise seemed critical to me, too; if they knew I was coming, they'd either prepare for me in advance, or split. It also occurred to me that surprise would probably only work with my first pigeon, since he'd warn the others before I backed out of his driveway. So it was important to choose carefully. I picked Cal Sepeta, Juky's best friend.

I didn't have any jeans with the knees ripped out of them, so I put on some sweat pants and a sweat shirt. But that didn't look right—too much like a suburban matron on her way to aerobics class. Sadie and Sophie were eyeing me critically, and I thought I heard a little sigh from one of them when I studied myself in the mirror.

"Okay, no go. I suppose you've got a better idea?"

Sadie stretched, yawned, and dragged herself to the closet. Humans can be so trying. When I'd stripped down to my undies again, I found her in the closet, sharpening her claws on an old pair of Fred's cords, wadded up and pitched in the corner. They were a little moth-eaten, stained with paint, and permanently crumpled. They were baggy, and I had to roll up the cuffs to keep from tripping over them. Perfect. I dragged out one of Fred's T-shirts, and a flannel shirt missing most of its buttons. A Cincinnati Reds cap trundled along the closet shelf and tumbled to the floor. This was Sophie's contribution. I laced up my Adidas, and I was ready to roll. No mirror sunglasses this time. Too intimidating.

For those of you who are wondering why I hadn't donated my late husband's remains to the Goodwill, I wish to clarify that the clothes I was wearing would not have been accepted by any reputable charity I know. Anything of Fred's that was still kicking around the apartment was truly the detritus. I think I'd been using the undershirt to dust, and the flannel shirt sported a suspicious-looking stain the color of kitty tuna. Smelled suspicious, too.

Cal Sepeta lived in an apartment complex right on Hamilton Avenue. I was curious about Cal, and his friendship with Juky. After all, Juky had his girl and the undying devotion of all Northside. Maybe LaTania and Cal had parted amicably; maybe the breakup was even *his* idea. And he was, according to my Rattlers program, a year behind Juky in school, so maybe he didn't resent playing a supporting role. But still. On the other hand, his game seemed to have caught fire when he moved to forward, so that now he was clearly more valuable to the team than Skuyler. Would a kid be able to pull that off with murder on his conscience?

I rang the bell at apartment 23. Nothing. I rang it again. Dead silence. The door looked like it could use a few coats of paint, and the whole building had a neglected, between-managers feeling about it. It occurred to me that I should have looked for his car in the parking lot. On my way there, I checked out the mailboxes, like all good detectives do. There were lots of fliers and papers and stuff addressed to "Occupant" and "Resident" crammed into the shallow bin below the boxes. Some of this stuff looked its age, and was held in place by spiderwebs. Either the building had no resident manager, or the manager was ignoring the rules as laid out in *The Landlord's Handbook*. I should know; I've ignored a few myself. Box number 23 looked pretty full to me, from what I could see behind the decorative carving. There were no Jeeps in the parking lot, and no cars parked in space number 23.

It was kind of depressing, to tell you the truth. This place made the Catatonia Arms look like the Beverly Wilshire. I couldn't help thinking that the people who lived here spent most of their time someplace else, because it sure as hell didn't seem like much to come home to. But I was probably being unfair; the apartments themselves were probably very attractive. And I am the Doctor of Dunk.

Butch was next on my list. He lived on Mad Anthony, one of those narrow Northside streets where you are always interrupting an athletic event when you turn down it and thread your way between the parked cars on either side. I bet if I left the bomber here for forty-eight hours, I could land an insurance claim, easy.

I found Butch before I found his house, but I almost

didn't recognize him from his backside. He and Reggie had their heads together under the hood of a Toyota Celica parked in the street. I heard them before I saw them.

"God-*dam* this motherfucker! It's so goddam motherfuckin' *tight* I can't get my hand down there!"

"Wait, man, lemme see'f I can push this sucker over."

"Naw, man, I'm *tellin'* you! This motherfucker won't budge. Why they make shit like this, anyway? You shoulda bought American, man. Them Japanese, they make everything little, man. Get they little hands down the goddamdest places."

"Yeah, but they smart. Sell this shit to the Americans, man, and we can't fix it, so we got to pay a goddammed mechanic."

"Need some help?" I asked. I'd sized up the situation in a second. Ever watch a great ball handler try to do detail work with his hands?

They looked up, startled, then heaved a joint sigh.

"Yeah, right, lady. You just what we need."

"I got smaller hands." I held them up for inspection. They were the smallest part of my anatomy by far.

They looked at each other. You could see them debating. On the one hand, they wanted this car fixed. On the other, Coach would shoot them if they were caught consorting with the enemy. Well, maybe not *shoot* them.

While they wavered, I made my move, stepping between them and peering down into the engine.

"What're you trying to do? Get that hose off?"

"Yeah," Reggie said grudgingly. "It's got a leak. But that air conditioner hose's in the way. Can't get to it."

I picked up the screwdriver Butch had laid down and slid my other hand past the upper hose to feel for the clamp on the lower one. When I located it with my fingertips, I slid the screwdriver down past the hose on the other side, guided it with my fingers, and unscrewed the clamp. Luckily, I didn't have to see what I was doing, because two heads were in my way.

"You got it?" Butch asked. "Now don't drop the screw down there. We never get the motherfucker back."

"I can't hold onto everything at once!" I snapped. "If I drop the goddam screw, you'll have to get a goddam magnet and fish it out."

For once, my goddams silenced my critics. I saw Reggie open his mouth to give me another piece of advice, but he thought better of it. As it turned out, I managed to bring up both clamp and screw, then repeat my stellar performance with the remaining clamp. They handed me the replacement part, and I suggested we have a little talk. That was when they realized I had them by the hose.

"We already done told the police all we know," Reggie said sulkily. When he pulled down his mouth in a pout, stretching the skin down along his cheekbones, his jug ears stood out from his head even more than usual.

He limped over to the curb and eased himself down.

"You injured?"

"Naw, i's jus' a little ligament problem I got with my knee. Didn't put no tape on it today."

"Rattlers have a lot of injuries this season?"

"Same as usual." Butch sounded a little defensive. "You play hard, you gonna get injured. Look, it's like Reggie said: we don't know nothin' 'bout Juky's death. We did, we go annihilate the sonabitch who did it."

"Several people seem to think he had something on his mind this fall."

"Shit, lady, he have a shitload of college recruiters on his case. What you think he got on his mind?"

"You don't know of anything else he was worried about? Any trouble he was in?"

"Trouble? Shit, man, Juky never got in no trouble. He a clean dude, dig? Mister Clean hisself," Reggie offered.

"Maybe it was somebody else who was in trouble, and Juky knew about it."

"Well, if it *was* somebody in trouble, it wasn't us."

"No, man, we clean, too."

"How about Sky Skuyler?"

"What about him?" Wary? Or just annoyed?

"Is he clean, too?"

"Why don't you go ax him?"

" 'Cause the hose I'm holding belongs to you. So I'm asking you." A hose in the hand.

"Aw, Skuyler's okay. His daddy Dr. Skuyler, the team doctor. Dr. S. and Coach, they big buddies, you know what I'm sayin'? What you think Skuyler can do with his old man around all the time?"

"And Corcoran?"

"He just hotheaded. Like Coach. Got girl troubles, too." Reggie shook his head. "Man, I wish him and Tina get back together before the playoffs."

"I heard he didn't used to be so hotheaded."

"Yeah, well, he didn't use to be involved with no Tina Vickery."

"Has the coach ever hit anybody?"

"Man, you crazy? Coach know better than that. He don't pull that kind of shit."

"Naw, he just yell and throw things, mostly not at you."

"So the night Juky died, Juky just looked at his watch and said he had to go?"

"Tha's right. Just like I told the police."

"And he was wearing his Air Jordans."

"Man, Juky *slept* in them shoes. Only time he took 'em off was on the court. Coach wouldn't let him play in 'em. Said they wasn't regulation."

"You both have a pair?" I looked pointedly down at their feet.

"I ain't wearin' mine," Reggie said.

"I ain't wearin' mine on account of I want to keep 'em clean. Don't want to mess 'em up with no grease and shit."

"You boys ever run into any drugs in the locker room?"

"You crazy? You know what Coach do to us he catch us doing drugs?"

No, I thought, but I wonder.

"What about Tower Hamburgers?"

"We done told you, we clean. It's some drugs going down there, sure, and maybe we seen some. But we ain't involved."

"Naw, man, we headin' to the NCAA."

"Tha's right. A year from now, I'ma be wipin' the floor with Butch's ass, man."

"Yeah, you be wipin' the floor, all right. You be third string, sittin' on the bench, doin' the clean-up duty, wit' your sorry-ass hook shot. But me? I'ma have my picture in Street and Smith."

"Shit, man, you get your picture in Street and Smith, it gonna say underneath, 'worse foul shooting percentage in the NCAA.' "

"Shit, man, if that happen, they ain't gonna take *my* picture, 'cause they gonna have a bigger picture, say 'worst rebounding in the NCAA,' and that gonna be yours."

"Well, it's been real nice talking to you boys," I said.

"Hey! Ain't you gonna put that hose in?"

"Why, I'd be happy to," I said, giving them a benevolent smile. I didn't even make them say "please."

Thirteen

It was late, close to midnight. Outside, buildings and streets melted into the black sky. A streetlight flickered in the distance, and went out. Somewhere a siren blared, and mingled with the muffled squall of a catfight.

Inside, the yellow glare of fluorescence cut through the thick miasma of smoking grease. Saturday night at Tower Hamburgers.

Leon was studying the menu unperturbed. I doubted, frankly, that he needed a menu; studying it was part of some arcane teen ritual. Al was holding hers by the fingertips, as if she suspected it of carrying unmentionable diseases. Moses frowned like a sommelier sniffing vinegar. Mel had refused to accompany us to this den of nutritional iniquity, and Kevin, of course, was working at a real restaurant, where if anything burned, it was unsalted butter or canola oil.

"How are the burgers?" Al asked Leon.

"They p-pretty good, but you k-kinda hafta be use to them."

"I see your point," said Al. "I'll have pie and coffee." She caught a look from Leon. "Okay, I'll just have pie."

"The p-pumpkin pretty good. Spices kinda c-covers up the taste of the c-crust."

"Okay, I'll just have coffee. How's that?"

"That sound good," said Leon. "I don't d-drink coffee."

We'd negotiated for a table in the corner with a good view of the whole place. This view included the counter, where Butch and Cal were sitting at the far end with their backs to us.

"Where are their girlfriends?" Al asked. "Don't guys their age go out with girls on Saturday night anymore? What's this country coming to?" This from the lesbian member of our party.

"They probably dumped their girlfriends at home already," I said. "A cheap goddam movie and a good-night kiss."

"Where you been, Cat?" Moses asked. "Ain't no cheap movies no more, except at the video store. Ain't hardly no good-night kisses, either, not the way *you* mean."

"Yeah, I guess the video stores are stocking condoms next to the Good-and-Plenty and popcorn." I glanced at Leon to see if his ears were burning, but he looked unperturbed. After all, he had four older brothers. Hell, for all I knew, he could have a sweetie of his own—or two or three.

The waitress delivered our coffee just as Sky showed up with Corky and another kid I recognized from the team. I let the waitress block for me, but I don't think they spotted me. They managed to rearrange the entire counter, as everybody got bumped over two stools. But nobody argued. Nobody was big enough to want to take on a Rattler, much less five Rattlers.

"How can they eat that much at this hour?" Al marveled.

"They growing boys."

"Are you kidding? If they grow any bigger, they won't be able to fit their knees under the counter," I said. "As it is, I don't know where they're putting their legs. Al, can you see? Anybody wearing Air Jordans?"

"Sky w-was wearing them when they c-come in."

"And I know Butch and Reggie both own them, and Atterbury."

"Who's he?" Moses asked. "He's not on the roster."

"Trainer," I said.

Leon nodded. "Eddie Atterbury. W-work out at the gym, him and Sky and s-sometime B-Butch."

"The gym? You mean a gym besides the school gym?"

"N-North Side Gym. Up on C-Colerain. I don't go there much." Leon was letting us know the limits of his information; the North Side Gym was out of his territory. Unfortunately, if it was where I thought it was, it was still within a half hour's walk of where we were sitting. *I* couldn't walk it in a half hour, but an athletic teenager could.

So some of these guys *did* hang out in one of those criminal breeding grounds Waltrip had described. That raised the question of drugs again—though I figured it could be gambling, too. Drugs seemed the obvious choice these days when kids were in trouble, and it could explain some things—like Sky's illness. But Reggie's knee? And Butch's ankle? I thought coke made your nose fall off, not your foot. And I admit it was hard for me to believe that high school sports could constitute a major source of gambling revenues, but Maury Schwab insisted they did.

As if on cue, Reggie hobbled in. Somebody at the counter decided he was finished, and gave up his stool.

Leon got excited and knocked over my drink, which was probably the best thing that could have happened to it. "Oh, look, M-Miz Cat! Reggie wearing his Jordans, too!"

So he was.

"What do *you* know about the North Side Gym, Moses?"

"Not a thing. Like I said, I don't *do* exercise."

"What are the chances that it's clean?"

"Oh, I'd say, roughly about the same as any horse track."

"That good, huh?"

"Why? What's wrong with them?" Al wanted to know. She belonged to the Downtown YWCA, so she'd had about as much exposure to locker room corruption as I had.

Moses shrugged. "They just attract a bad crowd, I guess. If you want to push anything, a locker room's a nice private place to conduct business, and the john's handy for any clients eager to sniff or shoot up. If you looking for sex, that's available, too, and you can inspect the merchandise before you buy. If you looking to bet on something, there's plenty of athletes available willing to make a little money on the side."

"Yeah, but these are *high school* kids."

Moses laughed. "So—they in training for big-time corruption."

"Lots of guys s-smokes in the bathrooms at school, and it's some d-drug dealing goes on there, too. They do all kinda things in them b-bathrooms, Miz Al."

I was gratified to read the disapproval written all over Leon's face. I had a lot of faith in his mother, but mothers seemed to need a lot of divine intervention these days to help them keep their kids straight.

The conversation at the counter seemed raucous enough. The decibel level never dropped into secrecy range. I admit I wanted to be a fly on the opposite wall so I could hear the account of my afternoon visit. One more fly on the wall in this place would hardly have been noticed.

As if on cue, Sky and Butch got up and headed for the men's room.

"Moses!" I whispered. "Go follow 'em to the john and listen in."

"But I don't have to go, Cat."

"Oh, hell, I have to do everything myself."

I hustled in the direction they'd taken, and found myself in a hallway, with a public phone hanging conveniently on the wall. I picked up the receiver and started talking, keeping my eye on the bathroom door. It swung open, and I lifted an arm to shield my face.

". . . get me some B-ball, man," Butch was saying.

Then they went silent, and I had my head turned away as I talked into the phone in a low voice, straining to hear. But that was it. Disappointed, I returned to our booth.

"So, you witness any drug deals, Cat?"

"No, what I heard just sounded like more basketball talk. I bet they never talk about anything else. Hey, see any other shady characters in the place, Moses?" I asked.

"Are you kidding? Every character in the place is shady, us included." Moses dropped his voice. "See that skinny white guy at the counter there, the redhead with the glasses? He's a regular downtown, but pretty small potatoes—mostly forged checks and stolen credit cards. The guy with him is Tom Gordy. He was stealing cars at sixteen. Never did talk him out of a life of crime. But if I had to put my money on the shadiest, I'd bet on the guy sitting alone in the last booth over there."

"Why? You know him?"

"No, but he looks like a sleazeball. And he's had two visitors since we been sitting here."

"You mean, he's dealing?"

"Either that, or he's loaning out his ketchup. And he don't look that generous to me."

"You gonna call someone and get him arrested?"

"Not me. I'm retired. Now, if he was dealing to kids, I might consider it. But you don't have to be a cop long to know that we ain't gonna solve the drug problem by arresting the small-time pushers one by one. Don't hardly pay. They're out on bail tomorrow, raising money to pay legal fees. If they serve, they don't serve long, and if they're lucky, they just take their business inside. Meanwhile, their customers find another supplier."

"So, if we're not going to clean the place out, can we leave already?" Al whined. "I got a date with an Alka-Seltzer."

"i don't want to leave before they do. Ask the waitress. I bet they stock Alka-Seltzer here." Another mountain of hamburgers, fries, and onion rings had just been set on the counter. "Besides, Leon hasn't had his dessert."

Leon popped his last French fry into his mouth and grinned.

"Ain't you-all going to h-have no ice cream? It c-comes right out the box."

We waited through the consumption of the latest delivery of hamburgers while Leon ate a hot fudge sundae. When the boys finally got up to leave, I followed them out at a discreet distance. Butch and Reggie were folding themselves into Reggie's Celica. Butch wasn't wearing Air Jordans, I noticed. The kid I didn't know vaulted into the back of Cal's Jeep, and Cal and Corky, neither of them wearing Jordans, climbed into the front seat. Sky climbed into a Mustang GT. I reflected on the advantages of being a doctor's son, but maybe Sky didn't need them, I thought, surveying the Rattler fleet. My first car had been a sickly green De Soto with sixty thousand miles on it, and that was a wedding present.

Fourteen

Mothers of babies awaken at the slightest whimper. People who sleep with cats can be propelled into consciousness by any low-level, repetitive sound.

My eye popped open and scanned the bed before my brain caught up with it. No cats in sight. If anybody was losing a hairball, they weren't losing it on the bed. I closed my eye and rolled over.

At first, I thought it was the blood pounding in my ear. But the hammering was too loud for that. I opened one eye again.

Something hit the building with a whack, and the windows vibrated like a cartoon coyote. I opened both eyes and sat up. There was some kind of commotion going on out back. Maybe Mel was building an attached garage, I thought hopefully.

I peeled back a corner of the curtain and looked out.

Mel was perched on a ladder at the periphery of my vision. I couldn't tell what she was doing, but she had plenty of help. Al had a hand on the ladder and was holding something I couldn't see in the other. Kevin, sporting sunglasses, had dragged out a lawn chair and was looking up at Mel, his mouth moving, as usual. Sidney was perched on his shoulder. Moses was there, standing with two friends of his I recognized, and they were all looking up, shaking their heads the way they do whenever white people are exhibiting their skills. There seemed to be some kind of dispute going on. Winnie was sitting on Moses's feet. Moses was holding a basketball.

No garage. Not even a goddam carport.

By the time I had dressed and emerged, fortified with coffee, there was a game of sorts going on. The reason I

knew was that I nearly got flattened walking out the back
door, which was located just below the new basketball net.

The day was unseasonably warm, and everybody had already peeled off their jackets. I heard the thwack of the
basketball on concrete, accompanied by grunts and calls
and swearing. Winnie was running up and down the sidelines, barking excitedly. I figured she was coaching. I sat
down in Kevin's lawn chair so she wouldn't be tempted to
throw it. Right in the middle of the commotion was my
boy Sidney, attempting to block and dribble at the same
time. It was enough to make a mother nostalgic. When he
was a little tyke, just a month ago, his idea of entertainment had been watching the toilet flush. Now he wanted to
play with the big boys, undaunted by a ball that was bigger than he was. Makes you wonder about male hormones.

It was Moses who finally scooped him up with the ball,
shouted, "We goin' all the way, Sid!", and went up under
the basket with Sidney in one hand, raised high overhead,
and the ball in the other. When it went in, Moses gave Sidney a high five, and everybody gathered around to congratulate him.

"Way to go, Sid!"

"Man, you was really smokin', Sid!"

Sidney wriggled delightedly in Moses's arms, and I
could hear his purr six feet away.

"So what you think of your boy, Cat?" Moses wheezed.

I wasn't fooled for a minute. I knew Moses needed to
break up the game to catch his breath.

"I think it's a mite early to bank on an athletic scholarship," I said.

"Me and the kids, we thought maybe you needed a little
inspiration for your case." Moses put Sidney down, and
the coach took him off by himself for consultation.

"That's right, Mrs. C.," Kevin added. "I mean, how can
you *really* hope to know the mind of a basketball player
unless you know the game from the inside?"

"You mean, the smell of basketballs and hightops does
something to your brain cells?"

"C'mon, give it a try, Cat."

"Course, it ain't regulation," mumbled Moses's friend George.

I suspected that this question of accuracy had been the bone of contention—the purists arguing for regulation height, and the others for something more manageable. It didn't look too goddam manageable to me. Moses tossed me the basketball, and to my surprise, I needed two hands to get a grip on it.

"Is this a regulation basketball?" I asked suspiciously. "It feels like a damn beach ball."

"That's 'cause you're not used to it," Mel said.

"They don't look this big on TV," I grumbled.

"The players don't look that big on TV, either," Al said. "But you've seen how *they* look in person. Come on, Cat, put it in the basket."

"What basket?" I squinted. "You mean way up there?"

"We lowered it a little for you," Mel said, giving George a look.

"You going to help me like you did Sidney?" I asked Moses.

"Now, Cat, you a grown-up. And I'm too old to lift that kind of weight. Move up closer."

"You mean, like on a ladder?"

I moved up. I tried to remember how Bill Walton looked when he was shooting. No good. How he looked was almost two feet taller than me. I hauled the ball up and pushed off with my right hand. It nicked the bottom of the backboard. I damn near broke my fingers.

"Hey! She hit the backboard!" Moses's friend Chuck had always been a fan of mine. "All *right*, Cat! Gimme five. You on the road to fame and fortune now, baby."

I sucked on my fingertips while Mel retrieved the ball. I needed elevator hightops. Or flubber. Maybe I'd been wrong all these years; suppose I was really left-handed?

The next three hit: the backboard, the rim, and the new floodlight Mel had just installed.

"I think I'm destined to be a guard," I said. "Or maybe

a coach. I see myself as kind of a Rollie Matsomino type, parading up and down the sidelines and yelling at the refs, shaking hands after the game. The handshake I can do."

"You'll get the hang of it, Mrs. C.," Kevin reassured me, applying suntan lotion to his nose.

So we played a game. Sidney got picked before I did. It was bad enough that I couldn't shoot, and my dribble drifted, but I couldn't even keep it straight who was on which team, so I practiced indiscriminate passing. Anybody asked for the ball, they got it. I was too damned relieved to get rid of it to care which team they were on. I suspected George of retaliating when he bounced a pass off my stomach that probably speeded up my menopause. I sneezed on his next free throw, and he scored a direct hit on the floodlight.

Then the inevitable happened. My team was down by 42, and I was beginning to get into the spirit of the game. Moses stole an inbounds pass and drove for the basket. I was hanging out under the basket, waiting for action. This was my big chance, and I was ready. I moved over and planted my feet.

"Look out, Cat!"

He couldn't fool me. I'd seen guys do this dozens of times. I'd be a hero.

Moses slammed into me, arm across my chest like a baseball bat, elbow rattling my rib cage. I heard the wind in my ears as something snapped in my right ankle, and I went down, arms spread as if I was embracing my fate. My back hit the cement, and my head followed with a bounce.

Darkness was closing in. The last thing I heard was Moses's voice.

"Goddam it, Cat! I'm on *your* team!"

I smelled bananas and coconut oil. It was nice. Maybe heaven was like Waikiki beach—warm, sandy, and crowded.

"Mrs. C.?" a voice said in my ear. I didn't think Gabriel—if I had my angels right—needed to be so formal.

I cracked open one eye.

At first, I thought I was having one of those out-of-body experiences—you know, when you are drifting above the scene, looking down, and you can hear the doctors directing the nurses to shut down all the life-support equipment so they can get back on the golf course. Then I realized I was looking up, not down, and that the shiny round thing I was seeing wasn't a surgical lamp or a halo but the sun over a basketball hoop. I was surrounded by worried faces. I felt like Snow White.

One of the dwarfs spoke.

"Are you all right, Cat?"

It must have been Dopey.

I took a tentative breath, but nothing moved. I groped for my chest and came up with a handful of fur. I plucked Sidney off my chest and tried again. It hurt like hell.

I closed my eyes to concentrate and tried wiggling my right foot. The pain shot up my shinbone.

"Shit!" I said.

The dwarfs helped me to sit up, and now I was beginning to feel more like Dorothy surrounded by Munchkins. They helped me inside, amid much profanity on my part and solicitous noises on their part—all except Moses, who brought up the rear, mumbling, "I can't believe she took that charge! Coulda had an easy two."

I sat at the kitchen table, my foot propped up like I had gout. Mel was applying an ice pack, and Moses kept insisting he should take me to the hospital for X rays.

"Are you kidding?" I said. "I was about to invent an illness, just so I could get in to see Skuyler, Sr. Now I'm legit."

"But you don't go see a GP for a bad ankle, Cat. He'll just send you to an orthopedist."

"But *this* GP happens to be team doctor to the Rattlers. He knows all about ankles."

"Yeah, but he's still going to send you to the hospital for X rays."

"That's right, Mrs. C.," Kevin put in. "And if he doesn't like your questions, he might set your ankle wrong just for spite."

"Yeah," Al offered, "or to put you out of commission."

"Hey, what do I know from X rays?" I widened my eyes at them. "I'm just a little old lady, tottering on the verge of senility, looking for a nice, friendly, neighborhood doctor to take care of my goddam ankle."

"Right," Mel said. "And I'm Kareem Abdul-Jabbar."

When Moses came downstairs that night to check on me, he found me lounging on the sofa under an afghan, watching television with a bottle of wine and a bag of Reese's Pieces at my elbow. Kevin had just collected the dirty dishes from his Basque chicken and rice, and retreated to his apartment to flambé the cherries jubilee. Moses narrowed his eyes at me.

"I do believe you're enjoying this, Cat."

I shrugged. "Well, it *is* my first sports injury. And now that Mel's wrapped it, I can kind of hobble around. I'm hoping for a crutch, actually. I've never had a crutch before. Or a cast," I said wistfully. "If I had a cast, you could all sign it. But I don't suppose they do that much anymore."

He shook his head. "Ain't going to help the investigation, though, you being on crutches."

"Oh, I don't know. I've already spoken to my operative, Leon, and he's offered to do all the legwork I need."

We were interrupted by the phone.

"It's Reverend Cain," Moses called from the kitchen. "You want to take it, or you want me to interrogate him?"

"I'll take it," I said, launching myself off the sofa with a shove. By now I had other muscles vying for attention with my throbbing ankle. I hopped kitchenward, muttering profanities. "Christ, I hope you had your hand over the mouthpiece," I grumbled, and took the receiver from him.

I collapsed in a chair and heard a yelp of protest from Sophie.

"Shit! I'm sorry, Soph. You okay?"

She switched chairs with an exaggerated air of martyrdom. She was doing her Greta Garbo imitation—one of her best. By now, the good reverend must have had an earful.

Sidney galloped into the kitchen, with Winnie at his heels, barking furiously. They skidded on the linoleum and crashed into a cabinet, dislodging the pots and pans within. The voice on the other end of the phone was talking, but I couldn't hear a goddam thing.

"I'm sorry, Reverend Cain, I can't hear you. Normally, of course, I'd take this call in my office, but I've injured my ankle and the kitchen phone is closer." I vowed to put one of those high-tech portable phones on my wish list for Mother's Day. Either that or have an extension installed in my closet.

"I don't know if Mrs. Kay spoke to you, but she's asked me to look into Juky's murder."

"Yes, Mrs. Caliban. I saw Mrs. Kay at services this morning, and she spoke to me about you. I assured her that I was only too glad to do anything I could to help clear up this terrible, terrible tragedy. I'll be honest with you, though; I don't think I'll be of much assistance."

"Well, I appreciate your cooperation, Reverend Cain. I'm sure you can at least give me a better picture of Juky. When would be a convenient time for me to come talk to you?"

"I'll be in my office tomorrow afternoon, if you'd like to drop by. I have a Ladies Aid Society luncheon until one, and a youth choir practice at four, but I'm free in between."

"Great. I'll leave it open, then, if that's okay with you. I have to try to get in to see Dr. Skuyler about my ankle."

No reaction. "That'll be fine, then. I surely do look forward to meeting you, Mrs. Caliban. Julius was like a son to me."

I almost made the mistake of saying, "Who?" Then I realized who he was talking about, thanked him, and hung up. Something I'd said had caught in my head, and I mentally called for the instant replay. Pictures, I thought. I needed to look at some good photographs of the two dead players—better likenesses than I could get from the newspapers. What did I expect to find? Shrunken pupils? Runny noses? The mark of doom on their foreheads? Doubtful, but I still shouldn't overlook the obvious.

Moses had helped himself to a beer and dealt a hand of solitaire.

"Red ten on black jack," I offered. "Tell me something, Moses." Moses was a deacon in his church, so I always referred theological matters to him. I figured he had a hot line to heaven.

"Hmm?"

"Do *you* think I could be on a mission from God?"

"Well, Cat, I tell you. On the one hand, the Lord moves in mysterious ways . . ."

I nodded.

"On the other hand, the Lord ain't no fool . . ."

I frowned.

"And on the third hand, I guess He got a sense of humor, same as everybody else."

Fifteen

Mel had wanted to tape my ankle, but I said it wouldn't look credible. Today I was posing as Miss Marple's evil twin—dithery but stubborn. I wound the Ace bandage around till it was a half inch thick, then stuck a safety pin through it, decorated with artificial flowers. I thought the flowers were a nice touch. I wore a bright green polyester pantsuit that my son Jason had given me under the mistaken impression that all women my age wore such things—or ought to.

I had battled my way to a spot on the doc's roster today, despite an impressive defense on the part of the receptionist—he's running late today, he's heavily scheduled, he can't do anything without X rays, etc. Now all I had to do was convert.

Mel drives like an inebriated armadillo, which may explain why she doesn't drive much at all if she can help it. Fortunately, we were only going four blocks.

The receptionist took her revenge by making me wait an hour. Mel went across the street to the building owned by Crazy Ladies, the feminist bookstore, where she rented a studio. She checked first to make sure I didn't feel endangered.

"I think it would be pretty damned suspicious if I expired of a stroke while being examined for a sprained ankle," I whispered.

"Just remember," she whispered back, "knee to the groin, elbow to the chin."

I settled in with *People* to read about how Charles and Di had spent their second honeymoon. By the time I was called, there was nothing I didn't know about the rich and famous. I practiced my routine on the nurse who took my temperature and blood pressure—how my doctor had re-

tired and I hadn't thought I'd ever trust anyone again, but
Mrs. Talbot and Mrs. Kay had both spoken so highly of
Dr. Skuyler, I thought perhaps I could risk it. This was no
mean feat, between the thermometer in my mouth and the
stethoscope in her ears. But it was a wasted performance;
I could tell she didn't give a shit why I was there.

Up close, the doctor was a distinguished-looking black
man, trim with a neat mustache, gray at the temples, and
a tasteful paisley tie under his white coat. To me, he
looked worn out—not the best recommendation for a
health care professional.

"Mrs. . . . Caliban? I'm Dr. Skuyler. You haven't been
in before, is that right?"

"No, and I do *so* appreciate your squeezing me in.
My—uh—son wanted to take me to the hospital, but that
seemed so drastic, don't you think? And at my age, why,
you never know what you'll catch at a hospital. Half the
seniors I know go in and never come out! So I didn't
know what to do, until I remembered what Mrs. Talbot
said about how you were the best doctor in Northside, and
I said to myself, well, I'll go and see Dr. Skuyler."

"Let's have a look at that ankle," he said, removing the
safety pin with a frown and starting to unwind the tape.
"How did you injure it?"

I was prepared on that score, too.

"Oh, it was so silly, but I was going down to the basement for a jar of pickled green tomatoes, and I guess I just
missed a step, and down I went! And when I think of all
the times I've been up and down those steps!"

"Hmm. It *is* swollen. Did you put ice on it? Keep it elevated?"

"Well, yes, I *did* put ice on it last night, but do you
think I need to continue?"

"Yes, you want to do what you can to keep the swelling
down. And you'll need to go to the hospital for X rays.
You go right to the X-ray department; my nurse will tell
you where to go and what to tell them. If it's just a bad
sprain, as I suspect, there's not much more to do except

tape the ankle, rest it, and keep it elevated. We don't want it to cause any additional injuries." He gave me the practiced look of a man intimately acquainted with pelvic problems in the elderly.

"Oh, my," I said. "I'd hate to be laid up for months and months like poor LaTania." He'd already glanced at his watch once, and I felt time slipping away.

"Well, a sprained ankle isn't mono. But there is always a possibility, of course, that it's more serious than a sprain."

"I do think LaTania is a sweet girl, don't you?"

"Mmm ..." He was writing in my folder.

"She's been so upset about Juky's death, and now, to have mono ..."

"Mmm ..."

"Didn't someone tell me that you have a son at Robertson, too?"

"Now, I'd suggest Tylenol 2 or something comparable for the pain—whatever you're used to. And this piece of paper you can take to the hospital with you when you go for X rays. They'll send the result to me, and we can go from there."

"His name isn't Jack, is it?"

"Whose?"

"Your son's. You see, my grandson Bill goes to Robertson, and now I think of it, he mentioned your son to me. A basketball player, isn't he? Jack Skuyler?" I was getting too desperate for subtlety.

"Scott. Scott Skuyler. Now, when the X rays come back—"

"Oh, X rays." I giggled. "I feel quite an athlete myself, having X rays! I don't know how many times I've read about young people injured on the playing field."

"Yes, so when the X rays come back—"

"Of course, that's not what happened to Juky, LaTania's little boyfriend. Such a sweet boy, I always thought, so polite. But there was that other boy, too, you know the one I mean."

"No, I'm afraid I—"

"Oh, yes, you do. I'm sure you do! That other boy who died playing basketball at Robertson. Now, what was his name?"

"Jackson Tucker."

"That's the one." I laid a hand on his wrist to prevent him from making any more notes. As much as he'd already written, he could have been making a goddam transcript. "Why, the coach murdered that child, if you ask me!"

"That's really unfair, Mrs. Caliban. The boy suffered from advanced atherosclerosis. Coach Biggs had no way of knowing that; the boy's family didn't even know. It's unusual in a person that young, of course, but not unheard of. He could have died during any strenuous activity. He just happened to die on the basketball court."

"Well, I suppose I see your point. But then that sweet boy Juky died not a year later. Two deaths on one little basketball team seems mighty suspicious to me. They ought to fire that coach!"

"Not every athletic problem can be solved by firing the coach, Mrs. Caliban. The world is a violent place, and much of that violence is random. We may never know why Juky Kay was killed, or by whom, but I doubt we can blame his death on Coach Biggs."

"I suppose you're a Rattlers fan, so you feel obligated to defend him. I suppose, too, your boy is pretty excited at the prospect of going to the state playoffs. I may be a dull old lady, but I make a point of keeping up with the local news so I can converse with the young people."

"That's good. Now in the meantime—"

"Isn't he?"

"Isn't who what?"

"Isn't your son excited about the playoffs?"

"Yes, of course," he said irritably, and crossed the room. "We'll call you when we've seen the X rays, Mrs. Caliban."

That sounded pretty final.

"But Doctor, can't you . . . ?"

"Yes?"

"Well, it *does* hurt terribly, you know. Couldn't you give me something . . . well, stronger?"

"Tylenol 2 should do the trick," he said. "We don't want to get you hooked on something, now do we?"

To tell you the truth, my ankle was killing me, and I was kind of hoping he'd play fast and loose with some prescription drugs.

"And in the meantime . . ."

He paused with his hand on the door and looked me straight in the eyes.

". . . *stay off* that ankle!"

Sixteen

"So was that a threat, or what?" Mel asked, as we sat in the Radiology waiting room at Good Samaritan.

"Hard to tell," I admitted. "By that time, he was so exasperated with me, it could have been anything. He could have been warning me off the case, or just telling me to stay out of his office. I'll bet you anything that before this is over he'll have one of his nurses call and pack me off to an orthopedist. I swear the nurse who rewrapped my foot took her degree from the De Sade School of Nursing. When she split a hair with the prong on the goddam clip, I thought my goose was cooked. I kept trying to remember whether there were any major veins or arteries running through the ankle."

"Just make sure the X-ray zapper is pointed at your foot when you go in there," Mel cautioned, "and that the rest of you is covered with one of those lead flak jackets."

But the X rays went off without a hitch, and they told me nothing was broken, but they did give me a crutch. Correction: they sold me a crutch for an amount that must have paid off the balance on the X-ray machine. I talked Mel into taking me to Burger King to celebrate. She had the salad bar, and I ate a Whopper with cheese. What with walking on one foot all the time, I felt ten pounds lighter.

"What this case needs," Mel said, "is some action."

"What this case needs," I said, "is some new evidence. Want to go undercover at the North Side gym?"

She shook her head. "No good. They'd never let me past the locker-room door."

"You could take my Mr. Microphone and pretend to be a reporter."

"That'll really boost their trust. They'll be falling all over themselves to confide in me. Ask Kevin."

"No, I believe you."

"I mean, ask Kevin to go undercover. He'd love it."

"Will he turn into a fitness freak?" I asked, eyeing her raw zucchini with distaste.

"Don't worry. The day Kevin stops cooking in butter, the ice caps will melt and oceans will rise and California will break apart and sink into the deep."

"That's already happening." I frowned. Sounded like a dangerous assignment.

"Just a figure of speech."

After lunch, Mel dropped me off at the Northside Holy Temple of God. I hopped around till I found the office and went in. Behind a desk and talking on the phone was a stunning black woman, tall and heavy, with short reddish hair and nails painted to match her violet chemise.

"Put the blue side down on the rack, Raymond. You got the blue side down? What's that noise? Did you take the plastic off first? Take the plastic off first, and put the blue side down. You got that? Okay, now turn the dial to three minutes. You got it on three minutes? Now you see that first little mark after three minutes? Turn it to that little mark. Line it right up with that little mark, hear? Don't you turn it past there. Now close the door."

"I'll be right with you," she said to me, and frowned in silent concentration. I eased myself into a chair.

Finally, she held the receiver out for me to hear the little. bursts of noise issuing from it.

"Sounds okay to me," I said.

"Raymond," she said into the receiver. "Baby, hang up the phone now, hear? Raymond? Raymond!" She listened some more. "Raymond, hang up the phone! You hear me? Raymond!"

She hung up with a sigh.

"Sometimes I think it's just as well the Lord Jesus didn't have kids. He said, 'Suffer the little children to come unto me,' but then He could always send them back. Are you Mrs. Caliban? I'll see if Reverend Cain is ready for you."

To tell you the truth, it made me nervous to be calling
on a minister, but I felt better now. God may have had a
sense of humor, like Moses said, but His earthly represent-
atives didn't always have one. I figured one little "goddam" and I was out of there.

The good reverend himself came out to escort me in and
fuss over my ankle. He was on the short side, paunchy,
bald on top; he wore a polyester suit, gold-rimmed glasses,
and a diamond as big as a basketball hoop on his right
hand. He sported a tie clasp that said "Jesus Saves." When
I had a chance to study him at close range, I could see he
wore the kind of lenses that magnified his eyes. He settled
me in one armchair and took the other. I gave him points
for not putting the desk between us.

"Now, what can I tell you about Julius, Mrs. Caliban?
Folks will already have told you he was a kind, generous,
decent Christian boy, and they're right. You'd likely walk
a long mile to find anybody with a bad word to say about
him. And yet"—he spread his hands palms up—"he's
dead. The Lord must have had some powerful reason to
take that boy so young. But He *had* a reason."

I wasn't going to contradict a minister. But if I ever saw
Him, I would have a few questions to ask about His reasons. Like why He took Juky and left Jesse Helms alone.

"Juky's mother seemed to think he had something on
his mind this fall—something besides college recruiting.
Do you have any idea what that might have been?"

He fixed me with his magnified eyes.

"Justice, Mrs. Caliban. Justice and mercy."

I guessed that eliminated nocturnal emissions and acne,
but it left a clear field for that old conundrum, The Meaning of Life—or, in its teenage version, My Place in the
Universe.

"Are you saying that he was considering whether to
bring someone to justice?"

"Well, I had that impression. You see, Julius attended
my Youth Bible Study class. He was very interested in

ethics, very interested indeed. Are you familiar with the Sermon on the Mount, Mrs. Caliban?"

"I'm a little rusty," I admitted. To tell you the truth, the only part I remembered had something to do with swearing, and I wasn't about to bring *that* up.

I guess he saw his opening, because he whipped out a Bible faster than you could say Armageddon.

"Here it is in a modern English translation, Matthew 7:1. Jesus has been speaking of the Law, by which He means, of course, not Roman law but the law of Moses and the Prophets. Now He is discussing right behavior. 'Don't criticize people, and you will not be criticized,' He says, 'Why do you look at the speck of sawdust in your brother's eye, and fail to notice the plank in your own? How can you say to your brother, "Let me get the speck out of your eye," when there is a plank in your own? You fraud! Take the plank out of your own eye first, and then you can see clearly enough to remove your brother's speck of dust.' "

He closed the Bible and looked up, as if to see whether I was following or not. Actually, I remembered the mote-in-the-eye bit from the good old King James.

"So you think Juky had seen some sawdust in somebody's eye?"

"We discussed this passage a great deal, Mrs. Caliban. Did Jesus mean that if you saw others doing wrong you must not correct them? Did He mean that you must purify yourself first, and then challenge the wrongdoing of others? Did law enter into the matter—whether Roman or Hebrew law, or as we would now say, American or Biblical law? The young people were profoundly perplexed by these questions."

"And you, sir? What position did you take?"

He surprised me with a chuckle.

"Well, now, Mrs. Caliban, I try to help the young people work these things out for themselves. I attempt to suppress any inclinations I have—and I do have them, I confess—to make pronouncements. The good pastor guides his flock to rich pasture, but he doesn't tell them which blades of grass to eat."

"Yeah—uh, yes, but you must have given them a hint."

He nodded and brought pudgy fingertips together. His diamond winked at me.

"I advised them to consider the harm. If a man sins against God and himself, then he and God are the only parties concerned, and he must make his peace with God. But you and I know that many crimes harm other people. Take theft, for instance. If your friend steals an expensive watch from another friend, and you know about the theft, what should you do?"

I had in mind a pair of sneakers myself, but I was willing to play along.

"Well, if I remember correctly, Jesus wasn't too keen on accumulated wealth. He would've counseled the victim to hand over his Walkman and his tickets to the NCAA playoffs, too. So maybe the thief was really helping him beat out the camel and enter into the kingdom of heaven." I didn't want him to think I was a complete ignoramus, Bible-wise. I also wanted him to know I could handle the King James.

He didn't bat an eye. Believe me, I would've noticed. If anything, his eyes got bigger. He raised a finger at me—an index finger, I mean.

"But now you are taking the perspective of the victim, and we were speaking about the perspective of the third party. Do our Lord's views on wealth and property influence your own decision to either confront the thief, report him in secret to the victim, or report him to the authorities, whoever they might be?"

I could see why the kids liked this guy. He was a real hoot when it came to rapping about right and wrong.

"I believe it was Julius who turned the conversation to murder," he said abruptly, and stood up. He turned to gaze out the window, clasping his hands behind his back. Take it from me, this pose only works if you don't have anything sticking out in front to spoil your profile.

"In murder, of course, the primary victim is dead. So where does your responsibility lie? Jesus says, 'You have heard it said in the old days, *"Thou shalt not murder,"* and anyone who does so must stand his trial.' But does that mean Jesus agreed with this statement? Does it mean we have a responsibility to bring the murderer to trial?

"Calvin was of the opinion that it depended upon the circumstances and whether the murderer might kill again."

"Calvin Sepeta?"

"Yes. He's been an irregular attender here lately, but I believe he came with Julius that day."

"So he and Juky disagreed about whether to peach on a murderer or not?"

"Oh, I didn't say that. I don't believe Julius had made up his mind. He was resolved to pray on the matter, a course which I approved."

"But you had the impression that it wasn't just some abstract moral question to him? That he might know of somebody who'd committed murder?"

"I didn't say that either, Mrs. Caliban. I believe it's accurate to say that this discussion seemed especially troubling and meaningful to him."

"Did you tell this to the police?"

"I spoke, yes, to a Sergeant Fricke, I believe his name was. I did not find him to be exceptionally interested in Biblical matters."

"No," I said, and shook my head sadly. "That's true. And this discussion you've told me about, it took place when?"

"I'd say perhaps a month before Julius was killed."

"Tell me, Reverend. Do you know any of Juky's other friends?"

"I know LaTania, of course. A sweet girl. Very bright, though she may not appear that way to the casual observer. Truly an excellent match for Julius."

"And Calvin? What is he like?"

He frowned. "Calvin is a good boy, at heart. He might

make a very good man, if he is not led astray by bad company."

"You mean, basketball players?"

"Perhaps."

"Who else?"

"Oh, I don't accuse any group in particular, Mrs. Caliban."

"After all, Juky wasn't led astray by basketball players, was he?"

"Ah, but Julius was a Christian soldier, wearing the armor of his faith up to the very end. No evil could touch him. And he achieved his Victory, Mrs. Caliban, and is undoubtedly reaping his reward."

I could hear that capital *V* in "victory." I wanted to hear a little more witnessing on the subject of murder suspects.

"Did you know any of the other players? Like Butch Frisby, for example? Or Sky Skuyler?"

"I met them all at one time or another, including the young man who died. What was his name?" He was pacing and stopped.

"Jackson Tucker."

"Yes, Tucker. I attend my share of sports banquets, Christian athlete prayer breakfasts, and, when time permits, basketball games. But I can't say that I know any of the boys well, except those who are members of my congregation."

"What about Coach Biggs? Do you know him?"

"Yes, Rex is an acquaintance of mine."

Rex? I'd seen fleas who looked more like Rexes than Biggs did. Horses, too.

"Our paths cross often, since we're both in the coaching business, you might say—I in the spiritual department, and he in the physical."

He glanced up to reassure himself that I'd appreciated this sally.

"Did you ever discuss Juky?"

I could not call him Julius.

"Oh, yes, often. But especially when Julius contemplated quitting the team."

"He did *what*?" I almost jumped out of my chair. What had he done—given up basketball for Lent and gotten carried away?

"Julius thought briefly of quitting the team last year. It was in the first round of the playoffs. A young man from Greenhills was seriously injured on a play. He was attempting to move into blocking position and was run over. He suffered a concussion and a serious neck injury that ended his basketball career."

"And Juky was the player who ran over him?"

"No, actually I believe it was Jackson Tucker. But Julius was considerably shaken by the incident. He went to visit the young man in the hospital. He began to wonder if basketball was an appropriate activity for a Christian. You see, he felt the injury had been deliberate."

"You mean, Tucker had nailed the guy out of spite?"

"Yes. And Rex called and asked if I would talk to Julius. I would have talked to him in any case, of course, if he asked, but I wouldn't tell him what to do."

"So you remained neutral?"

He sat down suddenly, folded his hands, and gazed at the ceiling.

"I told him that only he could decide how the Lord meant him to use his talents."

"So he stayed on the team?"

"Yes. I have wondered since . . ." He groped for words.

"Whether that decision led to his death?"

"Yes."

"We may never know, Reverend." I stood up, creakily. "I won't take up any more of your time, sir. But there is one more thing that's troubling me."

If I'd been Columbo, I would have left the room and come back, but it's tough to make a surprise entrance on a goddam crutch.

"What is that, Mrs. Caliban?"

"It's that thorny little theological question about murder, Reverend. I don't know where you stand."

His eyes met mine unblinkingly. "I have done my best to be helpful, Mrs. Caliban."

"And if you knew who killed Juky Kay, would you tell me?"

His expression changed. Now he looked kind of sad.

"That I don't know, Mrs. Caliban. It would depend upon the circumstances."

His ring left a crater in my hand.

I called Mel from the outer office and told her to pick me up on the side street. I hobbled around back and was rewarded by the sight of a dazzling cream-colored Lincoln parked in the Reserved space. Had I been had? It never does to be underly suspicious.

At home I dug out the Bible and perused the Sermon on the Mount. I also wanted to check that reference to murderers on trial, and it turned out to be in the same neighborhood—Matthew 5:17. This version didn't say anything about trials, though; it said, "Whoever shall kill shall be in danger of the judgment." Whose judgment? God's or Cincinnati's? The part about judges and prisons came later. But what worried me most was what I read a few paragraphs below that: "Therefore if thou bring thy gift to the altar, and there rememberest that thy brother has ought against thee; Leave there thy gift before the altar, and go thy way; first be reconciled to thy brother, and then come and offer thy gift."

But what if your brother blows you away before you get back to the altar?

Seventeen

"You sprained your ankle *making a charge*? My God, Mother, where?"

Did you ever suspect that your baby was swiped from the hospital by aliens and replaced with a pod person? I do, frequently.

"Not *making* a charge, Sharon. *Taking* a charge. As in basketball."

"You were playing *basketball*?"

She made it sound as if I had been bungee-jumping naked over the Grand Canyon. Okay, maybe I'm not Hakeem Olajuwon, but that doesn't mean that the only athletic competition I've ever engaged in is childbirth.

"I played basketball with you kids when you were younger."

"You threw the ball at the backboard, Mother, with nobody guarding you. If I remember correctly, you missed. That's not playing basketball."

"So? I'm refining my skills."

"Mother, you're sixty years old."

"I know, Sharon. Unlike you, I was around when I was born. And last I checked, I wasn't dead yet. So I'm refining my goddam skills."

The gin bottle was on the kitchen counter, more than an arm's length away, and I was beginning to think my drink wasn't strong enough, so I gripped my crutch at the base, hooked the bottle, wedged it between the crossbar and one of the verticals, and eased it onto the table. I was becoming more skilled by the minute. I poured myself a generous serving of Mother's little helper.

"So did you have a reason for calling, or were you just looking for a health bulletin? You know, if I were the suspicious type of mother I'd be tempted to suspect that you were after my money, if I had any money to leave you, which I don't."

"*Mother*, really! Actually, I was wondering if you were free on Friday night. Frank and I are going to take a client out to dinner, and we thought maybe we could bring Ben over for a visit."

Visit. Code word for unpaid baby-sitting.

"Actually, I'm going to a Rattlers game Friday night."

"A what?"

"A basketball game, Sharon. The Robertson Rattlers are only one game away from the playoffs. Don't you know *anything*?"

"Oh, that's great, Mom. Ben will really like that. I'll drop him off at six."

"But Sharon—"

"Oops! Gotta run, Mom. Ben's watering the plants with Kool-Aid."

I poured myself two more fingers of gin. I reasoned that the ice kept melting, so I wasn't doing *that* much damage. In front of me on the kitchen table was Juky's notebook. I kept staring at the page with all the numbers, waiting for the whole thing to make sense. I turned the notebook around. I picked it up and held the page up to the light. It still looked just the same to me. The first line read: 606 1919 72 180 400 650. I added numbers, subtracted numbers, divided them. Nothing. I tried numbering the letters of the alphabet, backward and forward, but I still came up with shit.

"It could drive a woman to drink," I said to Sadie, who had just polished off her tuna fricassee at Kevin's and waddled home to see if I was serving dessert.

The phone rang.

"Yel-lo?"

"That you, M-Miz Cat?"

"Yeah, Leon, what's up?"

"H-how you know it me?"

"Oh, just a lucky guess. We detectives rely a lot on our intuition." I doodled a little row of basketballs around my efforts to crack Juky's cipher.

"You 'member how you s-say I could be a ... a ... what that word?"

"Operative."

"Yes, ma'am. A operative. H-how you spell that?"

I spelled it.

"Listen, Leon, I'm pretty busy now with a chemical experiment. You got any information for me, or were you just calling for help with your Show and Tell report tomorrow?"

"Yes, ma'am. I g-got some information." Pause. "You want it?"

"Yes, indeedy."

"Skuyler gone."

"What do you mean, he's gone?"

"He gone, Miz Cat."

"You mean, he didn't come to school today? What is he, out sick or something?"

"Nuh-uh, Miz Cat. H-he gone. H-he ain't coming to s-school no more at all."

The gin sloshed around in my stomach. I sat up straighter.

"Give me this again, Leon. How do you know he's not coming back to school?"

" 'C-cause Jimmy Ray—you know Jimmy Ray, M-Miz Cat?"

"No."

"Well, he a friend of mine. Got a s-sister at Robertson, n-name of Sissy? Sissy, see, she w-work in the office, so she know *everything*. She say, C-coach come in this morning, and he be c-carrying on 'bout Skuyler, on account of S-Skuyler w-walked out on the t-team and all. And they say, S-Skuyler, he g-gone to live with his m-mother in Chicago. But S-Sissy, she say sh-she don't believe that."

"Why not?"

"Well, S-Sissy say everytime when s-somebody disappear all of a s-sudden, like that, it always mean s-something b-bad."

"What do you mean, something bad?"

"Well, S-Sissy say, if it's a g-girl, she going to have a

b-baby. And if it's a b-boy, he on d-drugs, maybe b-been arrested or s-sent to the hospital." He gave me a minute to allow me to absorb this scrap of adolescent wisdom. "But s-sometime, girls be on drugs, t-too. Or sometime, they just r-runs away."

"And Sissy thinks Skuyler was on drugs? Is that what the other kids think?"

"Well, J-Joey brother Mark say S-Skuyler have a f-fight with his old m-man. He mean S-Skuyler father." Just what I needed: a translator of teenspeak.

"Why does he think so?"

"I d-don't know. He n-not the only one, though. But C.J. and Bo, they think it's d-drugs, 'cause they s-say Skuyler been s-sick a lot."

"Sick with what?"

"Jus' out sick. G-got lots of h-headache. But then Jasmine say if S-Skuyler was on drugs, we see the n-needle tracks in his arm and all. But then C.J. say, nuh-uh, you d-don't need to use no n-needle if you d-doing some kind of d-drugs, 'cause he c-could be p-popping pills or sniffing, though ain't n-nobody notice he g-got a runny nose or nothing. M-maybe his eye look f-funny, but ain't nobody n-notice that, neither. Then Bo s-say, he think it affect S-Skuyler brain. But then Jasmine say n-no, he just d-dumb. Then C.J. s-say he s-seen this movie one t-time, where a g-guy die of a overdose in the garage, and d-didn't nobody find him for a whole w-week. Then Jasmine, she s-say C.J. as dumb as S-Skuyler he think Skuyler d-daddy didn't think to l-look in the garage. Anyway, S-Sissy say, Skuyler d-daddy gone to s-school already to c-clean out Skuyler locker."

Clearly, I didn't have to do any thinking for myself. The kids had already worked all the angles. Still, I found it mighty suspicious that Dr. Skuyler had taken time out of his busy day to clean out his kid's locker. Sounded to me like he busted his ass to get over there before somebody else did. What did he not want somebody to find?

In a way, though, I was relieved. I'd been waiting for

the next kid to drop dead. But if Skuyler's father wasn't worried about him, then probably the kid was still alive.

"That's a great report, Leon. You're doing a terrific job. Keep your ear to the ground, will you? And call and report in again tomorrow night."

"Yes, ma'am, Miz Cat. Hey, M-Miz Cat, you w-want me to d-do any 'vestigating for you? I g-got my bike. I c-can ride over to the h-high school, you w-want me to. I be real g-good at following p-people, too."

This was a questionable assessment of Leon's talents. The flattest city street was laden with objects for Leon to trip over, knock over, fall against and into, and generally disarrange. Grace was not his strong suit. But his social skills made him worth two of Barbara Walters. People would tell him damn near anything.

"Not yet, Leon. Just see what you can find out from Sissy about where Skuyler went. And—keep in touch."

I hung up and drained my G&T. I had this sudden overwhelming desire to kibbitz with Cal Sepeta. So I dragged myself to my feet, limped out to the beige bomber, and headed for Cal's apartment complex. I had a suspicion I wasn't supposed to be driving—a suspicion encouraged by the shooting pains in my ankle as I worked the pedals. I didn't have far to go, and maybe I'd get lucky and not have to brake till I got there.

Where the hell was Sky Skuyler? I didn't believe for a minute that he'd willingly walked out on the team this close to the playoffs. I should have asked Leon what time the good doctor had shown up at school to clean out his son's locker. Was it before I'd visited, or after?

Maybe I was having delusions of greatness. Could a Caliban investigation really stir things up enough to cause witnesses to vanish into thin air? If it could, then I must have pushed somebody's button. But whose? And how?

What did Skuyler know about Juky's murder? Was he the murderer? A witness? Or just somebody who'd figured it out before I did? No, axe that; the kids said he was dumb. He *couldn't* have figured it out before me. That left the first two options, plus a third. Skuyler might or might not know or suspect who killed Juky, but he might know what Juky had known, either because Juky told him, or because he was implicated. Say Juky knew about a drug ring operating out of Robertson. Skuyler might have been involved in drugs, either as a buyer or seller, without having been directly involved in Juky's murder.

The front steps of Cal's apartment complex were as well lit as the inside of a Frigidaire with the door closed. The stairs in the inner court were bathed in the light of three forty-watt bulbs, one of them flickering like a goddam strobe light. Two kids sat on the top step and watched me hop up, one step at a time.

"I got a Slinky move faster than she do," I heard one of them stage whisper to the other.

I rang at the Sepeta apartment. I knocked. I felt four eyes glued to the back of my head. I rang and knocked again. Nothing. Dead silence.

I hobbled back over to the top of the stairs and steeled myself for the descent.

"Who you looking for, miss?"

"Cal Sepeta. You know him?"

"Uh-huh." He cut his eyes at the other kid, a little girl whose tights were puddling around her ankles.

"Is he a friend of yours?"

"Uh-huh. He give me tickets to the game sometime."

"Does he have a lot of friends coming here to see him?"

"Nuh-uh. He jus' come by hisself."

"Oh. So his friends don't come here?"

He shook his head and meditated on the flickering light bulb. I started my descent, hippity-hop.

"He don't live here."

I was halfway down, and damn near twisted my good ankle. I turned awkwardly.

"Lonso! You don't supposed to tell nobody!" The little girl's voice quivered in righteous indignation.

"He doesn't?"

Lonso gave her a defiant look and shook his head. At

least, that's what I thought he did. I sighed, and reversed
my hop to get a better look.

"Where does he live?"

"Beats me." He shrugged.

"But the name is still on the mailbox downstairs."

He shrugged.

"And you say he still comes around?"

"Yeah, he come by sometime to pick up the mail."

"Lonso, I'ma tell him you told!" the little girl said sternly.

"So?" The standard comeback line.

"When did he move?"

"He din't."

Now I was baffled.

"You mean, he stays at somebody else's house?" A
girl's? The coach's?

He shrugged.

"Where do his parents live?"

He shrugged.

"How come you're not supposed to tell anybody that he
doesn't live *here*?"

He shrugged.

"But he specifically asked you not to tell anybody that
he didn't live here?"

"He sure did! And when he finds out Lonso told somebody, he's gonna *kill* him!" She glared at the miscreant
and added spitefully, "And he ain't gonna give him no
more basketball tickets, neither!"

"Well, I can see Cal at school tomorrow," I improvised.
"But I had something I wanted to ask him about tonight. Do
you guys have any idea how I could get in touch with him?"

Both heads shook.

"Maybe the manager knows where I could find him," I
suggested brightly.

"We don't have no manager," Lonso said. "My daddy
say, we have a manager, we could complain about this
dump. So they don't send no manager, and we can't complain."

I nodded, looking around.

"Does anybody else ever come to pick up Cal's mail?"
I asked.

"Nuh-uh. Jus' Cal hisself."

"Well, thanks, anyway. You've been a big help."

I was halfway down the steps again when I heard, "Boy,
are you gonna get it now!"

I drove home in a snit. It was raining goddam toads from
heaven. Now I had, not just one, but two, count them, two,
fucking witnesses out of pocket. Okay, so maybe nobody
had cleaned out Cal's locker yet. But what the hell was going on? Had somebody paid off Cal with a mansion in Hyde
Park? Or a condo on the river? Or maybe it wasn't a payoff.
Maybe Cal earned that much money selling drugs. Or
maybe he was stealing. I thought of going back to ask the
kids if he ever moved things in and out of his apartment, but
I couldn't face those goddam stairs again.

I pulled into my parking space, braked, and cursed my
athletic injury. I climbed out, balanced on my crutch, and
slammed the door. I was pissed off. Plus, I kept hoping the
door would fall off and I could collect enough insurance to
buy a new car.

I was maybe three yards from the back door when I
heard a delayed echo from the door slam. I never heard
that before, I thought; must have bounced off one of the
church towers.

Two hops later, I heard it again, and something hit the
brick in front of me. Okay, so the old gray cells slow
down a bit with age. But cut me some slack—I'd only
been shot at once before in my life.

The third bullet hit my crutch, making my arm vibrate
like a goddam tuning fork. I hit the pavement—by choice,
sort of. My good ankle registered a complaint.

I'd just found the next victim: me.

I was lying maybe three yards from the back door,
bathed in the floodlight Mel had so considerately installed.
I didn't want to raise my head and provide a better tar-
get. The temporary silence did nothing to comfort me, but
the background noise of passing cars was worse, since it

drowned out the noises I needed to hear. I pictured my assailant moving into better position. How close was he, and what was he firing with? I thought longingly of the unregistered firearm I had ditched at the climax of my last case, but if he was using a rifle with a scope, it wouldn't have made any difference. I began trying to ease myself forward, propelling myself with my good knee and pulling with my hands. Behind me I heard an ominous click.

The fourth bullet hit the brick, and a spray of shrapnel bit my hand. I was a little more than a yard away from the back door. From the other side came a frantic barking that now made it impossible for me to hear anything behind me. I surged forward and covered the distance. Panting from the effort—or maybe I was just hyperventilating—I reached blindly for the handle. I kept my head down and used my left arm to save my right hand. There was a loud crack, followed by a hiss I couldn't identify, as my fingertips grazed the knob. On the other side, the barking grew louder and more frantic, as Winnie began trying to scratch her way through the door.

I grabbed the knob and gave it a sharp turn. Locked.

Then footsteps and commotion. Al threw open the door. With one arm, she was restraining Mel.

"I don't give a damn if you're all organic," she was shouting. "You're not bionic, and that bastard has *bullets*!"

"Get down!" I shouted. In the confusion I felt a rush of air from a beagle flying low. It was either Winnie or Superdog.

"Winnie! You get back here this *instant*!" She minded as well as my children always had.

In the distance, the baying of beagle, the slam of a car door, the squeal of tires.

"Are you all right, Cat?" Al was bending over me.

I was so pissed off I was cross-eyed. I was holding a limp piece of rubber on my lap.

"Goddam sneaking sorry-assed son of a bitch plugged my basketball!"

Eighteen

"Al, if I ever get my hands on that guy, you can be my lawyer! I want to sue that shitheaded, weasel-bellied bastard for all he's got! And P.S., what took you so long?"

They were dragging me in, pulling me to my feet, checking for damage.

"Sorry about that," Al said. "We were watching a cop show, so we thought it was on the TV."

"I don't know, Cat," Mel said. "You can probably get a new basketball out of him in small claims court. And maybe a new crutch. I don't think you need a lawyer."

"You don't know shit about the law, Mel. What about mental anguish? Huh? What about that? What about my goddam mental anguish?"

"There's also the little old lady angle," Al said reflectively as they helped me to the kitchen, stumbling over the three cats who were circling our ankles protectively.

"Yeah, right," I said to the cats. "Where were *you* when the shooting started?" They had the grace to look sheepish.

"The little old lady angle?"

"Yeah, you know, fragile little old lady, a heartbeat away from death, that kind of thing." Al was really getting into this.

"That's *right*! I coulda had a heart attack and died! In fact, I feel a fainting spell coming on. Mel, Sweetie, why don't you fix me a little G and T? That ought to perk me right up—if anything can, which I doubt."

Moses was out, of course; there's never an ex-policeman around when you want one. But I drowned my sorrows in gin, and permitted my lawyer to console me with visions of a vast out-of-court settlement.

Winnie returned with the air of a bird dog carrying a condor and deposited at my feet a limp scrap of cloth.

"Hey! Look at that! Winnie must have got a piece of him!"

"Way to go, Win! Good dog!"

"Yeah, Win, you were really something, girl. Made the goddam hound of the Baskervilles look like a Pekinese with a head cold."

I joined in the fuss and patted her head, while she preened, but I was already dubious. When I scrutinized Winnie's treasure, my fears were confirmed. I held it out to Al and Mel.

"Aww! It's blue denim!" Mel couldn't keep the disappointment out of her voice. I nodded at Winnie and cleared my throat as her eyebrows wavered and one ear drooped.

"Yeah! But look at the size of it!" Al enthused. "Boy, Winnie, when you set out to do something, you don't mess around! Blue denim, too! That stuff's hard to get your teeth into!"

"That's right, Sugar Plum," I said. "And when you're bigger, your Auntie Cat will teach you how to go for the ankle as well as the pants."

"Speaking of teaching, Cat, maybe this would be a good time for me to teach you some self-defense."

"Mel, honey, get real! Cat can't get any leverage on a guy standing thirty yards away shooting a gun at her! You want she should tell him to come closer?"

"Yeah, what I need is a fucking bulletproof vest. But at least, you know, this attack means I'm rattling somebody's cage. That's one of the first principles of detective work: as soon as you get close to the truth, people start shooting at you. You don't even have to know that you're close to the truth, which I don't, by the way, except that I learned something interesting tonight."

"You mean about not walking across well-lit open spaces so somebody can take a potshot at you?" Al asked brightly.

"No, before that. I learned that one of the Rattlers players doesn't live where he says he does."

"Well, maybe he's moved in with his girlfriend, and he

doesn't want his parents to know. Believe me, I didn't want *my* parents to know when I moved in with my first girlfriend."

"That's because she was such a bitch, Allie," Mel said sweetly.

"No, it's not that," I said. "Or at least—I guess it *could* be that, but would you pay rent on an apartment you weren't living in?"

"I might now, if I were desperate. But in high school—no way I could have afforded it."

"No, but this kid isn't just an average high school student, is he, Cat?" Mel mused. "I mean, if he's a Rattlers starter, he has all of Northside in the palm of his hand. Who said he's paying rent? He probably just mentioned his little problem to a property owner or three, and they fixed it up for him. Boys will be boys, and all that."

"Yeah, maybe his girlfriend is an older woman—a career woman with a lot of dough, and they're holed up in some condo somewhere."

"In *Northside*?" Mel and I stared at her incredulously. Looking for a condo in Northside was like looking for holy water at a convention of Southern Baptists. Worse— more like looking for a martini at a convention of Southern Baptists.

"That brings up an interesting question, though," Mel said. "What if he doesn't live in Northside?"

"What difference would that make?" I said, frowning.

"Well, look, Ohio isn't like some states, where kids can go to school anywhere they want, and athletes can district-hop like crazy. If you want to play for a particular school, you have to live in the district."

"What happens if you don't?"

"You're ineligible."

"So you can establish residence by renting an apartment in the district?"

"No, not really, not unless you're living in that apartment with your parents—I mean, really sleeping there and everything."

"So what happens if you've been playing for a team, and somebody finds out that you don't live in the district?"

"Could be serious consequences. Not just for you, either, but for the whole team. A team that's been playing with an ineligible player could be barred from post-season play."

"So no playoffs, no championship."

"Right."

"Gee, Cat, that's heavy," Al said. "Just think, with what you know now, you've got the opportunity to be the most hated person in Northside. You think that's why you got shot at?"

"I don't know, Al. I guess somebody *could* have seen me at Cal's apartment house tonight. They could even have seen me talking to the kids. But it doesn't seem like enough, somehow."

"Maybe not to you," Mel said, "but you're not an eighteen-year-old basketball player about to see his high school career go down in flames. Or even, say, a coach who needs a winning team to advance his coaching career. Or a basketball-crazy parent who wants to see his kid in the next Olympics. I mean, this may not be Indiana, but it's the next state over, and some people take basketball pretty seriously."

"Yeah, I know, but if Cal's ineligibility is the issue, why has Skuyler disappeared? You think *he* was about to blow the whistle on his own teammate, and ruin the team's chances for a championship? And what about Juky? I can't see somebody blowing the star forward away to protect the team's shot at a championship. If Juky raised the issue of Cal's eligibility, don't you think they would have settled things quietly? I mean, they *could* have just had Cal move in with the coach, or with somebody else, declared somebody his guardian during the school year, couldn't they? Juky died in December, so the season hadn't even started yet; they had plenty of time to arrange something.

"Anyway, I'm still trying to sort out something Reverend Cain said about Juky's interest in justice, mercy, and murder. Of course, he could have been leading me down the garden path, but if he wasn't, Juky was interested in murder, not violations of district boundary rules. Of course, Juky's interest could have been academic, too, but if it wasn't, who got murdered? And by whom? The only candidate is Jackson Tucker, and every official connected to that case says Tucker died a natural death."

"Maybe the murderee isn't directly involved with the team, Cat," Mel suggested. "Or maybe he never got hit. Maybe Juky knew somebody was planning to kill somebody, and when he went to confront the murderer, he got bumped off instead."

"Or maybe," I said glumly, "the original intended victim was the mysteriously missing Mr. Sky Skuyler."

"Yeah, but Cat, I thought you said that his father, the doctor, had confirmed that Skuyler went to live with his mother?"

"Leon says that Sissy says that the principal says that. So?"

"So . . . if the kid were really missing—oh, I get it. What if dear old dad's the killer?"

"Cat, you have *got* to change doctors," Al put in.

"Well, girls, don't let this get around, but I am, as the kids would say, totally clueless on this one. It's heartening to consider that somebody out there thinks I'm so fucking brilliant that I have to be deep-sixed, but I wish I could figure out what the hell it is that he thinks I've figured out already."

"Oh, cheer up, Cat. Maybe it was just random violence."

"Great. My daughter already thinks I injured my ankle when I was stampeded by wild shoppers on the scene of a blue-light special. She is not going to understand this at all."

Nineteen

"Mother, I could never figure out why you moved into that neighborhood anyway. You know what I told you when you bought that place. And now look—drive-by shootings, for God's sake!"

"It *wasn't* a drive-by shooting, Sharon, it was a walk-by shooting. The guy was on foot when he fired the fucking gun. Give us some credit, for crissake. This is Northside, not L.A." My head hurt the way it usually does when I talk to my daughter—not a full-blown migraine, just a dull throb like somebody was running some heavy machinery in the basement, backed up against my skull.

I hadn't intended to tell her about the shooting incident. Normally, I am pretty good at lying to my children, or just keeping things back. But she'd caught me off guard when she asked out of the blue, "What were you doing at nine o'clock last night?" and it had just slipped out. I never did find out why she wanted to know.

Suddenly, I saw a flicker of light at the end of the proverbial tunnel.

"Does this mean you're not bringing Ben over here on Friday night?"

Silence.

"Well, of course they won't be back, now that you called the police," Sharon demurred.

Silence.

"You *did* call the police, didn't you, Mother?"

"Of course I called the police! What do you take me for?"

Besides, Moses had made me call them when he had arrived home from his poker game at eleven. In the end, I realized that I was curious to know if the bullets buried in the brick of the Catatonia Arms matched the bullets that killed Juky, but I figured I'd have to apply to Moses's pal Randy Waltrip for that information.

"Well, I'll bring him, but on one condition."

"Hey, don't do me any favors, kiddo. I got a basketball game to watch, remember?"

"You can't, under any circumstances, show him the bullet holes in the wall."

"Fine with me. He doesn't even have to *see* the fucking wall. He doesn't even have to see the fucking *house*, for crissake, or the neighborhood. He can go visit his Grammy Grant."

"She lives in Pittsburgh, Mother."

Silence.

"It'll be good for both of you, Mother. He can help you out, with your ankle and all."

And maybe King Kong could help out the window washers at the Empire State Building. Don't ask me where she gets this stuff.

"I'll have him there around six-thirty."

"Tip-off is at seven, Sharon. If you make me late to this game, I'm going to be real surly."

"I *said* I'll have him there at six-thirty."

She hung up, and I headed out for the mailbox to check and see if my mail-order copy of *Sneaky Techniques for Super Surveillance* had arrived yet. I'd given up looking for my P.I. license. Like my mother always said, a watched pot never boils.

I damn near broke my other ankle tripping over a little basket that sat in front of my door.

Tied to the handle of the basket was a note in a familiar handwriting: "Please take care of me." Inside the basket was a soft pink baby blanket, and inside the baby blanket was a gun.

"Where does he *get* these things?" I asked Sidney, who was camped in front of Kevin's door, smirking as if he knew all about it. "You'd think he worked at the Long Branch Saloon, not Arnold's Bar and Grill."

I took the basket into the kitchen so that I could examine its contents in the light. The gun was so small that at first I thought maybe it was a toy, but it looked real enough close up, and nestled in the folds of the blanket were five little bullets. Sadie climbed to the top of the refrigerator and regarded me anxiously.

"Her name is Diane," I said, reading it off the side of the gun. (I don't know what you call it, but there's this kind of flat metal part over the trigger where somebody with good handwriting had etched a few words.) "And she comes from Covina, California. I wonder if I have to lubricate her with wheat germ and canola oil."

"Please take care of me"—that was no doubt Kevin's little joke. The last time he gave me a gun, I lost it. Well, I didn't exactly lose it; I ditched it just as the cops were arriving to take credit for my collar. Unregistered handguns have a way of slowing down the licensing process for aspiring private investigators.

The last gun he gave me had been a revolver—the kind where you could see where the bullets were supposed to go. With this one, you could see where the bullets were supposed to come out, but that was all. I looked around, and finally decided to point it down at the crater in the linoleum where the microwave had landed when Ben was conducting his gravity experiment. Sure enough, there was this doohickey on the bottom of the handle that made the inside of the handle slide out, and you could see where the bullets were supposed to go.

I didn't load it up, though. I'd wait for Kevin to show me how. You know how it is these days. Nothing is as simple as it seems.

Meanwhile, it was getting on toward noon, and I had work to do. I pulled on some khaki pants, a turtleneck, and boots, and drove to Robertson High, trying to ignore my ankle's objections.

I hopped purposefully past the principal's office and the sign instructing visitors to check in there. It's hard to look purposeful on crutches, so I just fixed my gaze on a distant bulletin board and propelled myself forward. I had never

met a high school principal I didn't mistrust, mostly because they were all ex-coaches who reminded me of boot-
camp drill instructors crossed with FBI informants.

The school had that fusty, distinctive high school smell
that mingled drugstore cologne and after-shave, chalk dust
and pencil shavings, gym socks and spoiled sandwiches,
sweat and hormones. In the main hall, gigantic spirit post-
ers hung from the second-floor stair rails. Enclosed in a
large glass case, a blue-and-white papier-mâché rattlesnake
raised its defiant head, as big around as a telephone pole,
its beady eyes fixed on the office door of the school nurse.
"Oscar Sez: Lets Do It!!!" some wag had scrawled on the
glass in blue paint.

The walls were a grimy institutional beige, lined with
beige lockers, but on this occasion at least they had been
covered with blue-and-white rattlesnakes, variously rendered depending on the skill and temperament of the artist,
making the hall look like Medusa's hideaway. To one
locker a bouquet of blue-and-white balloons and streamers
had been attached. Inside another locker, a phone was
ringing. Someone trying to reach their dealer? I felt like
I'd stepped into the Twilight Zone. This place was a lot
like the high school where my kids had gone to school, yet
something about it was radically, disturbingly different. If
I'd brought my gun with me, would mine have been the
only one in the building? Probably not.

Following LaTania's instructions, I reached room 204
just as the bell rang. I stepped to the side to get out of the
way, but I still took a book bag to the stomach as a short
towheaded kid slung it over his shoulder.

"Sorry," he mumbled, checking his bag for damage.

"Hey, look! It's the lady detective!" This from a tall
young woman with short, reddish-brown hair. I winced.

"Oh, sorry," she whispered, as twenty kids turned
around and gaped at me. "Were you whatchacallit—
undercover?"

"Hey, we'll screen for you," offered a blond girl whom
I remembered as one of a matched set.

"Hey, you catch the killer yet?" a lanky black girl wanted to know. "You know who he is, we take him out for you."

I was surrounded by Lady Rattlers.

"No, I haven't caught him yet," I said. "But I must be getting warm because somebody took a couple shots at me last night. You girls wouldn't know if anybody around here owns a gun?"

"Shit, man, half the guys at Robertson *say* they got one."

"Aw, man, you *know* they lie. You ever *seen* anybody pack one?"

"I bet some of 'em do—the ones that're dealin'."

"Trevor Kincaid has one. I saw it in his locker one time."

"Yeah, well Trevor Kincaid may be dealin', but Trevor Kincaid is a total dork. He doesn't know his trigger finger from his dick."

"How about the basketball team—the boys' team, I mean? Any of them packing heat?" I decided to impress them with a little professional jargon, in case I needed their respect later—or even their credulity.

"Probably. Those assholes think they are stud central."

"Yeah, once they done thinkin' 'bout basketball, they done used up all the brains they got. Course, Juky was different."

"Yeah, he was, like, this total brain."

"Cal's pretty smart."

"Yeah, but Cal don't study none, don't do none of his homework, so how smart can he be?"

"Listen, kids, I'd like to continue this conversation sometime," I interrupted. "But right now I want to catch Ms. Fisher before she goes to lunch. Can I drop by some time after practice?"

"Sure," said Blondie. "Like we said before, anything we can do to help."

"Yeah, you know where to find us."

"Hey, what happened to your foot? Did it get shot?"

"No, I, uh, was playing a little basketball, and I, uh—took a charge."

"All *right*! Give me five, girl!"

Marge Fisher, the ogre who insisted that even basketball players read an entire Dickens novel, had just set down the eraser and was turning away from the blackboard. She had that glint in her eye that said lunch hadn't arrived a minute too soon. She was a middle-aged woman with graying brown flyaway hair, a thin face, bifocals, and a penetrating look. *I* wouldn't have liked to be the one to explain why I didn't think there was anything wrong with reading the Cliffs Notes instead of the novel.

I explained who I was and why I was there. As a rule, I preferred to do this in person, so I could be reassuring or intimidating as the occasion seemed to demand.

"I wanted to catch you now and introduce myself. I was hoping you'd be willing to talk to me about Juky, and anything else you might think was relevant. I don't want to keep you from your lunch, though, so maybe you could suggest another time—"

"Well, if you're willing to put up with Tuna Hawaiian, you can come with me to lunch, Mrs. Caliban. That way, you can meet some of Juky's other teachers. We all talked to the police, of course, and I don't know what we could add at this point, but I'm sure we'd all be happy to talk with you."

As we promenaded down the hall toward the cafeteria, she made a more or less successful effort to slow her usual pace to mine, but I had to hobble pretty fast.

"I don't think any of us who knew Juky will rest easy until we find out what happened to him."

"So you don't have any ideas?"

"Not one," she said, losing some time on the turn, and then picking up speed again on the straightaway. Then, suddenly, she pulled up short. "It's as if . . . as if . . . as if someone told me that Mother Theresa had been gunned down in a vendetta. *That's* how much sense it makes."

Twenty

Maybe you never thought of putting tuna, mayonnaise, pineapple, and baby marshmallows together. Take my advice: don't. If God had intended such a dish to be created, He or She would have put pineapple plantations off the North Atlantic, where mayonnaise wouldn't spoil so quickly.

No wonder kids were hanging out at Tower Hamburgers every night. Of course, most of them were wise enough to avoid the cafeteria line and buy hamburgers at the snack bar. No wonder kids were dropping dead of heart disease after twelve years of schooling—and school lunches.

I was sitting with four of Juky's teachers—well, three, really, since Barbara Anthony only had him for homeroom. Jerry Finkelstein had taught Juky in chemistry class, and Veta Paul in algebra and trigonometry. They all agreed that Juky Kay was one smart kid.

"Mature, too," said Veta Paul. "Most kids don't know what they're doing tomorrow or next week, much less a year from now. But Juky had it all planned out: a biology major at Indiana, then a career in the NBA, then medical school."

"Yeah, I asked him if he'd consider turning pro before he finished his degree, and you know what he said?" Finkelstein cocked an eye at me. "He said he probably would turn pro, if he had the opportunity, and would finish his degree in the off-season. Most kids would say that and never do it, but with Juky, you knew he would."

"I asked him if he wanted to specialize in sports medicine," Fisher put in. "He said no, he wanted to work more with kids—in pediatrics. He showed me an essay he'd written for his college application, all about why he wanted to be a pediatrician." She shook her head.

"And some smart ass with a gun and an attitude took it all away from him, and probably never gave it a minute's thought," Finkelstein said glumly. "And we're supposed to help the kids deal with Juky's death, as if we knew what to say about it, or how to deal with it ourselves."

"So none of you has any idea who killed Juky or why?"

Barbara Anthony shook her head. "The only thing that makes any sense is drugs. Not Juky, of course, but some kind of drug dealing he knew about or saw."

"Involving kids from Robertson?"

"Oh, I don't know, I didn't say that. It's hard to believe anybody who knew him could have killed him."

"But there *are* drugs at Robertson?"

"Drugs are everywhere, Mrs. Caliban, so of course they're here as well." Fisher sounded a little defensive.

"Well, but have you noticed any particular kids who act like they might be on drugs?"

"Good heavens, woman!" Finkelstein exploded. "These are teenagers we're talking about! They *all* act like they're on drugs!"

He had a point.

"What about the basketball team? Any rumors of drugs involving basketball players?"

Finkelstein shrugged. "Rumors are a dime a dozen around here, Mrs. Caliban. Anybody who acquires expensive stereo equipment gets a reputation as a pusher."

"Or expensive tennis shoes or cars?"

"That's it."

"Where the basketball team is concerned, certain parties would rather entertain rumors of drug involvement than guesses at the truth," Fisher commented acerbically.

"Now, Marge."

"And the truth is—?"

"It's hardly a mystery, Veta, and hardly a vice limited to Robertson. If the team were three-and-seven, those kids would be walking to school or driving the kinds of jalopies *most* high school kids own, if they're lucky enough. But nothing's too good for our Northside heroes. And I'm sure you'd have a hard time proving anything amiss."

"You mean, dealers just hand over a brand new car? That doesn't seem to make much business sense," I said.

"It probably doesn't work quite like that," Finkelstein said. "Some money probably changes hands, though not much, and the cars may be demos headed for a tax write-off anyway."

"Maybe. But a tax write-off is a tax write-off. You can't write off a gift."

"Not a gift. Just a car you had to take a loss on."

"Yes, and not one of them a car you could afford on a teacher's salary," Paul observed wistfully.

"I know," I said. "I've seen them. So tell me something: anybody notice that Juky had his mind on anything in particular this fall?"

"You mean, besides college and recruiting? Not really." There was lots of head shaking all around.

"So tell me about the other kids on the team."

"What do you want to know, exactly?"

"I wish I knew exactly. Let's start with Cal. Was he really Juky's best friend?"

Everybody looked at everybody else in apparent surprise.

"Why? You think he was harboring some secret grudge against Juky?"

"Not really. I'm just trying to get a handle on all these relationships. Juky had Cal's girlfriend, and a lot more fame than Cal. Friendships have broken up over less."

"I suppose that's true," Fisher considered. "But you'd have to know Juky to understand. Except on the basketball court, he didn't have a competitive bone in his body. He was the soul of graciousness. It was hard for anybody to resent him. He worked hard, and he was just so—so damned nice."

"As far as LaTania Talbot was concerned," Veta Paul picked up the thread, "I think she and Cal had already separated when she and Juky got together."

"What's Cal like?"

"He's smart," said Finkelstein, "but he's a lazy son of a gun. Insecure, too, I'd say. Or maybe it would be more fair to say he's an average seventeen-year-old male. Easily influenced by his pals. If studying is uncool, Cal won't study."

"They're all like that, really," said Paul. "Or mostly. The Jukys, who really value education, are few and far between. The rest of them you've got to trick into learning something. On the other hand, they'll practice free throws for hours at a time, so they can be disciplined when they want to be."

"Is Scott Skuyler like that?"

Barbara Anthony heaved a huge sigh. "I don't think poor Sky can even be tricked into learning anymore. You see, Mrs. Caliban, I teach the remedial English class, so Sky's one of mine."

"We've been kidding Barb that Sky's departure has relieved her of the moral responsibility of deciding whether to pass him or not," Finkelstein said. "But seriously, Barb, would you have passed him?"

"I don't know. He's still got a year to graduation, so he could have gone to summer school. But it wouldn't be enough. He'd probably mug, cheat, and fake his way through it as he does everything else. That's how I know he's not as stupid as everybody makes him out to be. He's extraordinarily ingenious and resourceful when it comes to covering up for what he doesn't know. I might be inclined to pass him on and hope he ends up at a college with extensive tutoring for athletes."

"And what doesn't he know?"

"He doesn't know how to read, for one thing."

"A serious detriment," Paul noted, "to his making any kind of academic progress."

"You mean, he doesn't read very well?" I tried not to sound skeptical. I could recite in my sleep some of the books my kids had been required to read during their years in school. "He couldn't get through ten years of schooling and not have *any* reading skills. His father is a doctor, after all."

"Oh, you'd be surprised, Mrs. Caliban," Fisher confirmed. "A really clever kid can go a long way in school without learning the basics, especially if he or she has some other talent."

"Like a formidable sky hook," said Finkelstein.

"But a *doctor's* son," I said incredulously.

"Doesn't matter. Might even have made things worse. Maybe he didn't want to be like his father," Finkelstein pointed out. "Or maybe his father wanted an athlete, not an intellectual. Maybe his dad wanted to live vicariously the life he never got to live. Who knows? Anyway, a single parent who's also a busy professional man may not take the time to notice or care how his kid's doing in school."

"Okay, point taken. Now tell me what you think about Skuyler's withdrawal from school. Did you expect it?" I addressed the last question to Barbara Anthony in particular.

"Certainly not," she said. "I would have thought the playoffs meant everything to Sky."

"So do you believe the official version?"

"That he went to live with his mother? Yes, I suppose I do. I believe his relationship with his father was . . . well, troubled. I can imagine a quarrel that ended with his being thrown out of the house. It happens all the time."

"Yeah, well *I'd* believe it if he got a better offer to play basketball in Chicago, with a full athletic scholarship to Northwestern in the offing," Finkelstein said. "After all, in Chicago, you can play for any school in the city, no matter where you live. They don't have the residence restrictions we have here."

I opened my mouth, and shut it again. I was about to say something I would have regretted.

"Do you think he'll be back?"

"I really don't know," Fisher said.

"Okay, how about this one: what was Skuyler's relationship to Juky like?"

"Oh, they were friends, I guess," Fisher responded. "Good friends because of the team, but not best friends, if you understand the distinction."

"I guess so," I said. "Does that mean they had a personality conflict?"

"No, just some different interests," Fisher said.

"Skuyler was interested in body building," Anthony offered. "He and Eddie Atterbury spent time over at the North Side gym, while the others mostly trained here at school. Well, I guess Butch spent some time at the gym. Skuyler trained here, too, of course; Biggs wouldn't have it any other way. But I got the impression he liked to hang out with the older men. Who knows? Maybe he just did it to impress girls. Or maybe he wanted to go somewhere where he could be the only basketball hero for a change."

I could think of a few other reasons, too, but I was running out of time. Most everybody had polished off the Tuna Hawaiian and was working on the fruit Jello.

"Tell me about Corcoran," I said. "Has he always had a bad temper?"

They had to think about that one.

"It does seem like he's gotten worse," Finkelstein admitted slowly. "But most athletes undergo a personality change when they hit varsity. Hard to know if it's the fame going to their heads or the late adolescent hormones kicking in."

"Has he ever been violent?"

"I think he's seen his share of fights," Finkelstein said. "But if you have him in mind for Juky's killer, think again. He's a hand-to-hand combat man, a loose cannon but not a loose gun."

"Anybody have him in class?"

Finkelstein nodded. "He's an average student. If he studied his chemistry as hard as he studied Coach's playbook, he'd maybe pull a B minus."

"Popular?"

"Yeah, lots of friends and fans. And more than a few enemies."

"Listen, Mrs. Caliban," Fisher said, "I'll have to excuse myself. Let me know if you need anything else."

I panicked, but nobody else made a move to leave.

"Smoker," said Paul enigmatically.

"Corcoran?"

"Fisher. No more smoking in the building, so she has to retire to the parking lot with the kids. That would make me give it up if nothing else did."

"Okay, I've got two more team members to discuss: Butch Frisby and Reggie Odum."

"They're both good kids," said Anthony. "Butch is probably smarter, but they both live for basketball."

"They've both been injured recently. Has the team seen lots of injuries lately?"

"Yeah," Finkelstein said. "They've been playing their hearts out, of course, but sometimes you've gotta wonder if they're going to make it to the NCAAs."

"And Skuyler's been sick a lot. Is it an unhealthy team, would you say?"

"Well, as Jerry says, they've been playing hard," Paul said. "As for illness—I don't know if you've ever lived with teenagers . . ."

I nodded.

"Well, then, you know how it is. Somebody gets sick, they pass it around the whole school. Some kids get whatever it is two or three times. It doesn't help that they eat the kind of junk they eat."

"So would you say that everybody on the team gets along pretty well?"

"Thick as thieves." Finkelstein grinned, making me wonder if I was supposed to read something into that.

"No racial tensions, for example?"

Now that Fisher had left, I was talking to two black faculty and one white one. But they were all shaking their heads.

"We're not saying they don't exist at Robertson," An-

thony explained. "But they don't seem to affect the team
at all. Oh, the blacks on the team seem closer to the other
blacks, but they all get along."

"But Skuyler hangs out with the trainer—Atterbury.
Isn't that what you said?"

"Yes, that's true," she conceded.

"What's he like?"

"Bright, ambitious, vain, not very popular," Paul put in.
"He's the kind of kid that might blossom after high school,
you know what I mean? High school is so . . ."

"Damaging to the ego," Finkelstein offered.

"Well, I guess that's one way to put it. High school kids
aren't really very flexible, and it's easy to get categorized
early on. Ed's like a lot of kids who aren't big enough or
quick enough to play sports."

"So he makes up for it by being a Rattler groupie,"
Finkelstein added, "and basking in the reflected glory."

"But, as I said, he's smart. I could see him as a head of
a multinational corporation some day, wearing Armani
suits over his tanning-bed tan."

"Or head of an international crime syndicate,"
Finkelstein muttered.

A bell rang and made me jump a foot. My elbow landed
in my Tuna Hawaiian, cushioned by tiny marshmallows.

"Ten-minute warning," Finkelstein explained. "We have
time for Final Jeopardy."

"Okay, so tell me about Biggs," I said, swabbing down
my elbow with one of those anti-absorbent institutional
napkins.

"Biggs? He's made for his job. He's a real son of a
bitch, who eats, drinks, and breathes basketball. Probably
why his wife left him."

"Is he ethical?" A trick question. I'd already heard a
sample of his tactics with Marge Fisher.

"Is a rattlesnake friendly? Of course, he's not ethical!
He's a high school coach, in training to be a college coach,
in training to be a pro coach, if he lives that long, which
is highly unlikely at the rate he's going."

"The boys say he wouldn't tolerate drugs."

"Probably true, and about the nicest thing you could say about the guy, unless you live for basketball championships."

"Is he any good as a coach?" I noticed that now that we were talking sports, the two women had dropped out of the conversation altogether. Had they tuned out, or were they biting their tongues to keep from saying something?

"Hell, he's brilliant. No argument there."

"But he's not hot on academics?"

"No."

"So tell me this: what would he do to win a state title?"

Finkelstein grinned at me and leaned back in his chair.

"If you're asking me if he'd kill to win a state title, the answer is yes. But he wouldn't kill Juky Kay. He may be brilliant, but nobody wins a state title without a star athlete."

Twenty-one

"So Finkelstein thought I was barking up the wrong tree with Biggs—or driving for the wrong basket, not to mix my metaphors. He's probably right. After all, Juky and Cal were best friends, so obviously Juky knew where Cal lived, and had known for a while. So my idea that he threatened to expose Cal, and get the team disqualified from post-season play, doesn't really fly."

"He doesn't seem to have been the threatening type, anyway," Kevin observed, splashing a little sherry on the mushrooms he was sautéeing. He was wearing pajama bottoms and a ratty blue terry-cloth bathrobe—the kind of item your mother always tries to throw out when you're not looking.

"Well, 'threaten' is probably too strong for what I mean. I just thought maybe Juky had some ethical crisis, and when he took it to the Lord in prayer, the Lord told him to sit down with Cal for a little heart-to-heart about the league rules. He may not have meant it as a threat, but somebody—Cal or Biggs—heard it that way. Or else maybe he 'threatened' to quit the team again rather than play on a team that was violating the rules."

"So, to keep him from quitting the team, Biggs killed him." With a flick of the wrist, Kevin slid the eggs around in his omelette pan. "It's original."

"Yeah, well, I'm nothing if not original."

"Well, what the hey, Mrs. C., as long as we're inventing, try this one: threatened by Juky's conscience, Biggs arranges to meet Cal on the pretext of discussing the situation. Cal freaks, and gets Juky to go instead, so Juky can talk things over with Biggs and get Cal off the hook. Meanwhile Biggs has decided that the easiest solution is to eliminate Cal. The meeting place is dark, and Biggs plugs

Juky." He aimed his spatula at me and fired. "What do you think?"

"I think that if you want to hide the address of an ineligible player, the last thing you want to do is murder him. Hey, how do you get that to cook evenly? Doesn't it stay gooey in the middle?"

"Voilà." He slapped a lid on the pan. "Evens out the heat."

"Say, speaking of heat, I found the gun. You know, you shouldn't leave those things lying around like that."

"I had solemn promises from all minors on the premises that they would leave it alone. Right, Sid?"

Sidney had just clambered up the back of the terry-cloth robe, leaving a trail of pulled threads in his wake, though I didn't think Kevin would notice. Now he was sitting on Kevin's shoulder. He loves to watch Kevin cook, and he is too short to look over Kevin's shoulder. This would drive me nuts if I were cooking, but he doesn't do it to me. Sid appreciates style, something my culinary technique is lacking.

"So do the bullets go in that doohickey that drops down from inside the handle?"

"Yes, I'll show you. But not until brunch is over."

"It's so cute. I like it lots better than the last one you gave me. That one was so damn heavy."

"Yeah, but that's the point, Mrs. C. This one is only .25 caliber, which means it's not going to stop anybody dead in their tracks."

"I don't want to stop anybody dead in their tracks. I just want their goddam respect."

"Well, you might not get that with a .25 caliber, either. They might be disabled by laughter. But it was the best I could do on short notice."

"So what are you telling me here? I might as well go buy a squirt gun?"

"Not exactly." Sidney wobbled as Kevin's shoulder dipped. Kevin was in that tricky stage where you slide the omelette onto the plate and fold it over. That's why I eat my eggs scrambled.

"A .25 caliber like the Wilkinson Diane can do some damage, and it's damage most people won't want done. Its ... uh, previous owner probably just wanted it to scare off potential muggers and rapists. It works fine for that, especially if the other party isn't armed. The down side is it's mostly going to weaken the other guy by causing internal bleeding, maybe slow down his getaway. The up side is that if the other guy takes it away from you, and shoots you with it, you won't be too bad off. Want some of this omelette?"

"Thought you'd never ask. Say, Kevin, did you ever hear of putting tuna and—never mind. Not while you're eating. So once I find Juky's killer, I plug him with my pal Diane, and he staggers off slowly enough so's I can limp after him and finish him off with my crutch?"

"No, you limp in the other direction and call the cops. They've got bigger guns."

"I could sic Leon on him."

"Or Winnie."

"Or Winnie. Then maybe *she'd* get a citation from the city."

"Moses would never have to pay another dime for puppy chow, as long as he lived in Northside."

"So, Kevin, how'd you like to go undercover?"

"I *am* undercover. I'm really a sixty-year-old former mob accountant with a face lift and a new identity as a charming gay bartender and gourmet cook."

Sidney, who had landed on the table, rolled over on his back and stuck all four feet in the air. He loves Kevin's jokes.

"No, seriously. You like to work out."

"I like to play games. I like my exercise to have a point to it. Mel likes to work out."

"Mel can't do this assignment. She nominated you."

"To do what? I don't think I'd fly as the Rattlers' new point guard, Mrs. C."

"I need you to check out the North Side Gym."

"What am I checking out about it?"

"Oh, the usual. Find out if there's any drugs, organized crime, or prostitution going on there."

"That certainly narrows the field. So, white collar crime I ignore, right? Along with failure to yield right of way and lapsed dog licenses?"

"Right. Two of the Rattlers—Skuyler, the missing forward, and Eddie Atterbury, the trainer—used to hang out at this gym. Find out if anybody else did—I mean, any of the other players, or if anybody knew Juky Kay, or if anybody knows where Skuyler disappeared to. Hell, while you're at it, find out if anybody knows Reverend Cain or Coach Rex Biggs."

"Do I know these guys, or am I just curious?"

"No, you don't know them. If we're lucky, maybe Atterbury will show up while you're there, and you can strike up an acquaintance."

"What's my cover?"

"Your cover? Your cover. Can't you just be a charming gay bartender and gourmet cook?"

"Oh, well, now you're going to take all the fun out of it! What's in it for me?"

"Okay. Who do you want to be?"

"Let's see. An airline pilot?"

"No way. You'd look suspicious if you were around more than three days."

"Well, how long *am* I going to have to hang around this place, lifting heavy objects and sweating?"

"I don't know, but the airline pilot is definitely out."

"Okay." He pouted a little as he speared his last mushroom. Then he brightened. "How about a cameraman for Channel 12 news?"

I shook my head. "They'd all be watching for one of those trucks with the satellite dish on top, and they'd get suspicious if you never showed up in one. Besides, you don't know enough about videography. Do you?"

"I could learn."

"No. Not enough time."

"Well, can I be a cab driver, then? You wouldn't let me be one on your last case."

"Sure, you can be a cabdriver. You can even be working on an alternative career—writing a novel, say, or whatever, as long as it's something you know something about."

"Do I have time to grow a beard?"

"No."

"Aw, Mrs. C—"

"No, Kevin. And that's final."

Twenty-two

It was one of those bright winter days after a snowfall, when the sun hits the snow and bounces back with such a blinding glare that it hurts your eyes. That was only one of the reasons why I was wearing my mirror sunglasses, especially since by five-thirty, the sun was pretty far down.

The other was mercifully absent when I showed up at the Lady Rattlers practice. I could hear his voice booming in the distance, bouncing off the lockers and echoing through the shower stalls down the hall, but I wasn't interested in a confrontation today.

Instead I bumped into Maury Schwab, tie clipped to his shirtfront about halfway down his chest.

"That you behind those Foster Grants?"

"Hey, Maury."

"Pretty good disguise. The crutch is particularly effective, I think. Makes you look like you've been playing for the Rattlers. Say, you missed a good one today," he said, nodding at the court.

"Why? What happened?"

"Corcoran collided with Shellenstein, and came up limping. I thought Biggs was going to tear them both limb from limb."

"Is Corcoran badly hurt?"

"Hell, he won't be by Friday night, whatever he is today. Old Doc Skuyler will shoot him up with a painkiller. Biggs will figure he can always have surgery later, but he's only got one more shot at a state championship."

"So Biggs was really pissed off?"

Schwab shrugged. "Put yourself in his shoes. Say you're obsessed with basketball—I mean, *really* obsessed. You lose one star player, then a second one quits. The few you've got left are trying to kill each other off on the court before the final game of the season.

"Anyway, I'm glad I ran into you. I was planning to call you. What have you got for me on this Skuyler thing? Kid really quit the team and leave town?"

"Shit, Maury, I was hoping you knew more about it than I did. Looks like you know as much as I do. Skuyler decided to go live with his mother. That's the official version."

"You talk to his old man?"

"Not since he disappeared. Or, rather, I *did* talk to him since then, but before I knew he'd disappeared, if you get my drift."

"So what's your reading, Caliban? Are we talking father-son blowout, or what? Kid's male, so he can't be pregnant, last I heard."

"Well, when I saw Skuyler, Sr., he didn't look happy. Somebody suggested maybe Skuyler got a better offer from a Chicago school, since the mother lives in Chicago."

"Better than a shot at the state championship? Not likely. You talk to the mother?"

"No. How could I do that? I mean, what would I say to her, even supposing I could track her down?"

"Jesus, Caliban, how're you ever going to make detective if you don't start sticking your nose into other people's business? Take it from me, you got to be obnoxious, absolutely-fucking-obnoxious, if you want to get the information you need."

"Okay, so *you* call the mother."

"Find me a phone number, and I will."

"Hey, I thought you were God's gift to investigative reporting. Why can't you find the phone number?"

"I am. I'm asking you. And I'll bug the hell out of you until you get it for me."

"Obnoxious is a two-way street, Schwab."

"That's the spirit, Caliban. Say, I gotta run. I gotta do one of my obnoxious, insensitive, hard-as-nails award-winning interviews with Biggs, and ask him what he's going to do without his two star players."

"Okay. See you at the funeral."

"Right. I'll be the one lying down."

"With the clip-on tie."

The girls were running plays as I clambered up the bleachers to watch. With my crutch, I only made it two rows, then gave up. My pal with the short reddish-brown hair waved at me. She was playing forward, and the black girl with the close-cropped Afro was playing forward, too. The blond twins were guards. But I caught myself staring at the center: a tall girl, slim but muscular, with jet-black skin and the most gorgeous headful of tiny black braids I'd ever laid eyes on. She had long fingers that made the basketball look more like a softball, and she moved gracefully, braids swinging.

The players made the coach look tiny, a Skipper to their Barbie. But she had a hell of a lot more energy than Skipper did, and I rarely caught her standing still. She had short brown hair and freckles, and a voice that contradicted her pixie look. She'd probably had a lot of practice yelling at Biggs, I figured. I didn't remember her name, since all the players called her Coach.

One thing I noticed right away was that she had a lot more praise for her players than Biggs did. She didn't throw anything, either, except the basketball.

Practice broke up about six-thirty, and my redhead climbed the bleachers in one step.

"Need some help, Columbo?"

"It's Caliban," I said. "And you're . . . ?"

"Turk. Nan Turk."

The other forward paused below us.

"Hey, Lady Detective! You goin' to come do some detecting on us right now?"

"If it's okay with you."

"It's okay wit' me if it's okay wit' you—if you can stand the smell." She took an ostentatious sniff at her jersey for emphasis.

"I'll hold my breath," I said. "Cat Caliban." I offered her my free hand.

"Terry Shipes. This here's Julie or Emmy Millikin." She grabbed one of the blond guards by the back of the jersey. "Don't matter which one. They answer to both."

"Yeah, we make it easy for you, Shipes," Blondie grinned, " 'cause we know how all whitefolks look alike."

This was probably a running joke of theirs, and everybody laughed on cue.

"Well, look at me and Ana." Terry grabbed the center by the waistband. "Colored folks got some di*versity*. Ana, say hello to Cat Caliban, the lady detective that's gonna catch Juky's killer. Ms. Caliban, say hello to Ana. You don't have to know her last name 'cause we can't pronounce it, anyway."

"Does the coach know I'm here?" I asked. I didn't want to sneak around. Unless I found out that was the only way I could accomplish anything.

"Hey, Coach!" Nan bellowed. "The lady detective is here!"

"Well, now she know for sure," Terry said, pounding her ear.

So, probably, did Biggs.

The pixie with the drill sergeant's voice popped out of her office.

"Barb Driscoll," she said, extending a hand.

"Cat Caliban," I said, shaking it. "You understand, I'm not official, Coach."

"Looks like you're on the injured reserve list." We pushed through swinging doors into the girls' locker room. It smelled of moldy showers and sweat socks.

"Coach, you got to show the lady how to take a charge so she don't keep getting her ankles busted."

Driscoll cocked an eyebrow at me.

"Yeah, I *could* use some pointers," I conceded.

"So tell me how you got involved with Juky's death."

She indicated a nearby bench, with the air of a business executive seating a client.

"Well, let's just say that Mrs. Kay asked me to look into it."

"Okay. Would that be true if we said it?"

"Oh, it's true, all right."

"So, how can we help?"

"Yeah," Nan said. "You find the perp, and we'll use his head for a basketball in our next practice!"

"To tell you the truth," I said. "I'm still trying to sort information. I've got a hell of a lot of it, and some of it must be useful, or somebody wouldn't be taking potshots at me. But I need some help from some insiders."

"Somebody shot at you?" one of the blond sisters asked. "That's so cool!"

"Yeah, so cool she might wind up dead," somebody pointed out.

"What do you want to know?" Driscoll asked.

"Well, let's start at the beginning. Were any of you here the day Jackson Tucker died?" I was determined to ask about Tucker, since I'd been cheated out of that particular question at lunchtime.

They looked around at one another.

"Most of us were here," Julie said.

"And Coach?"

She nodded.

"Can you tell me what happened?"

"Nan, you and Emmy were watching at the time."

"Well, it was real creepy," Emmy began.

"Yeah, Tuck was running up the court—"

"Yeah, and then he, like, stopped, and kind of bent over—"

"Like he was out of breath, or got a stitch in his side, or something—"

"And then—I don't know—he went down on his knees, and then he just, like, totally collapsed."

"He was clutching at his chest, and he said something—we couldn't hear what—"

"Yeah, and then, everybody kind of gathered around him, you know?"

"Was Biggs there?"

"Yeah, he went, like, 'For crissake, Tuck, get your ass off the floor.' "

"But when Tucker didn't get up, he kind of stood there and stared at him."

"I think it was Juky who told somebody to send for an ambulance. And then Juky, he started CPR."

"He used to work at this summer camp, so he knew all about first aid."

"So then *I* went and got Coach, 'cause you could just see that Biggs was totally clueless."

"So Coach came, and made everybody stand back and give Juky some room, and she had somebody get some blankets out of the locker room. And then the emergency squad came, and they worked on him awhile—not too long, though—"

"I heard them say they weren't getting a pulse," Driscoll said.

"Then they loaded him up on the stretcher, and put him in the back of the ambulance, and carted him off. And that was the last we saw of him."

"Where was Biggs at this point?"

"Coach made him move back, like everybody else. So he was just standing there, watching."

"Anybody notice his reaction when the medic made the comment about no pulse?"

"He looked very . . . um, scared. Very frighten." Ana spoke in careful, heavily accented English. "He lose color in the face."

"Other reactions?"

"Just shock, mostly. I mean, most of us never saw anybody die or anything. Not that we knew he was dead right then. I mean, who would have thought he *could* be dead? He was our age, and everything."

"How was Juky's CPR?" I asked Driscoll.

"Very competent. He obviously knew what he was doing, so I thought the best thing we could do was stay out of his way."

"You said when he collapsed he said something. Who was close enough to hear what he said?"

Nan and Emmy looked at each other blankly.

"Try to picture the scene in your mind's eye, and picture where everybody was on the court. Tuck had collapsed, he was clutching his chest, and he said something. Who was closest to him?"

"Corcoran, I think. He was kind of ahead of Tuck. Then off to one side was Skuyler. Then maybe two steps behind was Juky."

"Do you think they could have heard him?"

"I guess so. Everybody was watching him at that point."

"Was Dr. Skuyler around that day, by any chance?"

"No, he came while the ambulance was still there."

"And what was his reaction?"

"He say, 'There is not'ing wrong with that boy,' " Ana said.

"Was he angry? Upset? Frightened?"

Ana considered, and I waited for the words to catch up with her. "No. Shock."

"Why are you asking about Tucker's death, Ms. Caliban? The coroner said it was a heart attack brought on by hereditary atherosclerosis. What makes you think it's connected to Juky's death?" Driscoll asked.

"I don't know," I admitted. "I just don't like the odds that it's not, I guess. But I'm willing to entertain other theories, if anybody's got one."

Lots of head shaking. Since some of them had already made a trip to the showers, this caused considerable precipitation.

"Okay, anybody know where Skuyler is or why he left?"

Silence and more head shaking.

"Anybody care?" somebody quipped.

"Anybody know him well enough to know what his relationship with his father is like?"

"No, just well enough to know he ain't about to pass up no state championship."

"So, you think he'll be back?"

"He come back now, Biggs liable to kill him for missing practice."

"Yeah, shoot first, and ask questions later. Like, 'now where I'm goin' to find me a forward can shoot the basketball?' "

"Well, he got Shellenstein."

This pronouncement was greeted with laughter.

"I ain't talkin' 'bout no stand-still shooting."

"Aw, Shelly okay. He jus' wet behind the ears. Plus, Coach be all the time on his case, he can't hardly concentrate."

"Have you seen Biggs act violently toward his players?"

"Yeah, sure."

"Now, ladies," Driscoll said. "Biggs is not our favorite person, but if the point is to catch Juky's killer, we have to be scrupulously accurate in the information we give to Ms. Caliban. We've probably all seen Biggs grab a player, or whack him on the butt, or even jerk him around, maybe give him a shove. But has anybody ever seen him strike a player or knock him down?"

They shook their heads.

"I bet he's done it, though," came a small voice from the back of the gathering.

"I've heard that Coach Biggs and Dr. Skuyler are pretty close."

"Well, the doc gets free passes to all the games, and sits behind the bench and all, in case anybody gets hurt. They both like basketball, so I guess they're friends. Him and Mr. Odum are always hanging around."

"And Mr. Tucker used to."

"Yeah, he still comes around sometimes, though, to watch the team play."

"That's so weird!"

"Okay, I have one more question. Remember, now, I'm not the police. On the other hand, I intend to find Juky's killer, and sooner or later, that will involve the police." I hoped later rather than sooner. "Anybody know of any drug use on the boys' team?"

Silence.

"What you mean?"

I thought it was pretty obvious, so I wondered if they were buying time.

"Drugs. Dope. You know, cocaine, PCP, crack, pills, hell, even marijuana."

"No, nothing like that. Biggs would *really* kill them if he found out something like that was going down."

"Well, I guess that's it, then. I can't think of anything else to ask right now."

"Hey, Ms. Caliban, why don't you come to the spring formal Saturday night? You could, like, sneak around and observe all your suspects in one place. And we could, like, be your eyes and ears, too, and report back to you if we see anything suspicious."

"Are you expecting any more dead bodies to show up at this affair?"

"No, but then, we didn't expect the last two."

"I see your point." I did, too. Hell, I was more worried than they were. They had the confidence of the young that nothing bad could ever happen to them or anyone they knew.

"See, you could show up, and then the killer, if he's there, he'll get all nervous, and maybe take another shot at you, and then we'll nab him!"

"Sounds like a lovely evening, but I don't have a date."

"Neither do I," said Nan. "Pick you up at seven."

"Excellent," I said. "I can hardly wait."

I took Coach Driscoll aside a few minutes later and asked her if she'd ever entertained any suspicions about Tucker's death.

"To be honest, I really didn't, at least at the time." She fingered her whistle unconsciously. "I mean, it's highly unusual for a young person to die of heart disease, but not unknown. So I didn't think anything of it." She paused, and stared off into space. "Until Juky died. Then, I confess, I wondered."

"What did you wonder?"

"If there was something—something going on in the boys' locker room. Something dangerous. And if . . . anybody else could get killed over it. Our kids are so vulnerable, Ms. Caliban. Biggs runs a tight ship, but I don't think he recognizes just how vulnerable they are."

Twenty-three

Before I left the locker room, I'd arranged a date to the spring formal for Moses, too, with a second stringer name of Pearl. Driving home, I spent most of my time trying to figure out how I was going to persuade him to go, and how much it would cost me in the long run. A lot, probably, but I wanted him around in case anything developed that I couldn't handle. I planned to take Diane along, too, but from Kevin's account I was beginning to think I'd be better off bashing somebody over the head with her than shooting them.

I didn't have a goddam thing to wear to this gala event. The classiest place Fred ever took me was Bob Evans, and Bob didn't care what I wore as long as it included shirt and shoes. Maybe I'd canvas my friends and see what they had in my size.

I swung by the KFC and picked up some dinner for me and the cats—original recipe for me, and extra crispy for them—and went home determined to do what I'd been avoiding: call Jackson Tucker's father and arrange to see him.

Actually, I had a pretty good story cooked up, if I do say so myself. I told him I was a free-lance writer doing a story on great athletes dying young. He agreed to see me on Thursday night. He sounded impressed.

That gave me a few days to attend to my wardrobe and track down Cal Sepeta. As it turned out, finding a dress for Saturday night and finding Cal were equally challenging enterprises. Moses I didn't have to worry about, once I convinced him to go. Being a man with some class, he already owned a tux.

So far, I knew where Cal didn't live: he didn't live at the address given in the school directory. I called up La-

Tania and got directions to a house out on Colerain, almost
to the shopping mall. Still hoping to surprise him, I drove
out there. I found some kids playing basketball in the
driveway of a split-level ranch house, but they were all too
young.

Take it from me, it's damn hard to sneak up on anybody
if you're hobbling on a crutch. By the time I got both legs
out the door, and the crutch, everybody in the goddam
neighborhood knew I was there.

I waited until there was a break in the game.

"I'm looking for Cal. He home?" I wanted to make it
sound as casual as possible, so they wouldn't have time to
suspect I came from the athletic commission or whoever it
is that monitors high school sports.

"Naw, he ain't home." The kid who spoke inbounded
the ball and headed for the basket.

"Know where he is?"

"Maybe at Butch's." He caught a pass and went for the
layup without breaking his concentration.

I climbed back in the beige bomber and headed back to
Northside. This time there was no sign of Butch and
Reggie out front. A man about my age came to the door
holding a newspaper.

"Is Butch around?"

"No, he ain't here."

"You know where I can find him?"

"Lenora," he called, turning around. "Where Butch at?"

"Cal came by, and he went out. I think they over at
Reggie's."

"Thanks," I said, and made my way back to the car,
where I pulled out the directory and looked up Reggie's
address.

There was no sign of life at Reggie's, but out front three
young men were gathered around a car that was playing
loud rap music.

"I'm looking for Reggie," I said. "Anybody seen him
tonight?"

"Yeah, he was here. He gone with Cal and Butch."

"You know where they went?"

"Seem like somebody say they was going to pick up Corky."

"Thanks."

I was beginning to get cranky. Didn't these kids have any homework to do to keep them off the streets? In my day, back in the dark ages, we had Latin exercises and algebra problems and maps to draw and reports to write, and we couldn't do it in front of the television because there wasn't any television. No wonder they couldn't get through *Hard Times*. You can't read a goddam novel in homeroom.

Corky's mother wasn't sure where the boys were, either, but she thought they'd said something about Shelly's, by which I assumed she meant Shellenstein.

Shelly's mother thought Shelly was over at his girlfriend's, studying.

Shelly's girlfriend's mother thought they were over at Shelly's, studying.

I was sitting behind the wheel of the beige bomber reconsidering my career in detection when Leon sauntered up. He had a pencil stuck behind his ear, so my lightning-quick mind concluded that he was collecting for his paper route. Some mysteries are easier than others.

"Hey, M-Miz Cat. What you doin' sittin' in the c-car like that? Are you d-doin' one of them, one of them, s-stake things?"

"No, Leon, I'm not conducting a stakeout. Believe it or not, I'm looking for Cal Sepeta."

"He n-not here."

"No. I know that."

"Prob'ly, he over at the arcade."

"At the what?"

"The arcade. See, they got this place you can play all kind of computer games."

"What makes you think he's there?"

Leon shrugged. Almost as an afterthought, he added,

"That where they say they goin' when Corky get in the car."

"Where is this place?"

"You know where the Chuck E. Cheese p-pizza parlor is, up on C-Colerain? It back b-behind there, in the shop'n center."

I could probably save a lot of time if I went to Leon in the first place whenever I needed information.

Maybe it had something to do with being shot at, but dark parking lots were beginning to give me the creeps. Rationally, I knew that well-lit parking lots, like my own at the Catatonia Arms, were worse, but I still waited until a couple pulled up three cars away, then climbed out and followed them in.

Sure enough, the little arcade was overrun with hulking teenage mutant humans, gigantic hands wrapped around joysticks, stooping to watch little multicolored explosions on a computer screen. I'd never known computer games could be so physical. Shellenstein wasn't there.

Cal was in the corner, piloting a miniscule spacecraft amid meteor showers and enemy death rays. Every time he pushed the button on his joystick, the whole machine rocked.

He was talking to himself and anybody who would listen.

"Damn! Damn! Fucking meteors killin' me, man. Look at that motherfucker! Get him! All *right!* We on a roll, now. Wait. Where'd that sucker come from? Shit, man, this stick ain't workin' right. Oh, fuck, an asteroid! Aw, man!" "GAME OVER" appeared on the screen. "Fuck this machine, man! This fuckin' stick is all fucked up, man!" He gave the machine a vicious kick.

He turned around, and we were face-to-face at last. Well, let me rephrase that: he turned around, and we were face-to-chest at last.

"Eight quarters for five minutes of conversation, Cal," I proposed. Okay, I'm cheap, but I figured it was better than minimum wage, and he was just a teenager even if he was a foot taller than me.

"Aw, man, what you want to talk to *me* about, lady? I done already told you I don't know nothin' about Juky's death."

"Hey, Cal, you got another quarter, man?" Butch called.

"Five minutes. That's all I want."

"Okay. Five minutes. But that's all, 'cause I'm a busy man."

"I can see that."

"Hey, Cal, where you goin', man?"

"Hey, Cal, you know what Coach said about talking to her."

"I'll be back in a minute."

We went out and sat down in the mall.

"What happened to Skuyler?" I asked. With only five minutes, I couldn't afford preliminary niceties—how are you, are you looking forward to the playoffs, what do you think of the team's chances, what do you think of the teen-age drug problem, that kind of baloney.

"Look, I don't know what happened to Sky. If I ever see him, I'm gonna find out. And then I'm gonna whip his ass."

"What did the coach say happened to him?"

"Coach don't know nothin', man; he as shocked as the rest of us. Don't get nothin' out of Sky's old man. Coach wanted to talk to Sky, but the old man say he don't have no number, on account of his ex-wife don't want him to have it."

"Doesn't anybody have any theories?"

Cal shrugged. "We figure he got in a fight with his old man, and left. But that don't make sense 'cause we woulda heard from him. Somebody woulda. My old man threw me out, I go to Butch's or Reggie's, or maybe even to Coach's."

Now there was an angle I hadn't thought of. What if Skuyler *had* been thrown out, and picked the wrong person to run to. His father might be too embarrassed to admit they had a fight, and might assume his son had either run away or gone to live with his mother.

I switched tacks. "Juky have something on his mind last fall, Cal?"

"Recruiting."

"Besides recruiting."

"The championship."

"Besides that."

"What you gettin' at?"

"You remember a Bible study class when you discussed the Sermon on the Mount?"

"Yeah."

"You remember the part about sand in the eyes, and not criticizing other people?"

"Maybe."

"Reverend Cain said Juky was really interested in the ethical questions it raised, about when you had a responsibility to speak up and when you should keep quiet."

"Yeah. So?"

"Juky introduced the topic of murder. Do you remember that?"

"Maybe."

"Who was he talking about, Cal? Who was murdered?"

Cal rolled his eyes and hunched his shoulders, the way teenagers do when they're exasperated, except he had more to work with.

"He wasn't talking about nobody in particular. It was just a *discussion*, see? Juky was just asking a hypothetical question, like. He was all the time doing that. He was a real thoughtful guy, and that's why him and Reverend Cain got along so good."

"I don't think so."

"What you mean?"

"I don't think it was just a hypothetical question. I think he meant something by it, and I think *you* know what he meant." I was switching into attack Cat mode.

He moved into position, and took the charge.

"Oh, yeah? Well, who do *you* think got murdered? Anybody I know?"

"Yeah, as a matter of fact. I think it was Jackson Tucker."

"Aw, man, Tuck had heart disease. Everybody know that."

"I'm not interested in what everybody knows, Cal. I'm interested in what *you* know that you aren't telling me. And I intend to find out." That kind of shook him, I could tell.

"See, I don't think it's just a matter of district boundaries and where you live." His eyes shifted to look at mine. "I don't think anybody'd kill Juky over district boundaries."

"Well, you right about that, lady. And I tell you another thing." His voice was kind of choked now, and to my surprise, he had tears in his eyes. He stood up and towered over me. "Juky was my best friend, and you think I would've raised a hand to hurt him, you dead wrong."

The parking lot seemed darker and more deserted now, even though there were plenty of cars there. I surveyed them with dismay. Where the hell had I parked? Surely, I thought as I hobbled around, I would have parked closer than this.

I heard footsteps behind me, and headed for the nearest light, some thirty yards away. I'd never make it. I plunged my hand into my purse and felt desperately for the little pistol. It wasn't there.

The footsteps were catching up with me. I turned.

Cal stood there, hand extended, holding a gun, *my* gun. "Here, lady, you dropped this out your bag."

Twenty-four

I spent part of the next day making the rounds of my friends, and trying on a truckload of dresses reputed to be "just perfect" for me. Either they were too goddam tight to breathe in, or long enough to guarantee that I would trip and break the other ankle, or too full to allow me to maneuver with a crutch. Or else they were just plain ugly—and believe me, my standards plummeted as the day wore on and Saturday got closer.

I could tell Kevin was dying to go shopping with me. The way I could tell was that he kept dropping by to describe his latest fantasy dress for me.

"I see you in something very plain, very chic, perhaps black velvet."

"Is this number covered with cat hairs in your fantasy?"

"Maybe some white satin shoes—"

"Oh, no. Stop right there! I'll be damned if I'm going to invest in a new pair of shoes when I can only wear one."

"Okay. Forget the shoes. We don't want to draw any attention away from your décolletage, anyway."

"My who? Listen, Kevin, it's probably going to be ten degrees out and icy. When I'm not concentrating on my footwork, I'll probably want to be warm." He put on one of those wounded puppy dog looks. He does it better than Winnie, who's had less practice. "Okay, Kevin, I give up. Want to go shopping tomorrow?"

"Oh, I don't know, Mrs. C. I'm pretty tuckered out from all this weight lifting I've been doing at the gym. But if you need me to, I guess I could manage it." This was all an act. Kevin had been in good shape even before he started frequenting the North Side Gym, and we both knew it. "Maybe I'll go whip up a batch of granola bars to fortify me."

"You do that," I said. "By the by, have you uncovered any nefarious criminal activities at the gym yet?"

"No, but I think I'm about to be asked out."

"No drug dealing in the locker room? Numbers running in the whirlpool? Illicit sex in the showers?"

"What whirlpool? In this dive, I'm lucky they've got showers, and those aren't any too clean. This dump is a real he-man's hangout, Mrs. C. No aerobics classes, no health bar, no Muzak. The guy behind the counter cleans his fingernails with a switchblade, and the linen all looks like it was filched from someplace. My plan is to find out whatever it is I'm supposed to find out before I pick up some disease that my immune system never heard of before."

That night, armed with all this useless information, I went looking for Mr. Muscle Beach himself, Eddie Atterbury. Since he was apparently a particular pal of Skuyler's, I couldn't afford to leave him out of my calculations. Plus, he was also a North Side Gym regular.

Atterbury lived in one of your average Northside brick houses, on Fergus Street, maybe two blocks from Butch. I didn't see any fancy cars around, like the other kids had, but then, if I owned a fancy car, I wouldn't park it on Fergus Street either. I'd probably park it in a locked garage in Hyde Park and go visit it now and then.

Who should answer the door but Atterbury himself, holding one of those chest developer things with handles.

"Hi," I said. "Remember me?"

His face told me he did.

I planted one foot inside.

"Mind if I come in? I'm interviewing all the team members in the course of my investigation, and you're clearly an important part of the team, so I wanted to talk to you."

"I'm kinda busy, studying for a history exam tomorrow."

Yeah, right. The television was on in the living room, loud, apparently showing some MTV rockumentary. There was a Gatorade making rings on the coffee table. There was some piece of exercise equipment in the process of being assembled in the middle of the floor. Ditto a page of instructions, several plastic bags full of parts, and a tool kit. In the midst of all this confusion was what could well have been a history book, kept open by a mini-barbell planted on top of it.

The sad part was, he probably thought he *was* studying. In my observation, kids today think that if they just spend a certain amount of time in the same room with a book, they'll learn the material by some weird kind of osmosis. No wonder we're so far behind the Japanese in standardized testing.

"I won't take long," I assured him.

"Ed? Who was at the door—oh!" A washed-out blond with bright red lipstick and a June Cleaver outfit stood uncertainly in the doorway.

"This is . . . uh, some lady detective, Mom. She's looking into Juky's death."

"Catherine Caliban, Mrs. Atterbury."

Her hand went to her hair in that automatic gesture women make when they are suddenly confronted with someone and can't remember when they last combed it. "Oh. Pleased to meet you." She didn't look any too sure. "Ed, perhaps Mrs. Caliban would like some refreshment."

Ed looked like he could happily have made me a cyanide cocktail, but I graciously intervened.

"No, thanks, Mrs. Atterbury. I'm fine, really."

"Well, all right, then. I'll leave you two to talk. And Edward—you will clean up this mess before your father gets home, won't you?"

He didn't deign to respond, but slumped on the couch with a sigh.

"What'm I gonna tell Coach if he asks about you?" he asked me.

"Tell him I'm doing fine, thank you."

"I don't know why you want to talk to me, anyway. I mean, I knew Juky and all, and I hang out with the guys. But I wasn't there that night, and I don't know anything."

"What night?" I asked, just to keep him on his guard.

"You know, that last night the guys saw him. That night he didn't come home."

"You want to catch his killer, don't you?"

"Well, shit, yeah, I want to catch the guy. I mean, Juky was always real nice to me. He was nice to everybody."

"Where were you that night?"

"I was out with this girl I know." He gave me a sly little smile to assist my imagination.

"A Robertson girl?"

"No, she's not at Robertson. She goes to Seven Hills."

"So when was the last time you saw him?"

"At practice that day, like I told the police."

"And your friend Skuyler said he was sick that night. Did he miss practice that day?"

"No, he went to practice. You don't miss practice unless you're dying, that's Coach's rule. And then, he says, he'd better goddam well see the obituary notice in the paper. But Sky wasn't feeling good at practice, I could tell."

"How could you tell?"

"Well, he said he wasn't, and he was kind of clumsy. He kept missing his corner shots, and that's his best shot."

"Did he have a fever?"

"I don't know, do I look like a doctor? He said he had a bad headache. But he'd had all these headaches all fall."

"What did the doctor say?"

"I don't know. You know what they say about doctor's families—I think it was like that with Sky. His dad didn't really think there was anything wrong with him."

"What did you think?"

He shrugged. "Well, I don't think he's got a brain tumor or anything, if that's what you mean. Maybe he's just worrying too much about the team."

"Why was he worried about the team?"

"Oh, you know, just wanting them to do well and get to

the playoffs. Anyway, Coach is kind of hard to play for. He's a great coach, but he puts a lot of pressure on the guys."

"And on you, too?"

"Oh, sure. Everything has to be just right or my ass is grass."

"So, what happened to Skuyler? Are you suggesting he had some kind of breakdown?"

"No, I'm not suggesting anything. Way I hear it, Sky went to live with his mother in Chicago."

"You hear it from him?"

He shrugged.

"I thought you and Skuyler were pretty good friends."

"We are."

"So he must have told you where he was going and why."

"Well, if he did, he didn't invite me to share it with no lady detectives."

"What about the police? Will you share it with them?"

"The police didn't ask me. Why should they? His dad knows where he is. He's not missing or anything. So why do *you* care?"

"Let's say I'd like some reassurance that he's not where Juky is."

He gave me an incredulous look. "Who said he was? Look, lady, Sky doesn't owe *you* anything. He's got his own problems, and they don't have anything to do with Juky."

"What kinds of problems?"

"Family problems, okay? And that's all I'm saying."

"Have you heard from him since he left?"

"Maybe I have and maybe I haven't. That's none of your damn business."

"Well, maybe you'll tell me this. Were you around the day Jackson Tucker died?"

"What? You bringing *Tuck* into this? What's he got to do with Juky's death?"

"You tell me."

"Okay, lady, I'll tell you. Nothing. He's got nothing to do with Juky's death. I was there, I saw him collapse, I saw the ambulance take him away, and I read about the autopsy report in the paper. Nobody killed him."

"If you were there, maybe you heard what he said when he collapsed."

"He didn't say anything."

"That's not what I heard."

"Well, okay, then, maybe he said something I didn't hear. Big deal. You think he said, 'Biggs shot me, and he's gonna shoot you next'?"

I studied him a minute, just to unnerve him further.

"So you're telling me there's no connection between Tuck's death and Juky's?"

"No connection. Zero. None."

"And you're telling me you don't have any idea how Juky got killed or why?"

"I think Juky ran across some kind of drug deal in the street. If it's not that, then I don't know what happened."

"Well," I said, struggling to my feet and trying not to stub my toe on a barbell, "thanks for your time. I'd better go so you can clean up your mess. You don't have to see me out." I limped to the door, and looked back at him.

"Oh, by the way," I said. "Nice Jordans."

Twenty-five

I'll skip the details of the shopping trip with Kevin. Suffice it to say that I emerged from the ordeal with a smashing black velvet number, cut relatively straight but with a slit up the side to accommodate my game leg, and cap sleeves under a broad white satin collar kind of a thing that met my requirements for coverage and matched my white hair.

I balked when I found out it would cost me more than my last service agreement on the washing machine. I pointed out to Kevin that I got a whole year of service out of the contract, but would get only one night's service out of this dress. *He* pointed out that most years a washer doesn't break down anyway, so I was throwing my money away on the service agreement, and that now that I was embarking on a career in investigation, I would have to invest in expanding my wardrobe to cover all contingencies.

"Okay," I said. "I'll take it."

Take my word for it, I looked terrific.

But after four hours of shopping, I was in no mood to meet Jackson Tucker's father. If you've been there, you know what I mean. So I took a long bubble bath in the company of a gin and tonic, then ate a whole plate of macaroni and cheese with some garlic bread. Okay, I shouldn't have eaten the garlic bread, but what the hell.

Mel was accompanying me in the guise of a photographer. I thought it might loosen my pigeon up a bit if we posed him surrounded by mementoes of his son, and hinted at national circulation. Maybe you think I sound too callous about a father who's lost his son, and you're probably right. I admit I already held a grudge against him because of what Schwab had said about his wanting to return to the days of all-white college sports.

I reminded Mel that a photographer's role was to be seen, not heard. Usually, that's not a problem for Mel. Usually, it's like pulling fleas off a black cat to get a word out of her around people she doesn't know. But if somebody pushes her button, she may just skip the meditation and ritual bowing and rearrange his vertebrae.

"Hey, if Kevin can be a cabdriver, I can be a photographer," was all she said.

Richard Tucker lived in a little frame house that had that prefab look to it—plastic siding, plastic floors, a couple of dusty plastic plants, and Early American crossed with fifties TV tray. The dominant features of the living room were a trophy case crammed with trophies, faded ribbons, and framed photographs, and a television set tuned to a golf match on ESPN. The only thing I could think of more boring than watching a golf tournament on television was watching a rerun of a golf tournament on television. It gave me a lot of insight into Richard Tucker.

Tucker himself was an ex-tackle run to fat. He wore khaki work pants and a clean white polo shirt he'd probably put on for our benefit. He had what appeared to be a naturally florid complexion deeply tanned, and he was well on his way to going bald. He was drinking a beer from a can stuck inside one of those styrofoam holders, and he offered us each one. We declined. I introduced him to my photographer, Melanie Carter, who started wandering around the room with her camera.

"Listen, I think this is a hell of a story you're doing, Mrs. Callan. Not just for my boy, either, but for all those boys out there like Jackie, who never got a chance to reach their potential."

His voice quavered, and I kind of got a lump in my own throat.

My photographer muttered, "And girls."

"Why, sure." Our host was prepared to be generous. "Don't want to forget the ladies. Why, some of those little gals you see out there today—they aren't half bad, some of 'em. And, boy, they give it all they got. Oh, I'm a big fan of the ladies. And they're prettier to watch than the men, too."

"You were a college athlete yourself, weren't you, Mr. Tucker? Notre Dame, was it?" I didn't want to give Mel a chance to get a word in edgewise.

"That's right." He handed me a conveniently placed photograph. "That's me in the front row, missing a few teeth. God, I still remember the bastard from Auburn who knocked them out. 'Course, he went on to play pro ball, and I joined the service."

"Viet Nam?"

"No, I missed that one. Spent most of my time in Germany, facing down the Russkies over Berlin. But I learned a few things. If I'd met up with that big nigger from Auburn a few years down the road, he'da been lucky if I left him a few teeth, I'm telling you. But I was a cocky son of a gun in college—thought I knew everything."

There was a crash from the trophy case.

"Hey! Be careful there, honey."

"Sorry, *Dick*, it must've slipped."

"So how is it that Jackson became interested in basketball? Didn't you try to interest him in football?"

"Oh, hell, yes. You know how it is—a man likes to have his son follow in his footsteps." A thump from the trophy case. "But you can't tell your kids what to do. So I told Jackie, I said, 'Son, whatever it is, if it's basketball, or football, or baseball—whatever, just play your heart out and I'll be behind you one hundred percent.'" A scrape from the trophy case.

This line sounded rehearsed, so I wrote it down on my little pad, and he looked satisfied.

"'Course, now, Jackie, he was an all-round athlete. He could of played football. You don't see too many that can do both, but he could. But, like I said, I let him and the coaches fight it out in the end, and me—I just paid the bills." He took a swig of his beer.

"So at what point did it become clear that he was going to concentrate on basketball?"

"Oh, hell, that was . . . let me see . . . seventh grade. He was still playing the other sports, but I told him, I said, 'Son, you know eventually you're going to have to pick one thing, and do it well. You can't be a champion in everything.' So that was when he said he thought basketball was his favorite, so that was what we worked on."

"Then I take it you coached him?"

"Well, I don't know that you'd call it coaching exactly, me being a football player and all. But we set up a program for him—weight training and all that, and twenty baskets a day from the free-throw line we drew out in the driveway. Rain or shine, that kid was out there practicing." When he stopped to blow his nose, I caught a glimpse of Mel in the mirror over his head. She was sticking her finger down her throat.

"And this was in the seventh grade—the weight training and all?"

"Yes, ma'am. Jackie knew what he wanted even then. I bet you'll find a lot of those athletes that died young were like Jackie that way. Maybe they have some kind of . . . feeling . . . that they don't have much time."

"Maybe," I said.

"Makes me wonder if I should of held him back."

"How's that?"

"Well, I held him back in junior high. Red-shirted him, to give him a little more time to work on his skills. If I hadn't done that, he would of had a year in the NCAA. Well, I guess I . . . I took that away from him. I think about it a lot."

Another bang from the trophy case.

"But you didn't have any way of knowing." I was trying not to look appalled.

"No, that's right. But he could of got injured, too. Let's just say I took a gamble, and lost."

I wrote that down, too.

"I believe there was an autopsy, is that correct?"

"That's right."

"And they confirmed that Jackson had died of a heart attack?"

"Coronary thrombosis, yes, ma'am."

"And you were satisfied with the results of the autopsy?"

"Had to be. I saw that damn clot on the X ray myself. And the doctors showed me how the other arteries were in bad shape, too. I know it's hard to believe that an athlete who worked out the way Jackie did could have something wrong with him like Jackie did. Hell, I thought heart attacks were something you got when you sat around on your can all day. At least, for men. I knew it was different for women, 'cause they got all that fat to begin with."

"I wonder if you'd mind telling me when you lost your wife."

"Evelyn? Evelyn died seven years ago, when Jackie was twelve."

"And how old was she?"

"She was thirty-two."

"And do you mind if I ask you about the circumstances? Had she been ill? Was she being treated for heart disease?"

"No, Evelyn didn't go to the doctor much. Except for when she was pregnant, of course. She used to say doctors weren't really good for much, except to tell you what you already knew or could work out for yourself. So we didn't have any idea there was anything wrong with her. Well, maybe she'd had some chest pains—once or twice she mentioned heartburn. But she didn't talk about her health much. If you asked her, she was always feeling fine."

"And there was heart disease in her family?"

"Well, it turned out that her daddy died of a heart attack, but Evelyn was pretty young when he died, and I don't even know if she knew what he died of. So until Jackie died, it was all a big mystery."

"And nobody suggested that Jackson be tested when his mother died so young?"

"I don't b'lieve anybody did. If they had, why, we would of got him tested, him being an athlete and all."

"Do you have other children, Mr. Tucker?"

"Two girls. And you can be damn sure I've had them tested. One of 'em is what they call 'at risk,' and one of 'em isn't. Course, neither of them are athletes, so we don't have to be so careful with them. I guess Jackie—he just played so hard he used up his time fast."

A clank from the trophy case.

"Tell me, something, Mr. Tucker. Did Jackson have a lot of friends on the Robertson basketball team? I mean, is that where most of his friends came from?"

"Yes, that's right. They've always been real close, the boys on that team. And Jackie, he got along with everybody, even the colored boys. Of course, he could talk their lingo and jump as high as they did, so I guess they had to respect him."

I caught Mel's eye in the mirror and shook my head. She looked disappointed and set down the trophy she was holding.

"You know, these days, it's unusual for a white boy to succeed in basketball like Jackie did. Seems like the colored boys are just built for the game—"

Mel had picked up the trophy again.

I interrupted him before he said anything about "natural rhythm." "Was Juky Kay a friend of Jackson's?"

Mel put the trophy down again.

"Sure, like I said, they all liked Jackie. Kids like Juky, they really looked up to him. Say, that was a real shame about Juky. That kid was one hell of a basketball player. I feel real sorry for his mother. That kid could of made good money in the NBA, and a lot of these colored families, they really count on that."

The trophy was creeping toward the edge of the cabinet.

"I heard Juky tried to revive Jackson when he had his heart attack."

"Yes, he did, and I asked about that, of course. But everybody said Juky did it just like he was supposed to, and so I guess it just wasn't meant to succeed. And I'll always be grateful to that boy for trying. There's a lot that would've let a white boy die and never lifted a finger to save him."

The trophy teetered on the edge of the cabinet.

"Did Jackson have any particular friend on the team? You know, somebody who knew him better than the others? Somebody we could interview about him?"

"Well, let's see. Who could you talk to?"

He mulled this over so long I knew he'd overestimated Jackson's closeness to his teammates.

"I tell you, you could talk to Corky—that little red-headed guard? He could probably tell you a few stories. Coach Biggs could probably help you, too."

I didn't think so.

"Is there anyplace else I might find friends of his? I mean, did he have any other regular hangouts?"

"Oh, sure," he said. And I bet you can guess what he said next. "He used to go over to the North Side Gym all the time and work out. Especially in the summertime."

"Okay, I'll check that out. I'd like to see some pictures of Jackson if you have some. Is that a photo album there on the table?"

He nodded. "I got it out to show you. It's kind of an overview of Jackson's career." He handed it over, then came and stood next to my chair.

In the first picture, baby Jackson was chewing on a powder-blue rubber football. In the next one, baby Jackson, standing but not too steady on his pins, I'd say, was studying a soccer ball on the ground in front of him. The whole album was like that. The kid was in uniform by the time he was seven.

I studied the recent pictures carefully, then flipped back to junior high. I don't know what I was looking for, but I didn't see any obvious signs of drug use. I mean, his pupils looked normal to me, and his nose wasn't running in the pictures. In one picture, he was leaning over, getting ready to hike a football, and I scrutinized his arms. No needle tracks that I could see.

I asked if I could see his school pictures. I wanted to

see some photos in which his face, and not his athletic equipment, was the most important thing in the picture. Mr. Tucker brought down a box, and I looked through it. Still nothing obvious. And yet . . .

I couldn't figure out what was bothering me. The kid had changed over the years, but all kids do that.

"Mr. Tucker, could I borrow a few of these pictures? I'd like to take maybe three of the school pictures and a couple of the other ones."

"Sure, take what you want. The school pictures I got extras, so you can have those. The others I'd like to have back, seeing as how they're all I got left of him."

"Well, thanks, Mr. Tucker, that's been real helpful," I said.

"Cat, I'd like to get a few pictures," Mel said.

"Oh, sure." I'd almost forgotten what my photographer was really supposed to be doing.

She had him sit in his recliner and gaze pensively at a picture of his son.

"Now I'd like one in front of the trophy case. If you'll just go stand in front, Mr. Tucker."

"Is this okay, honey?"

She studied her viewfinder.

"Step back, please."

"Like this?"

"Step back, please."

He bumped into the trophy case. And every last trophy came crashing down, shattering two glass doors, showering him with glass, raining heavy metal down on his unprotected head.

"Oh, gosh, *Dick*. Are you okay?" she asked innocently—but not until after she'd snapped a few pictures.

I honestly don't think he knew what hit him, so I got Mel out of there before he had time to think about it. Before he realized that she'd moved every goddam trophy to the edge of the shelves before she directed him to back into them.

Twenty-six

"Don't ask."

I was looking down at Moses, Mel, and Al, who were comfortably settled into their seats, awaiting the tip-off, which was sixty seconds away.

By the collar, I gripped a little kid whom I was pretending not to know. His face was streaked with turquoise Magic Marker. He was wearing milk on his upper lip and strawberry jelly on his lower one, and on his T-shirt, which read, "My Grandma Loves Me." His jeans were caked with mud. On his feet he wore Big Bird slippers. In his hand he clutched a ratty scrap of a blanket that had once been yellow. His other thumb was in his mouth. On his head he was wearing a helicopter, a remote control one which had crash landed there five minutes before game time and become entangled in his hair. He looked like an escapee from an Andy Warhol guest appearance on "Sesame Street."

"What's he want to be when he grows up?" asked Al. "A heliport?"

Everybody moved down two seats so Ben could sit on the end. That way, he might be able to see the court. It also ensured minimal exposure of others to any messes he was carrying that might be transferable.

He'd been working up to a tantrum because I'd rushed him past the concession stand, as much as anybody with a crutch can rush anywhere, but now he was distracted by the fanfare.

"Rat—Rat—Rat-Rat-Rat-Ratratratratrattlersssssss!"

It was not an especially edifying display of adult behavior.

Ben planted his Big Bird slippers on the shoulders of

the young woman in front of him, and settled in to watch the entertainment. Fortunately, she didn't notice.

"Here, I got you a program, Cat."

"Hey, thanks, Moses. Any surprises in the lineup?"

"Butch's on the bench. Got a kid named Masterson in at guard. Shellenstein in for Skuyler."

"Does Butch look injured?"

"Got his ankle taped."

"Schwab said he injured it at practice on Monday, but he expected him to play."

"He might. Then again, Biggs might be saving him for the playoffs."

"Hey, Cat, you see your date for tomorrow night, point her out to us."

"Yeah, me and Mel want to go check her out. We don't think you should be going out with somebody you barely know, much less somebody *we* barely know."

"So, how good is Wyoming?"

"I thought you used to live there." Moses was speaking of my former neighborhood, the one where I lived in my incarnation as a suburban housewife.

"I did, but it's been donkey's years since I paid any attention to high school basketball. I didn't know I'd need it in my future career."

"Wyoming's pretty good. They're 14 and 5 coming in, and they haven't lost in a couple weeks."

"In other words, with Skuyler out, and Butch on the bench, our guys might get trounced."

" 'Our guys'? I thought they were all murder suspects."

"Well, they are. And if any of them killed Juky, they deserve to lose. But if you think I'm gonna root for Wyoming, you got another think coming. Hell, I'm going *out* with a girl from Robertson."

"Yeah," he said. "Me, too."

So far, the team looked deceptively good. Shellenstein sank two long jumpers in the first five minutes; Reggie, who was wearing some kind of contraption on his knee, outrebounded everybody on the court; Corky kept his cool; and

Masterson turned out to be a good ball handler. Cal had trouble at first getting the ball to drop, but he didn't give up, and his shooting turned around about eight minutes into the quarter.

Ben cheered whenever anybody else did. I bought him some blue cotton candy during the first time-out, and he was happy as a piglet in a mud puddle. Mostly, he stood in the aisle, jumping up and down, his propeller whizzing around. Every now and then he'd try his hand at the play-by-play.

"Oh, look, Grammy, the red man's got the ball again. Oh, look, now he threw it away from the basket. Why'd he do *that*, Grammy? Grammy, I see two guys dancing in the middle. Oh, look, now one of 'em's got the ball! Oh, maybe he'll throw it up. Look at that other guy—he looks mean. What's he sayin', Grammy? Is he mad at somebody? Why'd that guy blow the whistle, Grammy? Is he mad, too? Maybe they not s'posed to run like that. When they blow the whistle at me at the swimmin' pool, it's 'cause I not s'posed to run. Oooh, lookit, Grammy, they're running again! They better not do that, or that stripey guy will get mad!"

Luckily, the people around us seemed to think Ben was cute. Me, I ignored him.

During the next time-out, I spotted Dr. Skuyler and the Reverend Cain sitting with Reggie's father. Maybe it was Reggie's parents, because the woman next to him looked like she might be with Mr. Odum. Butch's parents were sitting next to them. A couple of rows away my eyes landed on Mr. Tucker. Quite a contingent of suspects.

Masterson lost the ball twice when it was stolen on an inbounds pass, and Biggs sent in Schindler. Meanwhile Corky ran into trouble guarding a kid four inches taller than he was, and Biggs had the others try to double-team the kid. Reggie paid a price for his rebounding, too, when he was called for his third foul in the final minutes of the first half. Biggs was up off the bench and gave the ref an earful, but returned without a technical. Then, with thirty seconds left in the half, Cal moved in to take a charge. He went down hard, with another player on top of him. He didn't get up.

They went into one of those huddles around him on the court, and we could see him sit up and rub his ankle.

"Look like he need to borrow your crutch, Cat," Moses said.

That was the moment when Ben began to announce, loudly, that he needed to go to the bathroom. I figured it was better to beat the rush, so I took him.

Unfortunately, Ben chose the occasion to recount a long, involved tale of how the class turtle had been lost and found during three harrowing days that week, choosing to make a dramatic reappearance in the midst of his memorial service. So there I was when the crowds hit, parading around with a kid with a helicopter stuck to his head. I could tell from the expressions on people's faces that the news about Cal was not optimistic.

On the way back to our seats, Ben got his helicopter stuck in a young woman's loose knit sweater. As near as I can figure, he turned around and looked down at just the wrong moment. She bumped into him, and suddenly he was attached to her just below the bust. It was all I could do to hold him still in the hope that I could extricate him without scalping him or destroying the sweater. For one thing, he was grabbing hold of it with sticky blue fingers. She was really pissed off. It didn't help that her boyfriend was prostrate with laughter. And me with only one good leg, and one arm draped over a crutch.

In the end, it took five people to separate them. Ben screamed as if he were being tortured, and when a security guard showed up to help, he got kicked in the shins for his trouble. You wouldn't think a foot inside a Big Bird slipper could do so much damage, but the cop crumpled as if he'd been hammered with a Jordan slam.

Me, I kept yelling, "The teeth! Watch out for the teeth!" I knew from experience that they were little but razor sharp.

We left the young woman indignantly inspecting her sweater while her boyfriend tried to apologize between fresh bursts of laughter. Moses was hanging out on the fringe of the crowd that had gathered.

"Thanks for nothing."

"You was doin' all right, Cat. Wasn't no more room in the combat zone, nohow. Now, if she'd slugged you, I would've stepped right in and made a citizen's arrest."

"Well, shit, *that's* a comfort. How's Cal?"

"Had to be helped off the floor. Don't look good."

We went back up in the stands, where Ben regaled Mel and Al, and everybody within earshot, with his version of the fracas.

A woman behind me caught my eye and beamed at me. "He's *so* cute," she said.

Me, I thought kittens were a hell of a lot cuter.

Two minutes into the second half, Butch came off the bench for Masterson, and the crowd went wild. You could tell he was trying hard not to limp. I wasn't sure I wanted to watch.

But amazingly, Shellenstein's shooting streak held, and Reggie began to catch fire inside with a hook shot. Corky was feeding him at one end, and breaking up plays at the other; he had three steals in the first five minutes. The first time Butch went up for an outside jumper, the crowd held its breath, but when the basket counted and his ankle didn't buckle, the air went blue with streamers. With eight minutes to go in the half, Wyoming called a time-out, and then went into a zone defense, with the zone collapsing around Shelly. Shelly began to have trouble finding his shots. He kept passing back out to Corky, who was having his own trouble getting the ball in to Reggie. With seven minutes to go, a frustrated Reggie was called for his fourth foul. We were in a bonus situation, with the score at 40–38, our favor.

They made both free throws, and the score was tied. You would have thought the Rattlers had never seen a zone before. They wasted another two minutes trying to attack it, which resulted in one steal and one jump ball. Biggs called time-out.

When they came back, Reggie was gone, and Shellenstein was playing center. A new guy, smaller than Shelly, was playing the other forward.

"What's he doing?" I asked Moses. "He's crazy."

"He's saving Reggie, and putting in another good ball handler."

"But he doesn't need a ball handler, does he? He needs somebody who can score."

"He's got somebody who can score."

And before I could argue, Corky passed to Butch, who landed a jumper over the zone.

"Ouch!" I said. "I don't think I can watch this."

For the next four minutes we gave up a lot of points at the other end of the floor, but Butch kept us in the game shooting over the zone. It was a good thing, too, because we were getting killed on the boards, where Shelly didn't have the height or strength to match up. Biggs must have told him to use his small size to his advantage, because all of a sudden the refs were calling fouls underneath—and they weren't on Shelly. Of course, Biggs had been working the refs all half, so when Shelly started doing his dramatic interpretation of a David getting clobbered by Goliath, they responded. Fortunately for us, Shelly was one of our best foul shooters, and I guess Biggs kept off his back, because he sank one right after the other.

The score was tied at fifty all, with forty seconds to play. Ben again announced that he had to go to the bathroom. I told him he'd have to wait. He announced that he was going to pee in his pants, and clutched at his crotch for effect. I told him he'd have to wait. He started whining about it, but noticed he didn't have anybody's attention and kind of de-escalated into a grumbling pout. Corky had just trapped a guy in the corner and tied up the ball.

Wyoming got the tip, and ran fifteen seconds off the clock before scoring on a back-door move. Then, before anybody realized what was happening, Butch took the ball out and threw it long to Shelly, who put it in the basket before the Wyoming defense was halfway down the court. By now we were all on our feet, or rather, everybody else was on their feet, and I was on one foot and one crutch. Wyoming called time-out. Ben tugged at my arm.

With twenty seconds on the clock, Wyoming inbounded the ball and ran it down the court. It got passed inside to the center, the center went up for the jumper, and Reggie hammered him. A loud groan from our side of the gym registered that Reggie had just fouled out. Their center missed the front end of the two free throws. Our side of the gym was doing its best to be obnoxious, and Ben was contributing. Damned if the kid didn't miss the second free throw as well.

"I'm glad I don't live at *his* house tonight," I murmured to Moses.

Butch inbounded the ball to Corky, and Corky took it down. Butch was limping noticeably, but he only had thirteen seconds to go, unless we went into overtime. Our guys were running the four corners, trying to avoid Butch as much as possible, and the crowd was counting down the seconds. At five seconds, Reggie's replacement, a kid named Byers, was fouled—and made both free throws. The game was over.

I could still feel Ben tugging, but I couldn't hear him anymore. The band was playing the fight song, the cheerleaders were trying to build pyramids in the middle of a swarming crowd, we were pelted with blue-and-white confetti, and when I looked at Moses, he had a small blue-and-white paper snake dangling rakishly from his bifocals.

I grabbed Ben by the collar, and we joined the stream of merrymakers headed down. We pressed forward into the main ramp down below the bleachers along with a hundred jubilant fans.

"Moses," I shouted in his ear. "You ever seen slam dancing?"

"Yeah. It's a lot like this."

When we reached the bottom of the ramp, I suddenly

realized that I wasn't holding onto Ben's collar anymore. In fact, I wasn't holding onto Ben at all. Ben had disappeared.

I turned and scanned the crowd, feeling a rising panic that he had been trampled coming down the ramp.

"You seen Ben?" I asked my cohorts.

Everybody looked around.

"Did he come down the ramp with you?"

"I thought he did."

"Mel and I'll go back up and scout around. You guys stay here," Al said.

While they were gone, Moses snagged a security guard and explained the situation.

"You can't miss him," I said. "He's got this helicopter stuck to his head."

The guard looked up to see if I was putting him on, but apparently decided I wasn't.

"He was wearing Big Bird slippers," Moses added. "And his fingers were covered with blue dye from that cotton candy."

The guard nodded, and reported in on his walkie-talkie. He told me to stay put.

"I feel kind of embarrassed reporting him already, when we haven't looked around for him ourselves yet," I told Moses.

He shook his head. "Can't take chances, Cat. You got to have them watch the exits, the sooner the better."

Mel and Al came back, shaking their heads. Moses and I had been inspecting the crowd, realizing how hard it was to spot a pint-size person in a sea of teens and grown-ups.

"We'd better go check the bathrooms," I said.

"You stay here," Moses said. "I'll take the men's rooms, and Al can check the women's."

"Would he go to the women's?" Al asked.

"If that's where he went before, he would."

I nodded.

They went away and came back. Still no Ben. The crowds were thinning, and I was feeling faint from anxiety. I had a tank parked in my throat, and my eyes were about to explode.

"Goddam that little bugger. Where *is* he?"

Our security guard returned and now took us to an office, where we were introduced to an officer from District 5. They'd apparently called in reinforcements, and a major search was in progress.

Officer McMichael asked me for a detailed description of Ben and what he was wearing. It was Moses who told her that I'd been shot at a few days earlier.

I turned and stared at him. "You mean—"

"I'm just saying it's possible."

"You're suggesting, Mr. Fogg, that we may be dealing with a kidnapping?" Officer McMichael looked at him thoughtfully.

"Oh, God," I groaned. "I hope he has sense enough not to bite the bastard."

Officer McMichael asked if I could reach Ben's mother. I said I could, but did I have to? She said they'd need an article of Ben's clothing to give the dogs a scent, and I started to blubber. In the end, Moses called Sharon, since I had become unintelligible.

Sharon fainted, but I didn't find that out until later.

Twenty-seven

The phone call came half an hour later, as we sat with Office McMichael in my living room. Sharon and Frank were sitting glumly on the sofa holding hands, and Kevin had left work and come home to do what he does best in emergencies: cook. He had coffee on the stove and brownies in the oven. McMichael had already tapped my phone, so I waited until she nodded to answer it.

The voice on the other end was muffled.

"I have your grandson, Mrs. Caliban." It was a male voice, but beyond that I couldn't have said anything definite. "I have no intention of hurting him."

All of a sudden, a cold icicle of fury slipped down my spine, and I lost control.

"Oh, yeah? Well, you'd goddam well better not hurt him, you son of a bitch, or you'll have me to deal with."

McMichael frowned at me and shook her head, and Moses gripped my shoulder so tight it hurt.

"He is sleeping now, and he'll be released unharmed. I only wanted you to understand the danger in which you've been placing yourself and your loved ones."

"What do you mean?" I asked, but I was talking to air. He'd hung up. I yanked out the receiver, flung it against the opposite wall, and narrowly missed taking out Sophie and Sadie, who were huddled anxiously on an end table, like children at a wake.

"Now, Mrs. C., you mustn't take it out on the equipment. He might call again, and then where'll you be?" Kevin picked up the receiver and inspected it for damage.

"That voice was pretty muffled, Mrs. Caliban, but did you recognize it?" McMichael asked.

"No," I said. "But if it's somebody involved with this case that I *know* about, there's only two possibilities."

"Who's that?"

"It's got to be either Skuyler—the doctor, I mean—or Reverend Cain."

"Why is that?"

"You got a tape?" I asked.

She nodded.

"Play it back," I said.

She did.

"There!" I exclaimed. "That last sentence—the one that uses 'the danger in which.' I don't think there's a kid left on the team, now that Juky's gone, who could have used 'in which' correctly, or would have thought to, and the same goes for the coach. They're probably out of it anyway, because they had better things to do right after the game than kidnap five-year-olds. I'd say the same for Mr. Tucker's sense of grammar—wouldn't you, Mel? So unless it's somebody I don't know about—which is perfectly conceivable—it has to be one of the two professionals, unless a kid got somebody else to write it for him, which doesn't seem too likely. Or, for a long shot, I guess we could consider Maury Schwab. He doesn't talk like that, but he probably knows how to."

"But you can't tell which one?" McMichael asked.

I shook my head.

She turned to another officer and told him to send squad cars to both homes and offices of Cain and Skuyler.

"Do you really think he meant what he said about not hurting Ben?" Sharon asked tremulously.

McMichael nodded. "Probably. He didn't ask for money, so there wouldn't be much point, except to cover his tracks. And I'd guess that he chloroformed your little boy to get him out of the gym in the first place. Ben may well wake up someplace that he can easily walk out of, with no one around to identify as a kidnapper—*if* the kidnapper was sincere about his motivation."

The call had been pretty short, but it had been traced, thanks to the wonders of modern technology, to a phone booth on William Howard Taft in Walnut Hills, about fifteen minutes away from Northside. The police were already making the rounds there, to see if anybody had spotted the caller.

Within twenty minutes, all the squad cars had reported in. Dr. Skuyler they had found at home, apparently watching television. He had given them permission to search the house, and they'd found nothing. He had also agreed to give them a key to the office, and his permission to search it. An alert officer had pointed out that his car engine was still slightly warm, but Skuyler had admitted he'd attended the game, and the night was cold enough to make it difficult to assess how long it had been since the car had been driven. At the office, they had found no Ben. They had, however, found chloroform among the doctor's supplies.

The Reverend Cain had not been home, nor had he been at the church. The cars were instructed to stay put and watch the premises until further notice.

Maury Schwab was at the newspaper office, working on his story. Witnesses there confirmed that he'd arrived shortly after the game. He had seemed genuinely entertained by the notion that he might be a kidnapping suspect, and gave the police keys to his car. A search of the building yielded nothing, and he lived too far away to have stashed Ben there on his way to the office.

Sharon and I took turns pacing. Winnie paced with us. I was having third thoughts about my choice of career. How could I have endangered the people I loved? How could I have been so thoughtless? I kept waiting for Moses to tell me to relax and stop worrying, and when he didn't, I knew we were in trouble.

There was a commotion outside, and one of the squad-car officers entered the room. He bent down and spoke to McMichael in a low voice. I stopped breathing. McMichael nodded.

"We have Ben," she announced to the room in general. "He's on his way back. He's fine."

Thirty minutes after the kidnapper's phone call, Ben had been picked up in Eden Park, at the overlook. His hair had been hacked off. He was carrying his helicopter and his blanket and wearing his Big Bird slippers.

Kevin baked another batch of brownies. I discovered, to my surprise, that we'd eaten the first batch.

Ben arrived at the Catatonia Arms in style, in a police car with flashing lights that sent the kitties to the basement to hide out. Winnie, who had been as morose as the rest of us, dashed madly to the door, followed closely by Sharon and Frank.

They carried him in and set him down to inspect the damage. Most of it had been done before the evening began, as far as I could see. When I'd heard he'd turned up in Eden Park, I was worried about the cold, since I hadn't put his coat on before he was snatched. But except for a runny nose, I couldn't see that there was anything wrong with him—anything out of the ordinary.

"Look at your hair!" his mother wailed through happy tears.

Ben put a hand to his head in bewilderment, but upon discovering that he still *had* hair there, dismissed this complaint as one of his mother's vagaries.

It quickly became apparent that there was nothing wrong with his vocal cords, and given the size of his audience, McMichael had difficulty distracting him sufficiently to ask him some questions.

"Ben, do you remember what happened tonight?"

He nodded gravely.

"Do you think you can tell us?"

She had turned her tape recorder on, and an officer in the corner was taking notes.

"My helicopter landed on my head, and Grammy yelled at me."

"Uh-huh, but after that. You remember when you and Grammy went to the game?"

"Yuh-huh, and Moses was there, and Al was there, and Mel was there, but Winnie wasn't there, and I ate blue cotton candy." He considered a moment. "And Grammy yelled at me some more."

Goddam kid was setting me up for charges of child abuse.

"And then everybody was yelling, and jumping up and down, and me, too, I was yelling and jumping up and down."

"Yeah, I bet it was real exciting, wasn't it? And did anybody talk to you at the game besides the people you mentioned—Grammy, and Moses, and Al, and Mel?"

"There was this lady that telled me not to put my hands on her pants."

"Okay, that's good, Ben. Anybody else?"

"Well, there was a bunch of people yelling at me when my helicopter got stuck in this lady's sweater."

I had forgotten all about that. Moses and I explained to McMichael what had happened.

"My goodness, Ben," she said. "You had an eventful evening! So, think hard, now; did anybody else talk to you?"

"At the park."

"Okay, I'll ask you about that in a minute. Now I want to know how you got to the park. Remember when the game was over, and the band was playing?"

"I had to go to the bafroom."

"That's right. And Grammy was going to take you. And you were walking down the ramp with Grammy, and then what happened?"

He frowned and thought. He worked his lip and thought some more. He scanned his audience, and saw his opportunity.

"A bear grabbed me."

"A bear grabbed you?"

"Yep."

"Now I think you're fooling us, aren't you?"

"Nope."

"Oh, I think you are. I think maybe somebody else grabbed you. Do you think so?"

"Nope."

"Didn't you talk to a man when you were coming down the ramp? Maybe it was before the bear grabbed you."

"Nope."

I had to hand it to her; she was a master of child psychology, but even the masters sometimes fail to get results.

"Did the bear wrap you up in something warm?"

"Uh-huh, in a bear coat."

"That must have been nice. What did the bear coat smell like?"

"Like the doctor's office."

"Uh-huh, and that's not a very nice smell, is it? Here, let me see if you still smell like your bear coat."

He leaned forward and she sniffed.

"Uh-huh, you do, but you smell nice, too. So the bear who grabbed you must have smelled nice."

I leaned over and caught a faint trace of chloroform and English Leather.

"So what happened then?"

"Um, the bear taked me to the woods, and, um, all the teddy bears were having a picnic, and they said, um, 'Oh, hello, would you like some honey?' "

"The teddy bears were having a picnic in the woods at night in the cold?"

"They had their bear coats on!"

"Oh, sure, I forgot. That makes a difference. So after the picnic, did you take a nap in the woods?"

"Uh-huh, the bears said, 'Time to sleep!' so I just layed down and went to sleep. But you know what?"

"What?"

"The bears snored!"

"No!"

"Yep. They did. So then I waked up, and I seed some people, and they were kissing!"

"No! And then what happened?"

"They stopped kissing, and they talked to me, and then the policemen comed and bringed me back to Grammy's, and here I am!"

"How about that! Boy, what a night *you* had!"

"Yep. And you know what else?"

"What?"

He lowered his voice to a stage whisper.

"One of the bears wet his pants!"

"Well," she said judiciously. "That's okay. He couldn't help it."

And she gave him a hug, pretending to ignore the obvious: that it was the bear in the removable coat who had wet his pants.

Twenty-eight

"You think it's Skuyler?" Moses asked the next morning, when we sat down to hash things out.

"Well, Skuyler is the logical one. But maybe he's too logical. You know, maybe somebody's setting him up."

"You mean, with the chloroform?"

I nodded.

"Yeah, but looky here, Cat. What's somebody doing with chloroform at a basketball game anyway? The doctor got it, 'cause it's in his medical kit, maybe. If somebody else got it, they must be planning to use it. Now, who were they planning to use it *on*? They couldn't hardly know that you were taking Ben to the game unless they were watching the house."

"Maybe they were planning to chloroform *me*."

"And take you where? To the locker room? See, Cat, kids is easy. You knock 'em out, throw 'em over your shoulder, and carry 'em out. You can cut their hair, change their clothes, throw a blanket over 'em, bury their face in your shoulder—that's the way professionals do it all the time."

"They *do*?"

"Sure, at amusement parks and any place kids hang out. That's why the shoes are important—you can change a kid's clothes or hairstyle, but you can't always get shoes that fit, and most professionals don't bother, anyway. Unless the kid happen to be wearin' Big Bird on his feet. Then you take him out in his socks.

"But I like to see somebody try to knock *you* out, throw you over his shoulder, and walk out the place 'thout rousing suspicion. See what I mean? It couldn't be done."

"So you're saying that this kidnapping probably *wasn't* planned in advance?"

"Not unless somebody was watching the house, like I said. And we know they know where you live. They also know what a vicious guard dog you got." He reached down under his chair and gave Winnie an affectionate pat. She gave one of those cute little puppy sighs, and her sides heaved.

"Yeah, but you know what's bothering me about this, Moses? I can't make it come out right. I mean, sure, I'd like to take a swing at the bastard who snatched Ben, but I don't think he's the one I'm after."

"You mean, you don't think he killed Juky Kay?"

"No."

"You think a guy that kidnaps a kid and lets him go unharmed is not capable of killing another kid?"

"Something like that."

" 'Cept we don't know if Juky's killing was deliberate, Cat."

"What do you mean?"

"Well, the man we after may be a good-natured guy, on the whole. But one night he's havin' a serious discussion with Juky, and things ain't goin' so well, and next thing he knows, Juky's dead—maybe in the heat of the moment, maybe by accident, who knows? Fact is, our good-natured guy got a corpse on his hands, and he has to get rid of it, any way he can."

"Yeah, but the son of a bitch who shot at me in our parking lot wasn't a good-natured guy, in my estimation."

"He hit you?"

"Well, no."

"You assumin' he's a bad shot, or else he wasn't no match for your lightning reflexes. But maybe he just wasn't aiming at you."

"Goddam, you make things complicated."

"In my experience," said Moses, "things *are* complicated. Folks get themselves in the damnedest situations, and when you ask 'em how it happened, they say they don't rightly know, everything was an accident.

"Course, you could be right about the two parties; I

ain't sayin' you ain't. I'm just sayin' consider all the possibilities. And one possibility is that the man you want is
not the devil incarnate, but some poor bastard got backed
into a corner and reacted more violently than he intended."

"You think the doctor killed Juky. Or his son did."

"I don't speculate till all the evidence is in." If you believe that about Moses, I'll sell you a ticket to Northside's
world famous underground caverns.

Still, I was glad that Moses was attending the dance tonight. His police experience counted for a lot, and I was
hoping he'd pick up on things I couldn't see. Plus, I
wanted the police protection, and I'm not too proud to say
so.

I wasn't discounting the possibility that the kidnapper
was somebody I'd never even met. It occurred to me that
if the doctor might kidnap Ben to warn me off a case that
might implicate his son in murder, other dads might do the
same. It was hard to picture Mr. and Mrs. Odum conspir-
ing together to kidnap Ben, but I thought I shouldn't eliminate the implausible. And there were plenty of dads
around last night, I guessed, even though I hadn't recognized them all.

Then there was the Reverend Cain. He was there last
night, too. I thought about that Lincoln parked around
back of the church, and wondered if the ministry had become more lucrative in recent years. I'd always thought
the only ministers who were rolling in dough were the
television evangelists. Silly me. If Cain was the killer, then
all that business about Juky and the Sermon on the Mount
was intended to throw me off the trail. Oh, it had happened, all right, but maybe Cal's version was closer to the
truth, and Juky's interest in murder was purely academic.

But if Cain *did* have a racket, what was it? Selling in-
dulgences? I mean, you could think of things a doctor
could sell to make a little money on the side. But what did
ministers sell? Their souls?

Maybe that was it. Maybe it wasn't a racket, exactly.
Maybe Cain liked to bet on the ponies, and Juky found out

about it and threatened to go public with the information. But would a minister really kill to preserve his reputation?

But if you bet on the ponies, there was a chance you'd eventually lose, and if you lost, there was a chance you'd eventually borrow money, and if you borrowed money, there was a chance you'd eventually miss a payment, and if you missed a payment, there was a chance that somebody with a Sicilian last name would send some thug around to break your kneecaps. So you might not want your congregation to know about all of your business acquaintances, in case they objected and fired you, thus precipitating the missed payment and broken kneecaps. I hadn't watched the Million Dollar Movie all those years for nothing.

Maybe Cain had sent one of his mob pals around to silence me. No, on second thought, those guys don't miss. Plus, they carry heavy-duty automatic weapons like Uzis against which my lightning reflexes wouldn't have stood a chance.

All in all, you have to admit this was a pretty unlikely scenario. Which brought me back to the original question: if Juky knew about a murder, whose murder was it? The only candidate I had was Tucker, and everybody, from the coroner on down to his father, swore that his was an accidental death. Maybe I had to go looking for some more missing persons.

But I didn't really believe it—that there was somebody new in this case that I didn't know about. People don't start taking shots at you and kidnapping your grandkids unless you're getting pretty goddam close to the truth.

Twenty-nine

Somebody whistled from the hall.

"Boy, do you know how to pick 'em, Cat."

"The car's nice, too."

"I meant the car. Can you see the girls?"

Kevin, Al, and Mel were crowded in the hallway like younger siblings, ogling our dates. I'd talked Nan and Pearl into coming an hour earlier so Kevin could see them before rushing off to work.

"Check out that tux. Maybe she'll give me the name of her tailor."

Nan was, in fact, wearing a tux, and she looked smashing in it. She was toting one of those wrist corsages in a plastic case. Pearl, under her coat, was stunning in a cream-colored drop-waisted chemise that looked like it had been resurrected from the twenties, with elaborate beadwork in the bodice. Youth, it's wonderful.

Mind you, we oldsters were holding up our end with considerable class, if I do say so myself. I already told you how terrific I looked in my black velvet number, but did I mention how the black set off my brown eyes? Did I mention that I had to spend a half hour on it with the lint roller because the kitties discovered it lying on the bed? Moses was positively elegant in a black tux with a cream-colored vest that matched Pearl's dress beautifully. He impressed me by whipping out a wrist corsage of mixed red and cream-colored sweetheart roses.

He caught my look, and said, "I ain't stupid, Cat, and I ain't so old that I don't remember what to do."

We sat down and chatted for a while, ostensibly to be sociable, but really so that Mel and Al could grill our dates. The kids drank Cokes, Moses drank Scotch, and I had a G&T to fortify myself. Kevin went reluctantly off to work, after reminding Mel five times to take pictures. We talked about—what else?—basketball.

When we headed out, I discovered what the neighbors had been whistling at—a white Mercedes.

"It's my Uncle Pat's," Nan admitted. "I drive a bug."

For dinner they took us to the Celestial in Mt. Adams, where we had a great view of the city. Moses regaled us with stories of disastrous dates from his youth, and by the time we'd finished wrangling over the check, which we ended up splitting, I realized that I was having a much better time than I ever had going to proms when I was a kid. You can't enjoy things when you're worried about how you look and whether your damn strapless bra will defy gravity all night, and whether your date is going to hold you too close or try to kiss you or drink too much. Take it from me, youth is wasted on the young.

The dance was at the Netherland, and lucky for me we found the elevators so I didn't have to climb all those steps. The elevator had its drawbacks, though: the goddam air was so overloaded with cologne, after-shave, hair spray, floral scents and a trace of permanent wave lotion, you had to fight to breathe. We got the same scents when we stepped off the elevator, only more diffused.

Looking at all those kids in tuxedos and floor-length gowns gave me a wave of nostalgia for my children's teen years, and my own. Then I reminded myself how miserable they really were, what with the cliquishness, the competition, the anxieties about what people thought of you, the pressure to have sex and not to have sex, and the raging hormones. And to look at these kids, you'd think they were happy.

We got some startled looks when we entered. I like to think it was because the kids hadn't seen my Loretta Young imitation, and were dazzled, but that probably wasn't it. We nabbed a table, and I rested my ankle. The dance was still in its early stages, when people are milling around, listening to the band and feeling too embarrassed to be the first ones dancing.

Moses didn't have that problem.

"Come on, Pearl. Let's dance."

"Moses," I said. "Did we or did we not agree that you would try to remain relatively inconspicuous?"

"Yeah, we agreed, but we at a dance now, Cat. The only conspicuous ones gonna be the ones not dancing."

"You don't have to be the first."

"Well, somebody got to be the first, 'cause I'm ready to start bein' inconspicuous on the dance floor."

If Pearl had been the inhibited type, I guess she would never have agreed to this double date in the first place, so off they went. And damned if they weren't good at it, too. I don't know how Moses's dancing measured up against the kind kids were doing today, but for my generation it was first-rate. And Pearl looked like she'd been fox-trotting and jitterbugging all her life.

"Hey, look at them go!" Nan enthused.

Moses hadn't started being inconspicuous yet. Right now, he was drawing quite an audience. The only thing that distracted them was the entrance of Cal, on crutches, and LaTania. The seas parted, and they were escorted to a place of honor right next to the dance floor. I wondered how LaTania had bribed her way out of confinement. I wondered how she had hooked up with Cal. Maybe later I'd go over and swap crutch stories with him.

I'd already made it clear to everybody, Nan included, that they should dance and have a good time and not worry about me. To tell you the truth, I love to people-watch anyway, and this was a great place to do it. Nan said she wasn't a good dancer anyway, but after Pearl's first session with Moses, Pearl said Nan ought to dance with Moses, because he'd make her look good no matter how clumsy she was. So she did: Mr. Inconspicuous danced with the only woman in the room wearing an outfit that matched his, down to the garters and black dress shoes.

"Better sit down, Gramps, and rest your heart," I said, kicking a chair out for him.

"You just jealous, Cat," he said, grinning and breathing heavily.

"Don't kid yourself. I represent Winnie's interests when I say, remember your age."

There was a big commotion every time a member of the basketball team arrived—the boys' team, that is. Last but not least, Biggs swaggered in, and brought down the house. The band swung into a jazzy version of the fight song. The cheerleaders led a Rattlers hiss. You never saw anything like it.

Nan danced, sometimes with boys and sometimes with girls, and I got the impression folks didn't know which they were supposed to be more shocked by, so after awhile they gave up and got used to it. Pearl danced, too, and even taught Moses a thing or two. I was trying to remember which pocket his nitroglycerin capsules were in.

As the evening wore on, though, Moses went cruising around. I don't know what I thought he'd see, but it gave him a chance to scrutinize Biggs and the team at close range. I'd been watching Cal and LaTania, to see if Cal put any moves on her, but so far they were acting like good friends. I'd also already noticed that Butch and Corky kept disappearing. Either they had very small bladders for two such hulking kids, or they were up to something. I asked Moses to check on it, but he already had them under surveillance.

"They got a bottle," he said. "You can smell it on 'em. What I want to find out is if they got anything else."

A little while later, he returned.

"I found another bottle," he said, and passed a small plastic bottle to me.

"Tylenol 3," I read. "Prescription Tylenol. Says, 'Two every four hours for pain, not to exceed eight tablets in twenty-four hours.' It's Corky's prescription, from Skuyler. Where'd you get this?"

"Corky's pocket."

"You *picked* Corky's pocket?"

He shrugged modestly. "Us ex-cops got lots of skills

you ain't even begun to suspect. Anyway, I saw him take one, and I wanted to know what he was taking."

"What do you make of it?"

"I'd say Corky's got something wrong with him that makes him need painkillers. Codeine ain't hardly the drug of choice among the young. It's probably legit, but it's interesting."

"You going to put it back?"

"Uh-huh. Now I'm goin' for the *other* bottle. Want to come watch?"

"No way."

He melted into the crowd, and I waited for the fireworks to start. But to my surprise, he was back in five minutes. He slipped a flask into my bag.

"Now we'll see what kind of reserves they got."

The next time Corky and Butch left, they were gone for a while. When they returned, they both looked mad. You could see them making the rounds, trying to find out who'd taken the bottle, and the more kids laughed and shook their heads, the madder Corky got. They went out again.

I took the opportunity to hobble over to Cal and La-Tania's table.

"Hi, kids," I said, helping myself to a chair from the next table over.

"Hey, Mrs. Caliban," LaTania bubbled. "You look awesome!"

"You look pretty awesome yourself," I said. Cal was making an effort to be polite, but his frown was getting the better of him. "Does Doc Skuyler know you're here?"

"Yeah, he's so cool! He said I could come if I didn't dance and if I went home at midnight, just like Cinderella or something! And then last night Cal told Marilyn to find another date if she could, 'cause he didn't think he could come, but then we decided to come together! I'm so *psyched*!"

"How bad is it?" I nodded at his leg.

"Aw, i's jus' a sprain. We goin' to tape it up real tight right before the first playoff game, see'f I can run on it."

"Doctor give you anything for pain?" Subtle, Cat, very subtle.

"Jus' aspirin."

"You mean, regular aspirin or prescription aspirin?"

"Jus' regular ol' aspirin. Don't do much good, though."

"I know what you mean. Well, I don't want to spoil you kids' fun. Catch you later." And I trundled back to my table. It was filling up with Lady Rattlers and their dates.

Butch and Corky were back. Moses was gone. I spotted him on the dance floor with Ana, who was wearing a beautiful floor-length multicolored robe.

Maybe fifteen minutes later, Butch and Corky left again, and I saw Moses follow them. You couldn't hear the shouting at first because of the band. But when the music stopped, you could hear that something was going on out in the hall. A couple of men teachers had already headed for the door, and the other teachers were pushing the kids back into the room, trying to convince them, the way people do in emergency situations, that there was no emergency.

I made good time across the floor myself, and pushed my way through. I didn't know at that point that I was running interference for Biggs, who was right behind me. I was worried about what Corky had done to Moses.

But it was Corky who was sitting on the floor with his back against the wall, rubbing his chin. Butch was kneeling next to him, talking, and Moses was talking to a hotel security guard.

"What the hell's going on here?" That was Biggs, in my ear.

"Nothin', Coach. He's all right." Butch didn't seem eager to explain what had happened.

"Who hit him?" Biggs demanded to know.

"I did," Moses said.

Biggs swung around.

"Who the hell are you?"

"Just an interested bystander. Look, Coach, I need to talk to the boys in private, so if you don't mind—"

"The hell you will! You don't beat up on *my* kids and get away with it, you son of a bitch!"

Biggs took a swing at Moses, but Moses was expecting it, ducked, and came up with Biggs's arm, which he yanked behind Biggs's back. It was the security guard, though, who escorted Biggs away—where, I don't know, because they didn't go back to the dance and I couldn't hear Biggs's profanity once the elevator door closed on them.

Moses crouched down to take a look at Corky's chin.

"How you doin', son?"

Corky glared at him sullenly, and didn't answer.

Moses reached out and extracted the Tylenol bottle from Corky's pocket.

"You know, I'm gettin' to be quite a fan of yours," he said. "I'd kinda like to see the Rattlers go all the way to the finals. But I don't think they gonna get there 'thout you, and you ain't gonna be there if you keep mixin' Tylenol 3 with bourbon."

"Tylenol 3?" Butch asked. "Is that that prescription stuff? Aw, man, you *told* me you was jus' takin' aspirin."

"It *is* aspirin, man. It's an aspirin substitute," Corky said and sulked.

"Yeah, that's right," Moses said. "An aspirin substitute mixed with codeine. You know where codeine comes from, Corky? It's a derivative of morphine."

"Aw, they used to put it in cough syrup. It's no big deal."

"Well, it's true that all by itself, it ain't no big deal. But you been addin' bourbon to it all night. You keep doin' that, you liable to wind up in a stainless-steel drawer downtown with a tag on your toe."

"Aw, man, he's right," Butch fumed. "That's some serious shit, man. Don't you *know* no better than that? Who you think gonna replace you in the lineup when you in the morgue?"

Corky didn't say anything. He was cornered.

"What you need painkillers for, anyway, son?"

"I got some kinda liver thing," he said. "So I asked the doc for some pain pills to get me through the next couple weeks."

"Well, that's between you and your doctor. Does the coach know?"

"Yeah, he knows."

"He just doesn't know you're taking pills and drinking. Okay, I'm going to keep the bourbon. You can have your pills back. What you tell the coach is up to you. I won't tell him about the bourbon."

"Hey, thanks, mister," Butch said, obviously relieved. "Come on, Corky."

"Yeah, thanks," Corky mumbled.

"That's okay, son," Moses said. "I don't know who'd replace you in the lineup, either."

So Corky had a "liver thing," and Skuyler had given him pain pills for it. Did that mean Corky had been fingered as the next Rattler to bite the dust? And if so, who had fingered him? Skuyler? Or Butch, who may or may not have known that his old pal was mixing codeine and bourbon?

Thirty

I slept late the next morning. Okay, I sleep late every morning, but that morning I slept later after our late night. Me, I thought we'd worn out our welcome after Moses decked Corky, but Moses claimed he was just starting to enjoy himself, and Pearl and Nan were in no hurry to leave.

"Aw, I just gave him a little tap, Cat," Moses told me. "You didn't think I was goin' to pulverize a starting guard, did you?"

Actually, I had thought somebody was going to get pulverized, but I didn't think it was going to be Corky. For a while after that, I had wondered whether we were going to be jumped by outraged basketball players on the way to the car. But the basketball players seemed to be taking it better than their fans—with good reason, of course.

I got up and ate lunch—two aspirins and a glass of ice water. Why hadn't Moses confiscated Corky's industrial-strength painkillers? Why hadn't somebody stopped me when I'd claimed, sometime after midnight, that I could *so* break dance with a crutch? Must have been what Moses was adding to our drinks from the bottles he did confiscate.

After that, I spent a productive afternoon rearranging objects to hide the dust lying around.

"Why don't you just dust?" Al asked when she came down for a report.

"Please," I said. "I'm a sick woman, Too goddam sick to do housework."

I took a swipe at the end table with Sidney, who removed most of the dust and left behind a coating of fur.

"You're right, Mrs. C. Detective work is much too strenuous." Kevin slumped in the doorway like a collapsed beach ball, a gym bag in one hand. "It's a lot like bartending. You talk to people, you listen to people. Except with bartending you don't have to lift the bar while you're attending."

"Pull up a pew," I offered.

Mel showed up, holding an electric drill. I didn't even ask.

I gave them the highlights of our evening. I could see they were viewing Moses in a whole new light when I'd finished.

"So what about you, Kevin?" I asked. "Anything to report?"

"Maybe," he said. "The answer to your questions is yes. Yes, there are drugs available at the North Side Gym. Also you can bet on the races at Latonia. Also you can arrange a sexual liaison, though frankly it's unclear to me whether that involves an exchange of money. What *was* made clear to me was that the sex should be strictly protected—safe as houses, as the English say. And just to make sure, there's a condom dispenser in the locker room. I thought it seemed a bit forward myself, if practical, but today I was told, in the strictest confidence, what everybody in the place apparently already knew: that a former habitué had been hospitalized with AIDS. Clean needles, my confidant confided, could be purchased at the front desk."

Mel whistled.

"You mean, people are *shooting up* in this place?" Al asked incredulously.

"All the time, apparently. But not the way you mean, my innocent. It seems that there's a whole set of drugs we've left out of our calculations. It's not surprising, since the only weight lifter we hang out with is Mel, and she wouldn't be caught dead—"

"Steroids!" Mel slapped her forehead.

"That's right. My informant assured me I could get fabulous results, and pointed out any number of benefactors of a well-balanced steroid program. I asked if steroids weren't illegal, and he scoffed at the idea. 'You name me a major sports figure,' he said, 'and I'll show you a steroid user.' "

"Mary Lou Retton?" Mel offered.

"Back up, Kevin," I said. "Are steroids illegal or aren't they?"

"They're available with a doctor's prescription, and some doctors—say, sports medicine types—aren't that scrupulous. And they're available on the black market, which translates into every locker room in the country."

"And you inject steroids, you don't take them by mouth?"

"Some are taken orally, and some are injected. Most hard-core users do a little of both."

"Then wouldn't a user show needle marks on his arm?"

Kevin laughed. "That's not where they're usually injected, Mrs. C."

"So did you ask about any of the Robertson kids?"

"Yes, but my informant suddenly went all cagey on me. He said he didn't know about them, but most high school athletes did. That's all he'd say."

"Okay, so they're banned from sports officially, but everybody uses them. It doesn't seem like a serious threat to the Rattlers, if somebody found out and threatened to expose them—I mean, not if that many high school athletes are using steroids. And unless Biggs is their source, he might give them hell for shooting up. But I don't see the big deal, unless the mob is involved in black market steroid distribution."

"But steroids are dangerous, Cat," Mel insisted. "And they're so widely abused that everybody thinks they're like alcohol—you know, the dangers are overrated, and anyway nothing bad will happen to *me*. It doesn't help that we don't have a lot of conclusive evidence yet about the dangers, so everybody thinks somebody's just putting out rumors—either to scare the kids away, or to keep the stuff controlled and keep the price up. There's even an underground guide to steroid use that assures its readers that all the reported dangers are a myth."

"So what kinds of dangers are we talking about?" I asked.

"I don't know all the medical stuff, Cat. I just know they're bad news."

"But give me an idea."

"Oh, I don't know. But I think they've been linked to cancer and high blood pressure at least."

"How about blocked arteries?" Jackson Tucker was beginning to find his place in my puzzle.

"I don't know, Cat. You'll have to look it up."

"But I thought steroids were for weight gain, Mel," Al objected. "And body building. I mean, I guess I could see weight lifters taking them, but basketball players?"

"Well, some basketball players need to gain weight and improve their upper body strength, like Shelly and maybe Reggie, right, Mel?" I asked.

"Sure," she said. "I don't think steroid use is as common among basketball players as it is among other athletes, but I can see how it could help their performance. Maybe that's especially true when they're teenagers."

"Steroids are just hormones, right?" I asked. "Now that I think of it, I can imagine what it does to kids to add hormones to the ones that are already flooding their bodies during adolescence."

"Well, one thing it does, if I remember correctly," Kevin offered, "is make them bad-tempered."

"That's right!" Mel exclaimed, slapping herself on the forehead. " 'Roid rages!"

"Say, what?" I asked.

" 'Roid rages. When somebody on steroids loses control. The hormones probably screw up his emotional equilibrium. Like Corky, for instance."

"Hey, that's right!" I said. "LaTania told me he didn't used to be so volatile."

"Mornin', y'all." Moses strode in, looking fresh as a daisy. "Say, Cat, I been thinkin'. What about steroids?" Winnie was bringing up the rear, carrying something in her mouth.

"Welcome to the club, Moses. Kevin says the North Side Gym is thick with 'em. Park your carcass and tell us what *you* know about steroids."

"Well," he said, "first, we got all them injuries. Ligaments and tendons, mostly. When somebody's puttin' on weight with steroids, they don't develop their ligaments and tendons as fast as they do their muscles. So they're putting more stress on ligaments that aren't very flexible and tear easily. So, like I was sayin', the injuries are one clue. Then, there's Corky's technicals."

" 'Roid rages," I said nonchalantly. I was catching on fast.

"And there's that liver problem he mentioned last night. I bet that's related."

"So is that bastard Biggs on steroids, too?"

"Does Biggs *look* like he's on steroids?"

"Well, no. But he might be the supplier."

"He might be. If Kevin says they got steroids at the North Side Gym, then you got yourself another possible outlet."

"And Skuyler makes three," I said. "I wonder."

Winnie gave a little bark and pounced on something.

"Moses, Al wants to know how common it is for basketball players to take steroids."

"Well, it ain't unheard of. 'Specially if they takin' 'em with something else."

"Like what?"

"Like something to increase their height. HGH, say."

"What's that?"

"Human growth hormone. Doctors use it to treat kids who don't grow enough. Athletes can use it to grow taller. I could see where a basketball player might be stacking steroids and HGH—that is, like I said, takin' 'em together."

Winnie held something between her paws and tore it with her teeth.

"Doctors, huh? Say, where's my copies of Juky's notebook? Goddam, I bet it's all in there! The whole fucking enchilada!"

I jumped up and limped into the kitchen, where I'd last been working on it. Some photocopies were lying on the floor, and the rest of the papers were scattered, as if there'd been a jump ball in the middle of the kitchen table.

"Hey!" I said, stooping to examine them. "Where's my worksheet?"

I heard a yap from the other room.

"This what you lookin' for, Cat?"

Moses was holding a soggy, torn sheet of notebook paper.

"Well, great minds *do* think alike," I said, and gave Winnie a pat. "At least she didn't swallow it—uh, most of it."

We laid out Juky's notebook on the floor, and my worksheet, and studied them.

"Here's SS, for Sky Skuyler," Mel pointed out. "Nineteen-nineteen, that's SS."

"Hell, I was reading them as ones and nines."

"Could it be Shelly Shellenstein?"

"Maybe. I'll have to check his real name. Sky's real name is Scott, so SS would still work for him."

"What if seventy-two was his height?" Moses proposed. "Seventy-two inches is six feet. And one-eighty could be his weight."

"And what if we were right the first time, Mel, about the six-oh-six being June 6?"

"Hey, there's CS," Al pointed excitedly, "for Cal Sepeta. Three-nineteen."

"And thirty-three for Corky," Kevin said. "Or three-three, I guess it is. Unless—I wonder what his real name is?"

"They all look like they got heights and weights recorded, Cat," Moses said.

"So what's this other number?" I asked. "A measure of upper body strength?"

"You're probably right, Cat!" Mel said. "They look like

bench-press figures to me. And that last one—I'll bet that's a time on the mile. Basketball players have to be able to run fast, you know."

"Check down the list until we find another date," I said. "Do the numbers keep going up?"

"They sure do," Al said. "Look! A gradual but steady increase."

We looked at each other.

"Does this mean we've cracked the case?" Al asked.

"Cracked but not broken," I said. "We still don't know who was distributing the steroids, or why Skuyler's disappeared. It's beginning to look like Juky was going to blow the whistle on somebody, I'll admit that. But are we sure it was the dealer? Or was it one of his pals who was using the stuff? Or did Juky go to Biggs and threaten to tell the state sports commission, and get the team disqualified from the playoffs? Did Skuyler disappear because he was dealing, or because he shot Juky, or did the same killer get rid of both of them? And if so, why hasn't Skuyler's father reported him missing? Is it because he's the supplier?"

"You right, Cat. You still got a heap of unanswered questions to answer."

"Plus one more you didn't mention," Kevin put in. "Does the AIDS case at the North Side Gym have anything to do with anything?"

"And one more besides," I said. "Did steroids kill Jackson Tucker?"

Thirty-one

I slept on it Sunday night, and woke up with a headache Monday morning. I needed another goddam wrinkle in the case like I needed another suspect in the lineup. AIDS was just one too many diseases for me to handle. All I needed was for somebody to tell me that Tucker had been diabetic, or that Biggs's mother had been convicted of an axe murder.

So I went to the place I always go for answers: the library. I wanted to know more about steroids, and their role in high school athletics. But before I went, I called Mrs. Kay to ask about Juky's reading habits. I wanted to know what Juky had been reading the last few months of his life. It turned out that Juky had also put in some time at the downtown library. Great minds.

I picked up a note from Mrs. Kay on the way to the library, asking the librarians to give me access to Juky's records. They called her to double-check, which was okay by me. I mean, you don't want just anybody to be able to walk in and find out you've been reading about divorce law or poisons or alien kidnappings or sex; that would be just a hop away from mind reading. And if the FBI ever comes looking to add to my file, I hope the same suspicious woman is behind the desk.

It turned out that Juky had done my work for me: there, on the printout of his last six months of library records, was a goddam gold mine of information about anabolic steroids and HGH. Maybe if I read it, I'd be as smart as Juky. Maybe not.

The stuff I read explained a lot to me. Not just why kids were spraining their ankles all the time, or flying into rages. It explained Corky's liver problems, Cal's nosebleeds, and Skuyler's headaches. It even explained what had bothered me about Tucker's pictures over the years: he had looked progressively stupider because of water retention in his face, and what the books called a "coarsening" of his features. And it explained why a kid with a genetic predisposition to arterial disease could die of a heart attack at the age of nineteen.

I also learned that kids were taking steroids as early as junior high, and that if they planned college sports careers when they got to high school, they assumed that they would have to take steroids just to keep up with the competition. Experts estimated that around ten percent of male high school graduates had used or were using steroids. Although about sixty percent of the high school kids on steroids were buying them on the black market, another twenty percent were wangling prescriptions from their doctors—or at least, their parents were. In Ohio, it was perfectly legal to prescribe human growth hormone for athletic improvement, and steroids weren't even categorized as a "controlled substance." And I learned that basketball players accounted for almost fifteen percent of the high school steroid users, right behind football players and wrestlers.

I found out a lot about testing for steroids, and that led me to wonder about Tucker's autopsy. Maybe I didn't know shit about steroids, but surely a forensic pathologist with a dead nineteen-year-old on the table in front of him would know. Then I read that testing for steroids was not a routine autopsy procedure, that it wasn't part of the coroner's toxicology screen.

All in all, it was a pretty damn sobering trip to the library.

Your first impulse is to go out and grab these kids by the arm, do some kind of violence to them, chew them out. Didn't they *realize* what they were doing to themselves? Didn't they *realize* what they had done to Juky? Because the more I learned, the more certain I became that this was the reason for Juky's death. What kind of a fool injects hormones into his body under the delusion that it can only do him good?

But the answer was obvious: a teenager. Only teenagers were learning it from older athletes—maybe even from their parents and coaches. Jackson Tucker had been marked for death from his first little baby football. His athletic career had been planned before he could walk. No wonder he went looking for help. No wonder they all did.

And not one of them had been willing to come forward after Juky died and admit what had been going on in the locker room. But I couldn't really blame them. They'd probably convinced themselves it wasn't relevant—not nearly as relevant as the state championship they were planning to win in Juky's name. And Juky himself had probably not been in on the secret, or he wouldn't have kept a notebook full of evidence. They probably figured he wouldn't approve, and they couldn't predict where his disapproval would lead. Even when it led to his death, they invented another story for themselves—some drug deal he'd witnessed. Real drugs. Serious drugs. Not like "the Juice."

Eating helps me think, so I left the library, hobbled down the street, and parked myself in front of a five-way at Skyline Chili. It took me twenty minutes to find the bottom of the dish. By then, I thought I had my puzzle put together. The question was what to do with it.

The timing, as usual, was lousy. The first playoff game was two weeks away—not the most opportune moment to break a steroid scandal around the heads of one of the state's leading contenders for a title. And, like I said, I was sympathetic.

I was also without any substantial evidence of the identity of Juky's killer, and unlikely to get it without help from the inside. The best I could hope for otherwise was that he'd shoot *me* in front of witnesses, and get convicted of that. Not a happy alternative, from my perspective.

But I also didn't think it could wait for the playoffs to end. There was, or were, a killer and a kidnapper running around loose, and no telling when the war would escalate, even if I pretended to go away for a while.

Moses agreed when I laid my case in front of him. He was down in the basement trying to fix the chain on Leon's bicycle, so I sat on the workbench, fiddling with a pair of pliers and complaining about my options.

"So tell me I'm wrong," I pleaded.

"No, Cat, you right. Even if you wrong about Juky's killer, you right about confronting the steroid use now. What if another kid got hurt in the next couple weeks? I don't just mean heart attacks—that's a long shot. But an injury that could ruin a kid's athletic career is a definite possibility. From what you say, so is cancer, over the long run. But what if one of our boys attacked another player in a 'roid rage? What if we lose the next game? You said steroids contributed to mood swings and depression—what if somebody tries suicide? What if he succeeds? These drugs are just a powderkeg, waiting to blow. Things that seem crazy now could happen—*they already did.* Then how would you feel two weeks from now? Hand me them pliers."

I sighed.

"But if I confront the steroid abuse, I don't have any choice but to go after Juky's killer, and I don't have any evidence to convict him with."

He put the pliers down and turned around. He planted a fist on the workbench on either side of me and looked up into my face.

"Cat, more killers go free than get caught, baby. That's just a reality. Welcome to police work. You got to figure out what's important." He spoke softly. "You think Juky Kay would have any trouble figurin' out what's most important?"

I shook my head. I started to snivel. My eyes sprouted tears, and somebody drove a pile down the back of my throat. My upper lip began to feel moist.

"Well, goddam that bastard anyway!" I said. I did not mean Juky Kay.

Thirty-two

Mrs. Emma Shielding's College Hill living room had been swallowed less by the quantity of people than by their size. I am not speaking of myself, but of the Robertson Rattlers, squeezed in with their manager, their coach, their team doctor, and a spiritual adviser in case things got heavy, which I expected things to do. Also present was Randy Waltrip, who had been unable to persuade my favorite homicide detective, Sergeant Fricke, to take seriously this little gathering. I figured he was down at headquarters, checking back files on unregistered firearms. Moses was there, in the doorway, and Mel and Kevin were sitting in the kitchen with the door open between. By both doors stood uniformed officers Randy referred to as "backup." I guess he expected Mel to throw the first punch.

I'd told Randy that I doubted we'd actually produce an arrest tonight, but he said that was okay, the officers needed a break from traffic accidents and domestic disturbance calls.

Sitting in an armchair to my right was Marion Kay. I hadn't wanted to do it this way, but like Moses said, I didn't have a whole hell of a lot of choices. The others were here because she'd asked them to come, and they couldn't say no to Juky's mom.

"I came into this case because of a notebook—Juky's notebook," I began. I produced it with a flourish, courtesy of Waltrip, and threw it down on the coffee table. "In it is the evidence he collected of something seriously gone wrong on the squad. At least one of you knows of the existence of this notebook, even if you've never seen it."

I scanned their faces. Everybody looked either apprehensive or puzzled, except Biggs, who looked hostile.

"I've been going at this whole thing wrong, looking for a killer—somebody who'd killed twice. That was wrong. Because actually, there are two killers in this case."

Now I had them on the edge of their seats.

"But only one of the killers is human. See, Juky figured out that many of you were using anabolic steroids and human growth hormone to improve your athletic performance."

"Now, wait just a goddam minute!" Biggs exploded. "Who the hell are you accusing, lady? I don't know what you're trying to stir up, but my boys are clean and they've always been clean, so don't give me that bullshit!"

I leaned over and picked up the notebook and pretended to read. Actually, I had it memorized because I wasn't that fast at decoding.

"Cal gained thirty pounds between June and October, grew an inch and a half, and improved his bench press from 380 to 440. Is that normal?"

"Hell, he was working out every day!"

"Is that normal?"

Biggs stared at me.

"In the same period, Corky put on twenty-two pounds and grew an inch. Are normal high school seniors adding that much height that fast?"

"These are *athletes*, goddam it! They're not normal! They're working out to put on weight and improve their strength."

"And which piece of equipment do you use to add height?" I asked. I didn't get an answer.

"One night, at Tower Hamburgers, I thought I overheard one of you say that you needed to 'get some b-ball.' It didn't really make sense at the time, but I assumed you were talking about basketball, as usual. I misheard the comment, though. What one of you wanted was 'd-bol,' dianabol, one of the most common of the anabolic steroids."

Silence.

"Maybe Coach would like to check you guys for needle tracks. Any volunteers?" I looked around. "Butch? Cal?"

Biggs was looking at them, too, staring at them with his mouth hanging open. They were studying their shoelaces, faces as impassive as practiced athletes can make them.

"Well, *tell* her, dammit!" Biggs grabbed Corky's arm roughly. "Tell her what I'd do to you if I found out you were shooting up! Tell her what I've always told you about drugs! *Tell her!*"

He'd picked the wrong kid. Corky exploded. "*You* tell her, goddammit! Then while you're at it, you *tell her* what you'd do to us if we fuck up this championship! And you tell her how we're supposed to win it when every other motherfucker playing championship basketball is on the Juice, if we're not! And *you* tell her what the principal would say, and what the kids would say, and what the recruiters would say, and what our parents and families would say, and what the whole goddam neighborhood would say, if we fuckin' didn't win your fuckin' championship for you! Go ahead, tell her *that*, why don't you, Coach!"

Cal was pulling on Corky's other arm, but Corky had already run out of steam, and he was wiping tears away with the back of his hand.

He sank back down on the arm of a chair.

"I'm sorry, Mrs. Kay," he mumbled. "I'm sorry for . . . everything."

Biggs was too stunned to speak.

I let the silence hold a minute, then started in again.

"There are two major sources for steroids," I said quietly. "One is the black market. The other is through a doctor's prescription. I think most of you used a prescription. Maybe you were suspicious of the quality of black market or mail-order drugs, and you were right to be. Somebody persuaded you that he could ensure that quality by getting legitimate prescriptions—well, maybe not legitimate, but apparently so."

"They ain't drugs," Butch objected. "It's jus' hormones,

like we got anyway. They natural. Ain't nothin' wrong with 'em."

"Sure there is, Butch. Were your ankles as bad before you started taking them?" I looked around. "Anybody got bad acne on their back?"

They all flinched on that one—I'd said the A word.

"Did Corky fly into rages before? Did he have liver problems? Did Cal have nosebleeds? Did Sky get headaches as often?"

"Aw, man, that shit don't have nothing to do with steroids," Butch insisted. "All athletes got physical problems. It ain't like we girls, gonna turn into boys because we takin' male hormones."

Oh, the confidence of youth.

"No, you're not gonna turn into boys. But you're a good prospect to turn impotent. Anybody want to talk about that?"

Nobody did.

"Sure, every athlete has some physical problems. But some are more prevalent among steroid users. And if you guys keep taking them, it may get worse. Steroids have been implicated in cancer, high blood pressure, liver failure"—I nodded at Corky—"and heart attacks. Which brings us to Jackson Tucker."

I heard a few gasps, and saw some looks exchanged.

"See, I got off track because Reverend Cain here said that Juky had murder on his mind. But it wasn't really murder—not the first death. It was suicide. Accidental suicide. Tucker had inherited from his mother a tendency toward atherosclerosis—that is, obstruction of the arteries. But he probably would have lived a lot longer if he hadn't been taking steroids, which aggravated his problem. In Juky's mind, that might mean whoever provided the steroids was guilty of murder."

"If steroids killed Tuck, then how come the autopsy didn't show it?" Butch challenged me.

"Because most coroners aren't looking for them, I suppose. Like I said, I think you had prescriptions, and I think the name on those prescriptions was Dr. Skuyler's."

"Now just a minute," Skuyler objected hotly. "If you think I condone steroid use, or hand out prescriptions like lollipops, you've got another think coming."

"I said your name was on the prescriptions, Dr. Skuyler. I didn't say you wrote them."

His face registered shock, but he didn't say anything.

"I'd say your son was involved. Not in the actual forgeries, but in stealing the prescription forms for someone else to forge. And he received his share of the profit from sales of the prescriptions."

"I can't believe Scott would do such a thing," he managed.

"Yes, you can," I said gently. I didn't like the part that was coming next. "Dr. Skuyler, when was the last time you spoke to your son?"

"I don't know," he said. "A few days ago. I don't see what difference that makes."

"I didn't ask when you last heard from your son. That may or may not have been a few days ago. I asked when you last spoke to him."

"A few days ago," he insisted woodenly.

"No, I don't think so. I don't think you've spoken to him since the day he disappeared. Now, isn't that true?"

"Certainly not."

"How did you know he was going to live at his mother's?"

"He told me so."

"No."

"Of course he did."

"No."

"He did." He looked around at the others in disbelief, hoping they'd realize how strangely I was acting.

"I think somebody else told you."

"Somebody else?" Now he appeared genuinely surprised, which shook me a little.

"Have you talked to your son often since he left?"

"Once or twice. And he's written me, of course."

The light dawned.

"No, he hasn't."

"But he has!"

"Dr. Skuyler, your son is virtually illiterate. He can barely read and write. I know because I spoke to his English teacher."

"That's ridiculous."

"He's been passed through school because of his athletic ability, and because he's bright, he's managed to cover up his illiteracy. That's how I know he wasn't the one who forged those prescriptions."

"He wrote me a letter." This time it was almost a whisper, a plea.

"No, someone else wrote you a letter and signed his name. And you've been protecting your son because of what he told you in that letter. You even kidnapped my grandson to keep me from finding out what he told you in that letter."

He squeezed his eyes shut and passed one hand over his forehead.

"Here's what I think happened. I think Juky confronted your son about the steroid racket. I think Sky's partner was present at that confrontation. I think one of the boys, probably the partner, shot and killed Juky to keep him quiet."

Marion Kay gasped, and Mrs. Shielding went over to her, bent down, and spoke softly. I was watching the eyes shift around the room and knew I was right.

"I think your son was very nervous about the killing, especially since he probably helped to move Juky's body. I think it's possible that Juky was killed in your offices, Dr. Skuyler. The police investigation petered out, and Sky felt a little more secure. Then a new investigation started: mine. I don't think he could handle the pressure."

I took a deep breath.

"I think Sky disappeared. I don't believe that you know where he is. I thought maybe someone told you he was gone, and why, but now I'd guess you received a letter, maybe typewritten, maybe forged—it didn't matter, because by now Sky's partner was an accomplished forger.

"The letter may have confessed to Juky's killing—I'm not sure about that. I have a stronger suspicion, though, that in it your son told you that he had tested positive for the HIV virus. I think he probably explained that he must have picked it up from sharing needles at the gym. More than anything else, that was the secret you wanted to keep—not that your son had been using steroids, which you assumed he'd obtained at the gym, but that he'd been contaminated with the HIV virus. Because it meant your practice and your livelihood to reveal that a close family member, a member of your household, was HIV positive and might one day soon develop AIDS.

"I'm not saying you didn't care about your son. I'm sure you felt anguished for him. But if you wanted to be able to pay for his care, and live on after his death, you couldn't afford to let people know what he died of. People's fears of AIDS aren't very rational, and don't have much to do with how the disease really spreads. They wouldn't see a doctor who had AIDS in the household."

Skuyler broke down.

"My God! A dirty *needle*, for God's sake! Do you know, Mrs. Caliban, how many clean needles I keep in my office?" He took out a handkerchief and blew his nose. "I didn't want to kidnap your grandson, Mrs. Caliban. I love children. I would never have hurt him. I wrapped him up in a blanket so he wouldn't be cold. I just . . . wanted you to stop asking questions. Why couldn't you stop asking questions? But I accept that you couldn't. Steroids—my God. And AIDS. That's the one thing you didn't mention when you told them the dangers of steroids."

"No, that's one of the biggest, if they're sharing needles. But your son wasn't HIV positive, Dr. Skuyler."

"He wasn't?" His voice was sharp and incredulous.

"I don't think so. I think that was just part of the plot to make sure you cooperated and kept quiet. There *was* a case of AIDS at the North Side Gym where Sky worked out, and that's where the idea originated."

"Then where is he?"

"I don't know."

"Can you find out? Can I . . . hire . . . you to find out?"

"No, Dr. Skuyler. There's only one person who can tell you where he is—his former partner."

Dr. Skuyler searched the room until he found the face he was seeking.

"Eddie . . . ?"

Waltrip had Atterbury by the elbow, but he didn't look armed and dangerous. For all his muscle, he looked small in this room of giants.

He smiled a funny smile. "That's the biggest bunch of crap I ever heard. You can't prove a thing. Not a goddam thing."

"I plan to have a hell of a good time trying, you little b—" I hesitated a split second, discarded the profanity, and substituted the worst high school put-down I could think of. "Dweeb."

Under his tan, he flushed.

Thirty-three

"He's right," I said gloomily. "I *can't* prove a goddam thing."

Kevin had cooked a celebration dinner, but nobody felt much like celebrating. Only the fur people appeared contented, two on the heat vents, one on Kevin's lap, and one under Moses's chair.

"I mean, on the plus side, we got some kids off steroids for a few years—maybe until they get to college and start feeling the pressure again. We found out who killed Juky, but he can't be arrested because there's no evidence. On the minus side, Juky's dead, and Tucker's dead, and Skuyler's probably dead. If Skuyler's dead, it's because I went looking for Juky's killer. I'm not saying I'm responsible exactly, but there it is. We may never find Skuyler's body. And in the process of accomplishing all this, I had to do a lot of damage. Skuyler's father had to find out not only that his son might be dead, but that the kid was a thief, a steroid junkie, and a dealer, not to mention the fact that the kid was illiterate."

"Come on, Cat," Mel said. "You don't really think it was news to his father that Sky couldn't read and write, do you?"

"Well, I think he must've known it at some level, but he'd never confronted it. The teachers tell me that kids are amazingly good at covering up those kinds of deficiencies. You wouldn't think it would be possible, but I guess it is."

"On the minus side, you left out the part about getting Ben kidnapped," Al put in, ever helpful. "Which reminds me: did you know for sure that Dr. Skuyler was the kidnapper when you called that meeting last night?"

"I was pretty sure. Moses convinced me that if the kidnapping wasn't planned, the kidnapper pretty much had to be the doctor. Besides, how many people know about how easy it is to grab a kid? Moses tells me it's done all the time in amusement parks and places like that, but I'd never heard that before. Now maybe a minister would have heard it, but there again, a doctor who treated lots of kids would be a better bet to have that kind of information. Anyway, he was wearing English Leather last night, and Cain wasn't. That wouldn't have been conclusive evidence all by itself, but it helped to corroborate Moses's theory."

"Okay, but maybe I'm missing something. I still don't see why Skuyler had to disappear," Mel said.

"I guess he got nervous, and made Atterbury nervous. Maybe the steroids had something to do with it—with Skuyler's behavior and with Atterbury's response."

"But he needed Skuyler to keep his bogus prescription business afloat, didn't he?"

"All he needed was the printed forms, right, Mrs. C.?" Kevin asked. "Maybe he hoarded up a year's supply before he bumped off Skuyler."

"I thought if he'd forged everything else, he could have forged the forms too," Al said.

"That might have occurred to him, somewhere along the line, now that photocopying technology has gotten so advanced. I don't think he thought of it at first. But I also think he spotted bigger game when he came up with a plan to get rid of his nervous partner and increase his earnings at the same time."

"What do you mean?"

"I think eventually he would have started blackmailing Dr. Skuyler. That way, he could have all the forms he needed and a cash payment as well."

"You mean about the AIDS business," Al said. "That was really smart, Cat. How'd you come up with that?"

"I just asked why Dr. Skuyler would be shielding his son. The obvious answer was that Skuyler had killed Juky, and decided to disappear. But what if Skuyler *hadn't* killed Juky? I had to play out that scenario as well. Skuyler might have disappeared because he knew something about

Juky's death. If he knew something about Juky's death, then he was a threat to the killer. That could explain why his father was shielding him: they were both afraid the killer would come after him next.

"Once I thought that, I had to consider the alternative: what if the killer *had* gone after Skuyler? But that didn't make sense, because if Skuyler were dead, why was his father so eager to make us think he was in Chicago with his mother?"

"Well, it could have been because Skuyler—the doctor, I mean—was the killer," Al speculated.

"That's right. But after the kidnapping, I didn't really take the doctor seriously as a candidate for Juky's murder. I know, Moses; you told me the murder could have been an accident, but I still didn't think the kidnapper was the murderer. I thought the guy in the parking lot with a gun was the murderer, but I didn't think that was Skuyler.

"Then Kevin's information about an AIDS case at the gym added a new wrinkle. On the other hand, it provided what seemed impossible—a plausible reason why someone whose son had disappeared hadn't gone to the police to find him. Assuming Sky wasn't the killer, or that his father didn't think he was."

"Hard to believe Dr. Skuyler wouldn't do *anything*," Al said, shaking her head. "But I guess he just thought Sky had run away."

"So he was charged with Ben's kidnapping?" Mel asked.

Moses nodded. "He was charged, but they'll probably plea bargain. He might get probation, under the circumstances. He's takin' things mighty hard."

"Atterbury's parents, on the other hand, seem pretty unperturbed by all accounts—or rather, his father does. His father's an attorney, and is pretty pissed off that his son is even being questioned. I gather his mother is bewildered why anybody would even accuse her son of anything."

"Boy's gettin' more attention now than he has for a

while, I imagine. Don't strike me as a kid that anybody's paid much attention to before now."

"Yeah," Kevin said. "He's a classic case, isn't he? Too short and unathletic to play sports, socially graceless, no special talents except entrepreneurial ones, a forgettable personality. And high schools kids can be vicious. Girls turn you down, guys ride you, or worse—ignore you. So you develop your muscles, get contact lenses, spend hours in the tanning bed, and become team manager so you can hang out with the players. And still the only vote you can get for 'Most Popular' is your own. Not that I'm speaking from personal experience, you understand. But tell the truth, Mrs. C.: don't you feel just the teensiest bit guilty about calling him a dweeb?"

"Hell, no. So he's had a tough life. Big deal. Lots of people have, especially in high school. The bastard didn't have to take it out on Juky Kay, who seems to have been nice to everybody, as far as I can make out. Like the kids say, he should get a life, for crissake. And then to steal Juky's Air Jordans so he could make another hundred bucks—that's cold-blooded."

"The cops didn't find them when they searched Atterbury's house?" Al asked.

"Nah, those shoes are long gone. Little bastard probably even sold the goddam murder weapon. Entrepreneurial, the teachers said."

"That's your phone, Cat."

"I'll get it," Moses volunteered, stepping over my crutch.

"When are you going to get rid of that thing?" Mel asked.

"Maybe tomorrow. I've been practicing around the house without it. The cats get that disapproving look on their pusses, the way they do when they think I've been drinking too much. But I do okay. It still hurts, but that goddam crutch has worn out its welcome."

"You get rid of it too early, you'll be in worse shape than before," Mel warned.

"Hey, when I want to be told what to do, I'll go visit my kids," I grumbled.

Someone pushed open the door, but it wasn't Moses.

"Hey, Miz Cat. Hey, y'all. Can I c-come in?"

"Hey, Leon. Sure, join the party. Where you been?"

"I been d-deliverin' fliers, hangin' 'em on f-folks' doors. I been over on Fergus, and Chase, and M-Mad Anthony, and—"

"That's okay. We get the picture."

Moses returned, and stood in the doorway.

"That was Randy Waltrip. Atterbury's dead."

"He's *what*?"

"Dead. Found shot to death in his garage."

"When?"

"Late this afternoon."

"The po-lice, they b-been over there, investigatin'."

I should have known Leon would get the first news flash.

"Have they arrested Dr. Skuyler?"

"They picked him up. Apparently, Fricke went himself, presumably because he didn't want anything to go wrong. When Skuyler came to the door, he reportedly said, 'Now I can bury my son.' "

"What's *that* mean?"

"Well, he's directed the police to a place in Mt. Airy forest where he thinks Sky is buried."

"You mean, he made Atterbury tell him, *and then* he shot him?" Kevin asked.

"Looks that way." He got this funny little grin on his face. "But looks can be deceiving."

"What's that supposed to mean?" Goddam, Moses was getting to be as dramatic as Kevin. Why couldn't somebody in this house just tell a damn story, and tell it straight?

"Every player on the Robertson Rattlers swears that Dr. Skuyler attended a closed team practice this afternoon at the time Atterbury was killed. Coach says the same thing.

They all tell the same story, right down to the color of his socks."

I felt a smile breaking out on my face. "No shit?"

"Randy says Fricke's got 'em all in separate rooms—the place is overrun with Rattlers—while he tries to break their stories."

I started to laugh. I couldn't help it. I was picturing Fricke trying to intimidate Cal Sepeta. Or even Corky. He'd never succeed. Fricke was a runaway bulldozer, and you needed the soft touch of a Cat.

"You cryin', M-Miz Cat?"

I shook my head.

"Good," Leon said. " 'Cause I b-been thinkin' 'bout the way you found B-Blackie? See, b-back in the summertime, I lost my b-best baseball glove. You think you c-could find it for me?"

Author's Note

Two other sources useful to me in writing this book were William N. Taylor's *Macho Medicine: A History of the Anabolic Steroid Epidemic* (McFarland, 1991) and Bob Goldman's *Death in the Locker Room: Steroids and Sports* (Icarus, 1984).

The Steroid Trafficking Act of 1990 made steroids a controlled substance under the Federal Controlled Substance Act of 1970, over the opposition of league officials, coaches, and trainers.

As I was finishing this book, I read of the death of Lyle Alzado from brain cancer at the age of forty-three. Alzado, former defensive lineman for the Los Angeles Raiders, blamed his cancer on long-term steroid use, and devoted the last year of his life to publicizing the dangers of steroids.